Books by Bill Thesken

The Lords of Xibalba
The Oil Eater
Blocking Paris
Edge of the Pit
The Catalina Cabal
Exodus from Orion

Quick Read

Bill Thesken

ISBN 978-1-7329689-1-2
ISBN 978-1-7329689-2-9

1.

The gentle rocking of the boat nearly put me back to sleep. Despite the physical pain I was in, it was comforting to be in the cockpit of the Spice. A self-imposed coma might not be a bad idea at a time like this. But I still had work to do.

Anchored in the middle of the harbor in Avalon, off the coast of Catalina island I sat propped up on the lounge chair, cushioned on all sides by soft pillows, waiting for the big shot from the CIA to arrive.

Covered in bloody scrapes, steady throbbing from the top of my head to the tips of my toes, aware of the exact location of every bone in my body. The result of jumping from a speeding truck on the hill above the casino to the right of my vision. My body was busted and bruised, but my spirit was not yet broken.

Last night I got into a bit of a tussle with a couple of hitmen from China, professional assassins from the Triad based in Los Angeles and I rolled out of a truck before it went over a cliff with one of the assassins still attached to the surfboard rack. Every inch of my body felt like it had been hit with a baseball bat, but that's the outcome when you tumble over rocks at thirty miles an hour. At least I didn't keep rolling over the cliff like the other guy.

I could see the SUV truck, what was left of it, being loaded onto the flat bed of a semi-trailer by a bulldozer. It would be hauled away to the Coast Guard base yard and combed for evidence.

They'd probably find a few shell casings and bullet fragments. Maybe some leftover body parts from the Chinese hit man that tried to take me out.

Amber was sitting quietly beside me. Her back towards me, dark hair cascading over her shoulders.

She was facing north east, away from the truck loading the wreck, gently watching the morning light peeking over the hillside of the island.

"What are you thinking about?" I asked her.

I could see the side of her face and the corner of her mouth. She smiled slightly without looking back at me. "I'm trying not to think at all. I could be thinking about being at work at the hospital, about how many babies were born last night, who was working the night shift, and if they ever fixed the broken elevator. I could be thinking about what's on the menu at that restaurant on the dock over there, or how deep the water is underneath this boat, and whether there's any crabs crawling around on the seafloor. I could even be thinking about how lucky I am that you weren't killed last night, but that would just bring me out of my happy place. I'm just glad to be here right now, because nothing else matters."

"That's my girl." I patted her on the back with the tip of a finger.

Nothing else did matter. I had a close shave last night, but that was in the past. Where it belonged.

We heard the engines turning over, the deep rumbling of the Coast Guard cutter that was tied to the dock at the center of the harbor. Our quiet time would soon be over. The head of the CIA was coming out to pay a visit.

The steady rumbling large diesel engines increased in volume, humming now in perfect unison, then it came into view, the silver and orange outline of the fast patrol boat blocking my view of Catalina Island.

It slowed to a crawl as the engines were put into reverse, then idled as it gently floated towards our stern.

Lieutenant Myles Johnson called out. "Permission to come aboard?"

If only I was in a better mood and felt a little stronger I would have waved them off and told both him and his passenger to take a long hike down a short pier, but I was in a piss poor mood and it wasn't going to get better for a few days. I waved them on board with a tilt of my head, the best I could muster.

Two crewmen on the Coast Guard boat reached out with tender hooks, bringing the two vessels together, side by side. Two men were standing next to Myles and they stuck out like sore thumbs on the boat where all the crew wore crisp blue uniforms. These guys were wearing black pressed slacks, white button down dress shirts and suit coats.

The CIA was here for a visit. For what I had no idea. The guy who must have been the big deal shook the Lieutenant's hand thanking him for the ride and the two odd balls climbed over the railing onto my boat by the stern. I could tell by their faces that they were serious men, and the way they looked at my scraped and bruised condition their seriousness doubled though they tried their hardest to hide it.

The main guy, the bigger of the two reached out his hand, then thought better of it.

"Pardon me for being blunt, but you look like hell."

I was equally sincere.

"You should see the other guy."

"Thanks for agreeing to see us, mind if we sit down."

I nodded at the long seat next to the rail. "Excuse me if I don't get up."

He managed a slight smile. "That's okay, we know all about your adventure last night. In fact that's why we're here. I'm Jack Pellegrino, head of the Central Intelligence Agency, and this is my assistant, Bob McCade."

I was mildly shocked. I was obviously out of the loop as far as who was running the spy business in Washington these days. "I expected a little scrawny nerdy kind of guy with a bald head and horn rimmed glasses."

He laughed. "That was my predecessor, and I appreciate your candor." When his jacket moved I could see the handle of the gun in a side holster under his armpit. He saw my eyes and explained. "I always carry a gun." He nodded with no smile. "Always."

I nodded. "I also usually try to have one nearby." I thought twice about it, and then pointed under the chair I was sitting in, what did it matter if they saw my hiding place. "My old man had a saying, 'It doesn't cost anything to be ready, but it could cost everything if you're not.'"

"I have armed bodyguards, but you need to be able to take care of yourself. In fact Bob here is serving dual purpose as my assistant and bodyguard. Unfortunately, the way it is with the world these days, the time might come when you may need to save the bodyguard."

Wasn't that the truth. I was a professional bodyguard and could've used a little saving myself last night, though I couldn't complain too much since I was the only one that was still alive.

"Why don't we get down to business," I said. "I'm sure your time isn't cheap. This is my fiancé, Amber. We're getting married in a couple of months and I'd like her to sit in on our meeting if you don't mind. She's my designated driver today."

"That's fine, this is all going to be very informal. The way I like to work is to get to know each other first and foremost. Then we can talk business if we still see any point in it. You see even though we're in the intelligence gathering field, you can't really get to know a person from a file."

I shrugged my shoulders. This was their show. "Myles, I mean Lieutenant Johnson said you were in Los Angeles on business and decided to take a special trip out here."

"My Mom's ninetieth birthday party. That's why we're all dressed up. It was a formal lunch at a nice hotel in the city. I was born and raised in Orange County and my mom never moved. She still lives in the same house I grew up in. I try to get out here to California every chance I get, which isn't often these days. I'm usually chained to a desk in Washington."

He was a California boy. I never would have guessed it. Looked like he grew up on a farm in the mid-west.

He glanced around the harbor and took a deep breath of the salt air and smiled. "This brings back great memories. I love it out here on Catalina." He continued. "So when I heard your story in this morning's briefing I jumped at the chance to come out and have a little talk with you. I spent a whole summer out here on the island when I was ten years old with an uncle who had a construction business, fixing up old houses. I'd help him with the small stuff, the drywall and painting, and in the evenings I'd explore the coastline with my fishing pole. And then he passed away and it was too tough to get out here. I tried a few times, caught the ferry a couple of times, but money was tight and the ride out here wasn't in the budget. That summer is etched on my memory banks like gold bars in Fort Knox, you know what I mean? Timeless."

"I kind of like it here myself."

"Funny how times change though. Now I can catch a ride out here on a fifty million dollar Navy helicopter anytime I want, only problem is I don't have any spare time in my life to stay here. Duty calls."

"Head of the CIA, how in the hell did you get there from here."

He smiled at that.

"Well, I was a pretty good basketball player in my day. Power forward for our High School team, went to the State Championships all four years, recruited by West Point, graduated with a double degree in mechanical and electrical engineering. Spent five years with the US Army's Fourth Infantry Division with one of those years in a platoon in a war zone, got out of the military then started an aerospace supply company in Kansas with a couple of patents that I designed, then I went into politics, got elected to Congress and served four terms, and last year the President called me up and asked if I could help out."

"You've been busy."

"I like to have a full plate in front of me. As Director of the CIA, I oversee a few key tasks to keep our country safe. Intelligence collection, analysis, covert action, counterintelligence, and various liaison relationships with foreign intelligence services both friend and foe."

"That's a big plate."

"It's as big as the whole world."

Whatever they wanted from me, I knew it wasn't going to work out for them, so I decided to lay it on the line right then and there. No need to pussyfoot around, I needed to let them down hard.

"I like small plates, and my resume isn't that glamourous. I started running with a local drug dealing gang when I was seventeen, dropped out of high school, then got volunteered into the Army by my Grandpa dragging me to the recruiters office by the scruff of my neck. Spent four years in a platoon which was also in an active battle zone for a year, got out and worked for a big security firm for about another year, till I quit that and started my own little company. I'm a one man band. I'm a loner in a way. I don't like working for big companies, I get a little claustrophobic."

"I understand. We're one of the, if not the biggest companies in the world."

"Oh yeah? What's your budget, and how many employees do you have?"

"Classified."

"I agreed to see you, but I'll tell you right now that whatever you're here to sell me isn't going happen, I'm not in the buying mood."

"Just hear me out. The fact is that even though we are one of the biggest companies in the world, most of our 'employees' are loners, just like you. They're independent contractors, and work on their own. As far as they and the rest of the world is concerned, our relationship does not exist. It has to be that way. For a lot of them, if our relationship was discovered, they would perish. Most times in unpleasant ways."

I knew the business model that they ran.

Most of their employees were in fact hidden in the shadows, gathering information and sending it off to their contacts who in turn sent it farther up the chain. And that information would sometimes be the most mundane facts and figures, things they'd seen or heard. News clippings, or scraps of paper from a waste bin that ended up in the trash. And all the little facts and figures were gathered up and collected into a big vat and boiled till it was a cohesive blob that could be deciphered, and used by the powers that be.

"You want me to be a spy."

He nodded. "Something like that."

He watched me for a moment to see it filter in to my brain, then he continued. "I made the special trip out here to see you for a specific reason. I didn't come out here on a whim, or to shoot the breeze. I think you might be able to help us, and in the process help your country."

"What if I say no."

"You haven't even heard my proposal."

"I'm just wondering why me."

"We know a lot about you."

"I wouldn't expect anything less. Do you have a file on me, and one on Amber?"

"Official policy of the CIA is to monitor and gather information on foreign entities, and we are forbidden by law to gather intelligence on the domestic activities of citizens of the United States, unless those individuals are suspected of involvement in foreign counter intelligence or terrorist activities."

"You didn't answer my question."

Of course he had a file. It was sitting right there in his assistants lap. Jack reached out his hand and Bob handed him the file. It was pretty thin.

"We have one on you right here, not on Amber. We ran a check on her, she's clean, and if not we wouldn't be sitting with you right now. But you can rest assured that there is a file somewhere on her, just not with me. Badger, I'm going to level with you, and this is something you probably already know. Everyone in the entire country has a file on them somewhere. Me, Bob, Lieutenant Johnson, the guy filling gas at the local station. There are other companies in the information gathering business, and even though their employee base isn't as large as ours, they have farther reaching tentacles, and use the info to make decisions on marketing, sales. It's just the way of the world that we live in."

Somehow that didn't make me feel assured. Everyone was either a suspect or a living breathing credit card waiting to be maxed out.

I took a deep breath and sighed.

"Alright, let's see what you have in that file on me."

He pulled out an eight by eleven glossy paper with ten neatly sized photos spaced evenly down the length of it. The first five photos were of the Chinese restaurant in Chinatown, I was at the front door heading inside, then I was sitting with my friend, Wang Lei having a discussion. Wang Lei didn't have a happy face. The next five photos were of Wang Lei with some other

Chinese looking dudes in various locations around the city. At a park, in front of a store, in a car. Someone was staking them out with a telephoto lens.

"That's Wang Lei with you. We're sure you know that. What you might not know is that he's been promoted to the number two man in a section of a local Triad."

"He pulled me out of a building and saved my life last year."

"We know that."

"I went there a couple of days ago to see if he had any information on the dead girl I found in the water last week. As you can see from the photos he wasn't very happy to see me."

"We know that too."

"Is there anything you don't know?"

"We know that one of the assassins that you killed last night was the Triad's number one hitman, and he was going to be used for a big job. All the chatter we're hearing is that the Triad is in big trouble, they lost their big gun, and now that he's gone, they don't know who they're going to bring in to finish the job. They're scrambling to bring in a replacement, they're distracted and vulnerable."

They wanted me to get information from my Chinese buddy.

"I don't know if you noticed, but 'ol Wang Lei hasn't exactly taken a liking to me."

"That's his nature."

"You know a lot about him."

"We gather intelligence. And we're pretty damned good at it."

Amber was sitting silent next to me, and raised her hand like she was in a classroom. We all looked at her as she spoke up.

"Umm, excuse me for intruding on the conversation, but since you said it's okay for me to be here, I have a couple of questions, like how dangerous is this job, potentially, and what's in it for Badger? And why do you think he can do the job in the first place, whatever it is. And why don't you ask a Chinese looking person who would fit in and not stick out like a sore thumb?"

She gently patted me on the hand.

"Your fiancé has a unique set of skills."

He pulled out another paper and read down a list from my Army days and some of the action in the big security firm.

"The first part is from your Army record in the war zone: disarmed a suicide bomber, took out a sniper, saved a child from a burning building. That was all in your first night on the perimeter. Then on other nights you repelled a grenade attack, tracked down a bomb making facility, rescued a company commander, and on one occasion prevented an ambush just by observation. Do you remember that one?"

"Sure I do," I said.

I thought back to that night. I'd forgotten about that tiny singular moment with everything else that happened since clouding it out of my memory banks, but they had it on record to remind me. One of those instances that happen suddenly in a war zone, where your reaction can mean life or death.

I continued: "I remember it, but I don't know

what it was exactly that caught my eye and made me stop our platoon from going forward. Maybe there was a swirl of dust, a reflection off a window, a flying bug that suddenly changed direction."

"All this occurred in a foreign country where you stuck out like a sore thumb a hell of a lot more than you do in this country," he finished.

Something I knew for certain was that in a lot of ways, a perimeter defense was the same whether you were in the middle of the city, or the middle of a dense jungle surrounded by wild animals all which wanted to eat you. Stay alert, and have enough firepower.

"You're part American Indian," he continued.

That comment rattled me, though I never showed it throughout my life whenever it was brought up in conversation.

"Yes. Why does that matter?"

"They kept you on the perimeter because you were the best at it, you kept your platoon out of trouble."

"More often than not."

"You're part American Indian, and that's why your parents named you after an animal, it's a tradition."

"Yes. My mother was half Cree Indian, so I'm a quarter. Why do you keep bringing that up?"

He kept reading. "Then when you worked for the security firm you prevented violence against a certain high profile client on three separate occasions, working the perimeter security team, three individuals with hand guns that never got close to that client."

I nodded, those events were still clearly in my memory. One was a simple robber who had no idea what he was getting into and that he was going to get disarmed and have his hand broken in the process, one was a disgruntled former employee who wanted revenge on the rich boss, and one was a professional hitman sent by a rival.

"Two of those guys were easy to spot."

"I could go on, but I think you get the idea."

"You forgot Gale Nighting."

"It's right here." He looked back down at the paper. "Your security team was ambushed and Gale was abducted. Every government and private company in the country was looking for her. Within two days, working on your own, you were able to track her down and save her."

"I got lucky."

"And then there's the two assassins last night. We've been looking for them for two years. Was that luck?"

I shrugged my shoulders.

"And you say I've been busy. Compared to what you've been up to, I've been living like a hermit in a cave. We've talked it over with some our best people. You have what we call in this business a natural instinct. There's only so much you can teach and train for, and at some point in time, for specifically important cases you find that you need people with that extra something, that something that can't be defined, or trained for."

Sometimes the path chooses you.

"This a volunteer position. If you want in,

we'll set you up with all the tools and info you need to get the job done. We'll provide money, weapons, high tech equipment, transportation, anything you need."

"I have everything I need."

He continued. "If you decline, we'll destroy your file. You go your way and we'll go ours."

He was hiding something. All of the small talk about my past and the Triad was a bluff, a counter-feint. Like jabbing in a boxing match before trying for the knock-out punch. He was still feeling me out before leveling with me. I could see it in his eyes, the way he was tilting his head slightly to the right, tension in his jaw.

"What is it that you really want? And don't give me some BS about the Triad and some mysterious replacement hitman."

He understood that I knew, and leaned forward. His voice got lower, the tone more even, serious. "Somebody stole something from a research facility in Palo Alto last week. We need to get it back."

"What kind of something?"

His eyes hardened. "Something that makes normal people do things they wouldn't normally do. We're in a bit of trouble here and could use your help."

I turned my head towards the island, looking towards the casino. Both the semi-trailer with the wrecked truck and the bulldozer had disappeared. One mess was swept up and gone, and another was looming in front of me.

"How much time do I have to give you an answer?"

"In this business, a single lost minute could make all the difference in the world."

"I can barely walk, I hope you have someone else as a back-up."

I saw the look in his eyes change.

"You do have other people working on this, I hope."

"Of course. We have to cover all the angles. But for this specific role, we've chosen you. You're the perfect candidate for the job, but there is absolutely no pressure at all. If you don't want it. We'll find someone else who may be less qualified and hope for the best. Take some time to think it over, recover from your injuries and let us know. I have to catch a flight back to Washington in about an hour. Bob here will be your contact, he's our bureau chief in Los Angeles."

He reached into his coat pocket and pulled out two cards and handed them to me. One of them had no name, no address, just ten numbers centered in the middle of the card, the top left corner was torn off. "This is my private cell phone number. Call me anytime. And this is Bob's card, call him if you decide to take the job."

I didn't have a pocket so I handed the cards to Amber.

"Alright, I'll think about it."

"There's one other thing."

"What's that?"

"You haven't asked about compensation."

"I haven't decided whether to work with you people yet. But I charge a thousand a day plus expenses whether I succeed or not."

"We'll up the ante for you. Your thousand a day plus expenses, and if you do succeed we'll pay you a quarter million. Tax free."

Now if anyone could pay you tax free it was the government. A quarter million was nothing to sneeze at. Unless you were getting shot to pieces for it.

My expression remained unchanged. If my gut didn't tell me to take a job, he could have said a billion and it wouldn't have mattered. What's a billion dollars if you're on the wrong side of right? What's a billion dollars if you're dead.

I reiterated. "I'll think about it."

He nodded then got up and handed the file to his assistant who also rose to his feet, then they both climbed aboard the cutter, the engines rumbled to life, water churning from the back engines as it headed to the dock.

I watched them the whole time as the boat cruised slowly away. The drumming of the diesel engines fading into the distance. Neither one of them looked back at me till the very end of their little journey, when they were just about at the dock. The chief looked back, just for a brief moment ours eyes met, then they were onto the dock and bustled into a police car for the trip back up the hill to the airport.

Amber looked me in the eyes.

"What do you think?"

I shook my head and watched the police car weave through pedestrian traffic in the center of town then head up the hill and disappear behind a maze of buildings.

"I don't know. Why does the biggest spy agency in the world need a two bit bodyguard like me to help them find something?"

The two bit bodyguard crack was an attempt to make light of the situation, but she didn't smile.

"What are you going to do?"

I could see the concern in her eyes.

"Don't worry. I'm not going to make any rash decisions. Right now I just need a nap."

She patted my hand gently as I eased into a long slumber.

2.

It was a typical Monday morning on the outskirts of San Francisco. A middle aged man parked his lime green electric car, and walked briskly through the fog towards the entrance of the subway system that would take him to his office in the city.

Everything about this day was as ordinary as ever. He woke at six, coffee at six ten, breakfast at six twenty, shower and shave at six thirty, parked the car at the park and ride at seven AM sharp. Everything about this day was as predictable as the rotation of the earth. And that's the way he liked it.

Ralph O'Neil was a systems analyst for one of the top software companies in the world, and he thrived on predictability. From the moment he opened his eyes in the morning, until he closed them at night his goal was to compartmentalize the world and everything in it into neat little boxes that could be counted, and be counted on.

He wasn't just a systems analyst for his company; he was a systems analyst for his life.

He glanced quickly at his watch as he strode

confidently towards the entrance. "Seven oh three," he said to himself and smiled. In exactly two more minutes he would be at the gate with ticket in hand waiting for the seven fifteen train. And, as he always said: "If you're not ten minutes early, you're late."

He passed a row of neatly trimmed bushes and suddenly and uncharacteristically stopped, for out of the corner of his eye he spotted a small stack of white paper under one of the shrubs.

"That's odd," he remarked with a frown, and bent down to pick it up. He flipped quickly through the pages and looked around to see if he could spot anyone who might have dropped them. The misty fog swirled through the parking lot, there was no one in sight, so he continued walking and flipped through the pages again. It was only fifteen pages long, single spaced courier twelve point font with a staple at the top left hand corner holding the pages together.

"It looks like a short story," he thought to himself as he looked around again, then shrugged his shoulders, put the papers in his briefcase and continued to the entrance.

The train was crowded, but since he was early he'd managed to find a seat. Throughout the cabin his fellow travelers were reading and texting on their phones, all quietly enraptured by the silent digital communication. Not a word was spoken throughout the train.

Ralph remembered the papers and pulled them out of his soft case. A few people looked at him askance. One frumpy woman with her hair tied at the top in a bunch frowned at the sight of the papers. She narrowed her eyes at him, but when he stared icily back, she looked away.

He began to read.

The story started slow, but picked up speed as the pages turned.

The train burrowed under the bay, hurtling through the tunnel towards the city as he read, sometimes laughing out loud, sometimes wanting to cry, and wiping away a slow tear. It was a good story, and he almost missed his stop because of it. He looked up just in time to see the Powell Street station and hustled out the doors before they closed with a hiss.

Powell Street was crowded with people heading to work. He checked his watch while hurrying down the street. Seven Forty. Perfect timing. Seven minutes to walk the two blocks to his office building, a three minute elevator ride, and he'd be sitting at his desk ten minutes early as usual. It was a fairly easy walk through the streets since in this part of town no cars were allowed. He thought about reading the story as he walked, but decided it wasn't safe. There weren't any cars, but there were too many bicycles weaving in and out of the pedestrians, you had to be on your toes, or you'd get run over.

When he was safely situated in his office and sitting at his desk, he pulled out the papers and began reading again where he'd left off.

Since I'm ten minutes early, he reasoned, I'll read for ten more minutes, and start my work on time.

The office was quiet and he was able to read in peace, completely enraptured by the story.

The Pacific Coast Highway winds along nearly the entire California coast from Mendocino County in the north to Dana Point in the south. At one stretch of highway just south of San Francisco, the road edges precariously close to the cliffs with the ocean looming below. Motorists are protected from plunging off the cliff by a six foot thick concrete barrier that runs along the edge of the road.

The police car was parked by the side of the barrier, its lights flashing to warn approaching cars. On the other side of the barrier was a hundred foot sheer cliff that went straight down and ended on a boulder strewn beach. The heavy smell of salt, seaweed and fog filled the air. The tide was high and the kelp lined waves surged onto the boulders. When the waves receded, the rocks rolled with a crescendo.

Officer Macklin peered over the cliff at the scene below. It was a cold foggy morning and he could just barely make out the figures moving on the rocks. They stopped near a sprawled figure and his radio crackled with static, then a voice came across clear as a bell.

"You there Mack?"

"Right here."

"We've reached the victim, over."

"And?"

"He's definitely dead, no doubt about that. Severe trauma from the fall most likely."

"Any ID on the guy?"

"His driver's license says he's Ralph O'Neil, home address just outside Oakland. He's got a business card that says he's a systems analyst for a company in San Francisco."

"Ten four. Let's get the basket in there and get the poor guy out of there."

The Coast Guard helicopter that was hovering over the ocean slowly maneuvered until it was directly over the figures and lowered the basket.

"Poor bastard", officer Macklin muttered. "I wonder what happened."

He walked over to his squad car, opened the trunk, and pulled out a black case. Inside the case was a CSI kit, including a camera, fingerprint tape, assorted hermitically sealed bags and tools for retrieving evidence. He put on some new plastic gloves and got to work.

A lime green electric car was parked in front of his squad car.

Officer Macklin thoroughly photographed it from every angle, gently lifted fingerprints from every surface, then searched the perimeter for evidence. He bagged cigarette butts, candy wrappers, beer cans, soda caps, even an old diaper.

"Damn litterbugs", he muttered.

Once he had the evidence secure in the trunk, he turned his attention to the interior of the car. He saw that the latch was up, but before he opened the driver's side door he got his little mirror on a stick and looked at every nook and cranny under the car, the shocks, the wheels, the door hinges, everything.

"Can't be too careful."

Ten years ago some crackpot was booby trapping cars with C-4 explosives and leaving them abandoned in front of banks and police stations, blowing up unsuspecting tow truck drivers and traffic cops. They never caught the perp, and now this was normal operating procedure.

He got out the PBSD, the 'Portable Bomb Sniffing Device' and whiffed it around the vehicle. Finally satisfied that it was safe, he slowly opened the driver's side door and repeated the procedure with the mirror on a stick under the seats, and a PBS whiff of the interior. All clean.

A soft briefcase was on the passenger's seat and he opened the side flap. The usual. A cell phone, sunglasses, and a laptop computer. He opened the other flap.

"Well, what do we have here?"

He pulled out the papers neatly stapled on the top left corner.

"Looks like a story." He started to read it.

After a while the tow truck pulled up and backed in front of the lime green car. Officer Macklin was now sitting on the concrete barrier completely engrossed in his reading, and barely noticed the tow truck.

The driver whistled loudly snapping Officer Macklin out of his trance. He looked up with a frown.

"It's all clear, you can take it to the station."

"Must be interesting!" laughed the driver as he hooked onto the car's front bumper.

Officer Macklin didn't respond. He put the briefcase in the trunk of the squad car and drove off.

The story was sitting on the passenger seat as he headed back to the precinct station.

"Well it is an interesting story," he thought as he drove while glancing over at the papers. "And it's strange, since I'm not a real fan of reading stories of any kind. After a hard day at work all I want to do is eat, watch some sports, and sleep."

His eyes kept hovering over to the page on the passenger seat.

"I have to read the end of that story," he thought.

He pulled over to the side of the road.

The staccato clap of gunfire echoed through the city, broken at times by a loud explosion.

Golden rays of the impending sunset bathed the city in an unearthly glow, and the San Francisco Police Station was under attack.

Sirens filled the air as squad cars raced to the scene. A police helicopter circled overhead, while black smoke billowed from burning cars and buildings.

Officer Macklin sprinted from an alley and took up position behind an abandoned trolley car. The pop of large caliber weapons shattered the windows and tail lights of the trolley, and he crouched by the wheel well and covered his head with his arms to avoid the flying glass.

He counted to three, took a deep breath, and

then leaped into the open, his AK47 on full automatic spraying hot lead in all directions.

Bullets ricocheted all around him kicking up asphalt, metal and glass. He felt a sharp pain in his ankle and he rolled back under the trolley.

He clicked the mic on his chest and yelled into it. "This is Officer Macklin. I'm hit!"

His radio crackled back in return. "Mack, this is Captain Ross, do you hear me? It's Captain Ross! Give yourself up Mack! Lay down your weapon before any more people get hurt. Something's wrong Mack. We need to get you to a Doctor!"

Officer Macklin was sobbing and squeezing the tears out of his eyes as he re-loaded, the mic on his chest still recording.

"No, no, no, no, no, no, no, no, no."

Captain Ross switched channels on his radio. "Alright take him out."

The helicopter came low over a building and swung into position. The police sniper hanging out the window had a clear shot and squeezed the trigger.

Officer Macklin lay still on the ground. Swat team officers on the ground swarmed the trolley, the lead man kicking the rifle out of Mack's hands and checking his pulse.

"He's dead." Then he shook his head in disbelief. "What the hell happened?"

Dr. Herman Castle was on his way to his research lab when the shooting started. He was herded into a nearby bar and grill by the police who barricaded the door. He and about twenty others huddled under the pool tables as the carnage unfolded on the street outside. The staccato bursts of gunfire lasting over half an hour.

When it was finally over, they were led out the back entrance and offered counseling and coffee, and a ride to their destination. He declined. It was all quite a nuisance. He needed to get to his lab right away. A timed experiment was nearing completion and he needed to measure the data.

He walked briskly down the sidewalk in the deepening shadows when something caught his eye. Square and white sitting neatly against a wall was a small stack of papers held together by a single staple. With no time to waste he picked it up and continued on his way.

The environmental research laboratory was located adjacent to the Medical Center at Mount Zion just a few blocks to the west. Dr. Castle was recently awarded a research grant to study the Eisenia kelp. Certain enzymes in the kelp were showing potential building blocks for a miracle drug. This was a unique opportunity and he vowed to make the most of it. His lab was lined with the most advanced chemical and microscopic analysis equipment available.

He placed the stapled papers that he'd picked up from the street on his desk, and proceeded to measure the kelp data.

Twenty minutes later, the data input was complete and his eyes wandered to the stack of papers that he'd picked up.

"Okay, now what about you?"

He picked up the papers and leafed through them.

"It appears to be some sort of prose."

He read the first few paragraphs, and noticed something strange. The lights in the lab being very bright and monochromatic seemed to give a shine to the printed words. He held the first page up and rocked it back and forth under the lighting.

"What type of ink could they be using to make it shine like that?"

He opened a drawer in the desk and pulled out a magnifying glass, and studied some letters closely.

"It looks... metallic." He brought the papers over to a table with a laser optical microscope and placed it under the lens. "Okay, let's see what you're made of."

This particular microscope was designed to map the topography of the smallest of cells, and he had no doubt he could get to the bottom of the mysterious shine compound of this ink. He shifted the paper to line up one of the letters with the laser and locked it into place.

He peered through the eyepieces and focused the knob, and the image became clear at one thousand magnification. He was looking at a miniature structure, a myriad of odd shaped squares and rectangles that were filled with parallel lines and set together like an intricate puzzle.

"Why this is impossible," he muttered. "It's

some sort of microchip."

The man with a thick face, short white hair and wraparound sunglasses stared emotionless out of the mirrored glass window towards the city below.

"And the testing is going well?" he asked.

The darkened shuttered room was empty save for a large stainless steel desk in the middle. At the desk sat a small round man with thick reading glasses. A single laptop computer was sitting on the desk. The small man was staring intently at the screen.

"Very well indeed. We've had three subjects perform whatever task they've been instructed. And we've evaded detection so far."

"Let's keep it that way," replied the man at the window.

"Using paper as our testing platform was genius. We're off the grid. Out of sight," said the small man.

"Yes, out of sight," repeated the man at the window.

"To think," said the small man. "It was only a year ago the development team created this electronic hypnotic device. And only last month they were able to create micro circuits using ink as the trace element. We've come a long way very quickly"

"Yes, we are moving quickly," agreed the man at the window.

"It's just amazing how the human brain

functions," continued the small man. "When a person is reading and concentrating, and the brain is interpreting words and symbols into a cohesive understandable language within their mind, it's like a window is opened in the brain, and subtle invisible suggestions from an outside source can be used to make that person dance like a puppet."

"Yes, that is amazing," agreed the man at the window.

"If we wanted, we could create micro circuits that are part of a viewing screen for computers, and reading devices. We could control the entire world."

The man at the window was motionless and made no comment.

"When are we heading back to DC?" asked the small man.

"For now, the less you know about that, the better," said the man at the window. "Let's concentrate on the task at hand."

"Right, right," said the small man as he continued to stare at the screen.

Compartmentalize. Do your job. Don't worry about the other cogs in the wheel.

He was only responsible for one part of the testing, and although he had an inkling of an idea who it was, he did not know for certain who was giving the subjects their final instructions.

Some psychotic masochist for all he knew, since they all ended up killing themselves, and sometimes everyone around them.

The man at the window shifted his gaze to a commotion on the street below. A crowd had gathered around the bank. He turned away from the window and walked towards the door.

"Keep testing. I want to see how far we can push this."

A young mother with a baby in a stroller and a toddler holding her hand are on the outskirts of a crowd that has gathered outside the Bank of America. A crazy looking man in a lab coat is standing on top of a cement wall throwing money into the air.

"Take it all! Take it all!"

He threw another fist full into the air while the crowd yelled with delight as the bills fluttered in the wind towards them.

"What's going on," the bewildered young mother asked a security guard standing nearby.

The guard shook his head. "Some poor nut that guy is. He emptied out his bank account about fifteen minutes ago, twenty five thousand dollars in assorted bills I heard. He's gonna get arrested for causing a riot."

"My goodness, twenty five thousand dollars? Can't anyone stop him?"

"Well I guess it's a free country Miss, plus that mob would tear anybody apart who tried to stop him. If you ask me I think he's lost his mind. You better stand back Miss, you and the little ones might get trampled by that crowd."

"Don't worry, we're not going anywhere near them," as she moved away down the sidewalk.

She stopped to pick up a five dollar bill that

had gone unnoticed from the crowd. It had floated down from the sky and was wedged in a small hedge. And that's when she saw the stack of papers under the bushes. She plucked the five dollar bill out of the hedge, quickly placed it in her purse, then crouched down and picked up the papers.

"What is it Mommy?" asked the toddler.

"I don't know. It's some sort of story."

"What's it say Mommy?"

She looked at the front page. "Well, the title says Quick Read."

She carefully wedged the pages into the back pocket of the stroller and hugged the toddler then kissed him on his cheek. "I'll read it when you two are napping."

A light rain began to fall. She saw the dark clouds forming towards the west over the ocean, heading inland.

"We'd better get going." She patted the toddler on the head. "Looks like a storm is coming."

3.

I slept for two days. It was all a blur. Every now and then I'd pry myself with Amber's help off the bed and hobble around like a crippled old man, use the bathroom, get a drink of water and a bite of food, then crawl back under the blankets.

By the end of the third day my kidneys had stabilized and I stopped pissing traces of blood. Most of the pain in my bones had seeped away, replaced by a strange deep itching.

"That's normal," said Amber, ever the nurse. "The injured tissue is replicating itself as scar tissue and the natural sensation makes you want to itch it. Don't, okay?"

I shrugged my shoulders and obeyed.

We sat in the cockpit of the Spice as the sun went down in the west and I had the first solid meal in what seemed like a week.

"Do you feel able to take the boat back to Dana Point," she asked.

I nodded. "Yes. I feel pretty much well enough to drive the boat back. But I think I'll stay here for another couple of days. If that's okay with you."

"It's okay with me. I should probably get back to work though if you're feeling able to fend for yourself."

"I can manage nurse." She loved her job at the hospital, and was good at it. And I knew the one thing she missed the most.

"I can't let all those babies be born without me."

"I guess I was your big baby for a couple of days."

"Big snoring baby with a beard." She was quiet for a moment, but the question had to be asked. "What are you going to do about the CIA?"

"That's why I want to stay here for a little while longer. I have a decision to make. I'm not quite sure what to do yet."

Not much more needed to be said. She knew what I had to do while I was still fairly young and able. I wasn't cut out for a normal nine to five job; Monday to Friday and the weekends off; a low paying but steady paycheck with health benefits and a company matching 401k, barbecuing in the backyard with my buddies on Sunday afternoons, slowly getting a sagging beer belly, drooping jowls, and grey hair, while my only forward thought was retirement and being able to take long naps every day. Aiming for the sublime.

I would make it on my own terms, or die trying. Maybe it was reckless. Selfish.

Whatever it was that drove me was relentless

at times. I was a loner there was no doubt about that, I had no need to confide in anyone about anything, except where Amber was concerned. I needed her in my life, but we had an agreement; I'd pursue the high risk cases only when my gut feeling told me I had to. She would let me do what I had to do. And I knew I got the better part of the bargain.

The money was no consideration to the need of the individual for my help. I would forego any pay, on any day of the year if my gut feeling told me it would help an individual or group survive.

None of us will be here forever anyways so might as well do the best you can while you're here was my motto. But it seemed that if there was ever money involved, the danger factor increased exponentially.

You could get robbed for a dollar in the middle of the city with your life at risk, and it might be just as dangerous as digging around in the muck of humanity trying to find stolen goods by the bad guys.

The United States Government in the form of the CIA was willing to pay me half a million dollars to find something that was stolen, and they wouldn't tell me exactly what it was until I agreed to help them.

Not exactly the ideal business relationship to get started in, but they were spies, secretive in nature and necessity. Their corporate strategy was in the shadows, and it worked for them.

Half a million in cash would go a long way to helping us get to the next level, Amber and I. We had the two boats but we needed a house. Then we might be able to think about settling down just a bit and have kids before it was too late.

I couldn't say without lying that I was the best guy in the world for her. She'd be better off in the long run with someone like a doctor from the hospital. Someone who mended people, not someone who put them there.

She could tell by the look in my eyes. She knew what I was thinking.

"Look Badge. We've been together for two years and it seems like forever. You don't have to tell me anything. Just tell me when you think you might be coming home."

"This one might be more than a couple of days."

"As long as it's not more than a couple of weeks, and as long as you don't get hurt again, okay?"

The next morning she was gone. She took a shore boat to the island and caught a helicopter back to the mainland. Back to the real world. Before she left she made a quick trip to the general store at Avalon, and stocked the fridge with fresh vegetables. I had enough canned food on board to last a year.

I got out my laptop and sat with it in the lounge chair in the cockpit. I had a satellite link with high speed internet. I started looking through the news stories of the past week. I'd been out of action for a while and need to catch up.

It was the usual stuff. Wars in the middle east. Gridlock in Washington. Disasters in Asia. Little stuff compared to the cities on the mainland USA. There were multiple shootings, robberies, crashes, mobs running wild through malls and public spaces. Tornados, wildfires, earthquakes, floods.

"I should have stayed in bed."

There was a voice in the back of my head: Someone stole something in Palo Alto.

I started looking deeper at some of the little stories in and around the bay area.

A well-known scientist emptied his bank account and threw it off the top of a building causing a riot. He was finally captured, sedated and taken to a hospital, unable to speak and in a walking coma.

A decorated cop and family man goes berserk and attacks his precinct with grenades and automatic weapons that he steals from the evidence locker, then is killed by a swat team sniper. The cause of his disturbance is under investigation.

A young mother leaves her children in their stroller and jumps two hundred and twenty feet high from the Golden Gate bridge into the San Francisco bay, and miraculously survives, rescued by a passing fishing boat. Witnesses describe the woman holding the children over the edge of the bridge, ready to throw them over, when she abruptly placed them back in their strollers and flailed in the air as though she was fighting off a swarm of bees, or something invisible attacking her. Restrained and sedated now in a hospital bed she claims that she has no memory of the event.

I looked up from the computer screen and

rubbed my eyes.

One of the rarest events in humanity is a mother harming her children. There was some inherent trait, a connection between a mother and her children that transcended everything. Carrying them in her womb for nearly a year, feeling their heartbeat along with her own.

And it wasn't a trait that was specific to humans either. Most animals on the planet, the mothers of the species especially seemed to have a protecting force surrounding her off-spring.

Try to get near a black bear cub with the mother nearby and see what happens.

I thought back to an event that I witnessed many years ago, and could never quite shake. I was driving on a semi deserted highway with just a few cars travelling in either direction.

On the other side of the road, just inside the opposing lane near the shoulder was a mother hen with a gaggle of little chicks staying close to her as they made their way to safety, just a few feet away.

Barreling towards them in the opposite lane from me was a car doing at least sixty in a forty mile per hour zone. The driver either didn't see the mother hen with chicks or just decided they weren't worthy enough to slow down or avoid. The car seemed to speed up.

The mother hen sensed immediate danger and rather than flee to save herself, gathered her little chicks around her folding her wings over them. A split second later the car ran them all down. In the rear view mirror all I saw was a burst of feathers. Yet in my mind I can still see the mother hen gently folding her wings over her chicks before they all perished into the abyss.

Somehow, the woman on the bridge was the mother hen, protecting her chicks.

I looked deeper at the three stories, pulling up different newspaper accounts of the events.

Taking a pen and my little pocket note pad from the side pouch of my chair I wrote down the times and locations.

I made a split screen and pulled up a map of the city, and zoomed in on the first location.

Officer Macklin broke into the precinct's evidence room at forty two fifty Powell street at around four o'clock on Friday afternoon. A half hour later at four thirty, after five officers were killed and fifteen wounded, he was killed by a swat team sniper.

Dr. Herman Castle withdrew twenty five thousand dollars in hundred dollar bills at five o'clock at thirty eight twenty Pine avenue, which is three blocks from Powell street. At five thirty he was arrested for causing a public disturbance and admitted to a local mental hospital.

Kimberly O'Donnell, twenty eight years old, threw herself off the Golden Gate Bridge over San Francisco Bay at six o'clock. She was over a mile away from her apartment and just two blocks from the bank on Pine street.

Three separate events. All within two hours of each other, and all within a few city blocks. A cop, a scientist, and a young mother.

Somebody stole something that makes normal people do things they wouldn't normally do.

It was the mother and her babies that got me.

If I could go back in time and stop that car that ran over the mother hen and her chicks I would try. Even though it was in the past it's something you don't forget.

If I could stop that car I would. I could still see it in slow motion. Gentle wings over the baby chicks. The burst of feathers. Anguish at the senselessness of it all.

Now, in a way, there was another car barreling down the highway, about to do harm to innocents. This time it was people in the way. This time maybe I had an opportunity to stop it.

I went downstairs to look for my phone and the business card with a ten digit phone number.

4.

I made a deal with the Coast Guard to leave my boat in the harbor at Avalon for a couple of days, or weeks if needed. They had a special rate they afforded me since I helped them solve a big case.

It would save a couple of days if I could just leave it there and fly straight to the mainland. I needed to get a jumpstart on these leads.

If anything happened to me someone could drive it back to Dana Point and Amber could sell it. I had a provision in my life insurance policy to pay for any and all equipment to be returned to my base of operations at Dana Point Harbor.

That provision, the so called 'just in case' provision was something that everybody needed, not just me. Even the guy going to work at his accounting job on the fifth floor of a nameless building in any town USA needed a just in case provision.

You never knew for sure when your time was up. And there was no need to unnecessarily burden those around you. Be prepared.

It was time to head into the unknown.

I had nothing to go on except for a couple of news stories that happened a few days ago.

That, and a gut feeling.

I double checked the anchor lines, buttoned down the main hatch and waited on the stern for the shore ferry to come alongside.

While I was waiting I called Amber on her cell phone. She answered on the third ring.

"Where are you now?" I asked.

"At work, making the rounds, checking on patients."

"Any new babies?"

"Yeessss."

I could almost see the smile on her face over the phone signal.

"How many today?"

"Two girls and one boy, and we have another due any hour now."

At the maternity ward they counted their time in babies and hours.

"Is the one you're waiting on a boy or girl?"

Two girls and one boy so far, I was hoping the odds would even out.

"They didn't want to know, wanted it to be a surprise."

Something I never understood. With all the technology in the world, why wouldn't you want to know what to prepare for. Pink walls or blue walls in the nursery.

"So why'd you call? Miss me?"

I could sense the tension on the other end of the line when she asked if I was going to miss her, the inflection of her voice changed. She knew exactly why I called.

"Yes, of course I always miss you. And I'm going to have to miss you for a little while longer I'm afraid."

"You're taking the job."

Resigned acknowledgement.

"Yeah, well of course I thought it over. I can't say no to this one. Did some research. Found out about some things that are happening." I didn't want to tell her bad things were happening, didn't want to pile on the worry. Kept it simple at 'things are happening'. "Maybe there's a slight chance I can help."

"Gotta do what you gotta do."

"Remember the talk we had."

I knew she was nodding her head on the other end of the line. We had plenty of talks over the past couple of years, endless long discussions, long winding eloquent journeys of ideas revolving around life, the universe and everything in between. The kind of talks you have with your best friend, all-nighters till the sun comes up, until the time comes when sometimes you really don't even need to talk anymore, silence between you is good enough and just being nearby is sufficient conversation.

Yes, we'd had plenty of talks. But there was one particular talk we had about what to do when I was ready to embark on a job. And what to do while I was away on that job. The precautions to take. The possibility that I might not make it back, or if something went wrong that someone may try to blackmail her, or worse.

The business I'd embarked upon was rough.

A walking talking, bomb sniffing human bullet proof vest. Private secret service protection without the frills. Bodyguard to the rich and famous. If I ever had to take someone under the radar to protect them, the unscrupulous characters of the world who would do anything, just might.

I owned the two boats, the Sugar, a thirty eight foot sailboat, and the Spice, the thirty two foot power boat, with two slips in my name at Dana Point Yacht Harbor.

Amber's apartment was in her name alone, so if someone tried to find me, they wouldn't find my name on the city ledger or in the phone book at that address. But she was a known quantity in my life, whenever I wasn't working and she wasn't at the hospital, we were together and you could not hide the obvious.

'The talk' centered on what to do if and when I disappeared for a while. Which was soon to happen. I was about to take a helicopter from Avalon, and had a flight booked from LA to San Francisco that evening. After that it was the great unknown.

I tried to prepare her both mentally and physically. Trained her in a few martial arts moves, a couple of simple arm bars and bone breaking twists, which was good to know regardless if I was going underground. We lived in Southern California for crying out loud. Took her to the firing range. Travelled to my old Kung Fu instructor who, over ninety years old , small and wizened did not teach us any physical defense moves, but instead taught us in the metaphysical. The strange realm beyond human understanding. He was always talking about the path, the golden or rocky road that you think that you, and you alone choose, to cast off your over-riding ego, that sometimes it's the path that chooses you.

I heard the tiniest of sniffles on the other end, then a calm voice. She laughed a bit at the absurdity of it all.

"I feel like you're a paratrooper getting ready to parachute behind enemy lines in World War Two."

"I'm flying to LA in just a while on a top of the line helicopter, then up to San Francisco in a commercial jetliner. After that I'm not sure. Maybe I'll find a used donkey and ride up into the hills."

She giggled. That was good.

"Don't worry. I'll be okay, I'm just going to go up there, catch a cable car, eat some clam chowder down at Fisherman's Wharf and look around a little. See what I can find. You never know, I might come across a big bag of gold just sitting in the street. All lonely and needing a home."

"I just wish you'd call me at least once to let me know you're okay."

"You have the phones I gave you tucked away?"

"Safe and secure."

"Get them out, make sure they're charged up, then tuck them away again. They're good for one call." Something I didn't need to tell her, and I wasn't sure why I even mentioned it. I bought three burner phones just in case. Use them once and throw them away. Untraceable. As long as you only used them once. Any more than that and you were a target.

"What about your other best friend?" I asked her.

"She's great. I called the other day. Misses me of course. When you get back we'll go visit."

Her other best friend was really her first best friend, her eighty year old Grandma who raised her from a baby. And Grandma's house was the safe house. Tucked into the foothills of the Sierra Nevada, the nearest home a mile away. Grandma was still a pretty good shot. Old school, she learned to hunt down in old Mexico to feed her family, and still kept a couple of long guns nearby in case a bobcat or coyote tried to hassle her.

If the stuff really hit the fan, Amber could drop everything, head straight there and be safe.

We had a little game, silly actually, like school kids.

"You hang up first," she'd say.

"No, you hang up first," I'd reply.

And it went on and on, but now with the shore boat laying alongside, it was time to go, and she knew it, could hear the motors and the squeak of the rail guards.

"See you later," she whispered.

I never said goodbye, didn't like it. She beat me to it.

"See you later," were my last words and I pushed the red button ending the call.

I threw my bag to the boat driver, then

climbed over the rail into the little dingy. Holding back my grimaces.

I patted the rail of the Sugar and shoved her away from us, the little motor of the dingy ratatattating towards the dock.

Like a one man troop transport, taking me to the airport.

I watched from the back of the dingy as the Sugar faded from view, getting farther and farther away till it disappeared behind the edge of the shoreline dock. I was leaving the safety and security of my home, getting ready to drop in behind enemy lines.

5.

"We have a problem."

The man at the window, looking out at the city spread before him nodded. "Yes."

"Our little experiment in San Francisco didn't go as well as planned."

"No it didn't."

"Two out of four are not very good odds. Not for what we have planned, are they?"

"No, they're not."

"Two out of four did exactly as they were told, and destroyed themselves. And then there's the other two. One of them, the scientist, was captured before he could throw himself off the building, so we don't know if that could have been a success. But the woman with her children. She was supposed to jump off the bridge while holding her children, wasn't she?"

"Yes, those were the instructions she was given."

"Something is missing in the inhibitor block."

"Yes."

"We only have one chance at this. If we fail, we'll both wish we'd never been born."

"We won't fail then."

"The first two are dead, so we don't have to worry about them. But what about the woman, and the scientist? Where are they?"

"The scientist is under sedation, in the psychiatric ward of a San Francisco hospital. He can't, or won't speak. He appears to be in a walking coma."

"And the woman?"

"She's coming in and out of an actual coma, head trauma. The report is that she's in serious yet stable condition and is expected to survive."

"I don't want either one of them to somehow remember what happened."

"Understood."

"Get a team over there and take care of the situation."

6.

The guard at the entrance to the hospital nodded acknowledgement as I limped through the front doors. With scuff marks on my face and hands, and the way I was hobbling, I still looked like I'd been run over by a truck, which was nearly true. By the look on his face he felt empathy for me, and probably thought I was going to see my doctor, or check in to the ER. He didn't bother me or ask me any questions, just let me keep going on my un-merry way.

I gave him a little salute and keep hobbling towards the bank of elevators. There was a large plexiglass covered black plaque next to the elevators containing an alphabetical list of departments, and locations in neat white letters.

There it was. Third floor. Psychiatric unit.

The elevator door nearest to me opened and a petite young nurse rolled out a white haired old man who was wrapped in a blanket. She nodded to me and smiled. Looked like the old man was going out to get a breath of fresh air before he expired.

I stepped into the elevator, pushed the

number three button and listened as the car gently rose up through the shaft.

One funny thing about hospitals is how brightly lit they are. At times it almost felt as though you were actually inside of a lightbulb. Even though you'd think that someone suffering a mental breakdown would need to have the lights toned down, the third floor psych ward was no different.

The nurse's station was front and center as you exited the elevator. The desk was empty. The corridors leading in both directions were also empty. I stepped over to the desk and looked over the edge. There was a list of rooms with the patients name written in ink.

Herman Castle. Room three twenty eight.

The way this hospital was set up, it was down to the right and on the left hand side of the hallway. I waited, and watched.

Three long minutes went by and still no nurse.

I considered just walking down the hallway and knocking on room three twenty eight, but thought better of it. Might as well wait. I heard the click of a door and saw movement. A man in a white lab coat, with a stethoscope hanging around his neck, pens and a laminated ID on his front pocket, and a clipboard in his right hand exited room three twenty eight. He moved smooth and methodical, gently closing the door behind him and glanced down the hallway at me.

He had black, close cropped hair, dark eyes, chiseled features. The glance was quick. He turned his back to me and wrote on his clipboard for a moment, then walked away down the corridor towards the end where there was a red neon sign above a heavy metal door that read: EXIT.

He opened the door and went down the stairs, his shoes echoing on the metal steps until the door closed with a click behind him, then all was silent again.

There was the rattle of a cart as it exited a room to my left and two nurses came into view, startled to see me waiting there.

Both nurses were middle aged with kind eyes and short curly brown hair that was held in check on the sides with bobby pins that had little plastic colorful flowers on them.

They could have been sisters for all I knew.

"I'm sorry sir, I hope you haven't been waiting long," said the taller of the two. She went behind the desk and checked the lights on the board. All were green. "I'm sorry usually we have someone at the desk at all times, but one of our patients fell out of bed and it took the both of us to help her back up."

"I've only been here three minutes at the most," I said.

"Are you here to visit a patient?"

"Yes, I'd like to see Dr. Herman Castle if that's okay."

"Are you a friend, or family?"

"We work together at the lab." I showed her one of my fake IDs. "Is he doing alright?"

"Well, he had a rough experience as you probably know. He's been pretty heavily sedated."

"Would it be okay to just pop in to take a look at him?"

Her eyes softened. "Why certainly honey."

This is the kind of attitude, I thought, that a nurse needs on a floor such as this, where a lot of the pain that someone is feeling, is on the inside, invisible to the rest of the world.

As we walked towards the door I noticed her white tennis shoes with the soft bottoms. They didn't make a sound.

She stopped at the door and turned towards me. "We have him on a vitals monitor, he's sedated and probably sleeping, but just in case."

She knocked softly on the door before opening it and walking into the room.

I waited till she was all the way through the doorway, then followed. He looked so peaceful. Eyes closed. The muscles in his face relaxed, head slumped back into the pillow. An intravenous tube snaked down from a bag of clear fluid hanging on a hook next to the bed and ended on his wrist. It was tightly bandaged.

"Oh my God," she muttered. "The monitor is shut off." She rushed into the room and placed her stethoscope on his neck. "He's not breathing." She pressed the big red button on the wall, the alarm that would ring at the front desk and in the Emergency Room downstairs. She pressed another button and spoke quickly into the intercom. "Stat, room three twenty eight." Then she tore the bedsheet off his chest and began to give him CPR.

Quick footsteps down the hallway and the

other nurse came into the room to assist. I could hear the ding of the elevator as it opened at this floor, then more footsteps as a three man army crowded into the room. I made way for them and backed out of the door into the hallway, while still watching the action.

They were quick and efficient, opening up his gown to expose the flesh on his chest, then placed one of the defibrillator paddles over the top left side of his chest, and the other on the right lower side, with the heart in the middle.

"Clear!" shouted the tech. A jolt of electricity bolted his body off the bed. The nurse listened through the stethoscope at the vein on his neck.

"No," she said clearly, then backed away to give the tech room.

He repeated the procedure.

"Clear!" he shouted, and the body jolted off the bed again.

The nurse listened for a moment and shook her head. "No."

It was time for me to leave. He was dead. Of that I was certain. The guy in the lab coat that looked like a doctor must have done something, and turned the vitals machine off so no one would notice. I took another close look at the bag of fluid that fed the tube into his arm. Something untraceable could have been inserted into the bag.

I headed for the red exit sign and pushed through the heavy door, carefully in case someone was lurking behind it waiting to ambush me.

The coast was clear and I limped down the

stairs till I was at the ground level. When I pushed out the door I was right next to the security officer.

He nodded at me, with a quizzical look on his face. "Shouldn't you be taking the elevator in your condition?"

"I'm trying to get back in shape."

"You're the second guy in the past three minutes to tell me that."

"That's my buddy. I was trying to catch up with him." I nodded towards the front door. "Did he go this way?"

"Yeah, it looked like he got into a car out in the parking lot and they took off. Looks like they left you behind."

"That's okay, I've got my own car. By the way, did you see what kind of car it was?"

He shrugged his shoulders.

"Looked like a big black SUV. But it's dark out there, it could have been brown or blue for all I know."

I continued limping out the doorway trying not to make it look like I was in a hurry.

I had to get to the other hospital with the woman who jumped from the bridge.

7.

Saint Mary's Medical Center is located on the corner of Fulton and Stanyan Street, about three miles as the crow flies from the Golden Gate Bridge. It took ten minutes to get there. I spent another two or three minutes looking for a parking space, then gave up and left the car in a tow away zone.

I was travelling light and had everything I needed. My watch read seven thirty on the dot.

Keeping to the shadows, pulling my cap down, and the collar of my shirt up, I found my way to the front entrance. There was a guard at the inside corner of the doors, he glanced up at me for a moment, then back down at the newspaper he was reading. A receptionist was sitting at a desk in the middle of the lobby. She saw me as I walked in and didn't take her eyes off as I made my way over.

She smiled uneasily, probably worried about my bruised face, and what type of trouble caused it.

"Can I help you?" she asked.

"Yes, I'm here to see Kimberly O'Donnell.

She's a patient here."

"Hmm," she whispered and scrunched her forehead. "That sounds familiar."

She typed the name into her computer. I saw her facial expression change. "She's..." She was unable to complete the sentence.

I leaned closer and spoke softly so my words wouldn't carry. "She's the one who jumped off the bridge yesterday."

She winced. "Oh."

"I'm her brother."

"Yes, let me call upstairs." She dialed an extension number on the phone. It was a four digit number that started with the number five. Most likely the fifth floor.

She spoke quietly into the mouthpiece, but just loud enough that I could hear.

"Is it okay to send the Kimberly O'Donnell's brother up to see her. Very well. Thank you, I'll let him know." She hung up the phone. "The nurse said to wait twenty minutes. A specialist is scheduled to visit her right now. She's in room five one oh two."

"Fine, thank you. I'll get a cup of coffee in the dining room. Where is it please?"

She pointed behind her. I thanked her and walked that way.

Twenty minutes. I didn't have twenty minutes. Margaret didn't have twenty minutes. I headed towards the dining room, glanced behind me to see that the receptionist had moved onto a new task and was busy looking down at her desk, then made a detour into the stairwell and started climbing up.

I had to stop for a moment on the third floor stairwell, with my heaving breathing the two broken ribs on the lower right side felt like someone was sitting on me. The next two floors went quicker.

As I popped my head around the corner to look down the hallway I could see a nurse exit a room and head back to the floor desk.

Someone was in distress nearby. The sound of a gentle moaning coming from a room two doors down. I walked over and looked in. There was an old woman lying in a bed. She must have been ninety years old if she was a day. Her eyes were closed, head tilted back on the pillow. Sparse white hair, brittle splotched skin. She was sleeping, and moaning in some sort of pain, maybe it wasn't actual pain, but a dream that she was having. I was praying that it was just a dream. Nothing I could do about it.

I could hear voices coming from the nurses station, then footsteps coming down the hallway. I stepped all the way into the old woman's room and peered with a sliver of my eye around the doorframe.

A doctor in a white lab coat was walking down the hall. Short black, close cropped hair, trimmed tight around the ears, dark eyes, chiseled features. It was the same guy at the other hospital, the one outside Herman Castles' door just before he went into cardiac arrest.

He had a clipboard in his right hand, stethoscope hanging around his neck.

The receptionist said a specialist was going to visit her. He was a specialist alright. Doctor death.

He closed the door quietly behind him, and I made my move.

I walked out of the old woman's room, then quickly towards the door where the good doctor went in, carefully tried the handle, it was locked. In my pocket was a slim yet sturdy plastic card shaped like a hook that was designed for this occasion. Placing it in the crack while holding the doorknob steady, it slid and curved in between the door and the frame and lifted the dead-latch away from the strike plate.

The door opened swift and silent.

He turned, startled. There was a syringe with a long needle in his right hand that was about to plunge into the woman's neck.

His eyes wide as saucers as he recognized me., then the eyelids hardened, his jaw squared as he gritted his teeth and lunged at me.

I closed the distance and brought both my hands up in a cross to block the syringe which he was trying to plunge down into my neck.

With his free left hand he made a fist and popped it up into my ribs. My broken ribs. I winced in pain then jackknifed his hand with the syringe around his back, turning him around and getting an arm bar around his neck.

We fell to the ground struggling for control, our feet sliding on the slick floor trying to find something to push against for leverage. I was trying to get my other arm around to put him in a rear naked choke hold, but his hand with the needle came free and he had it poised above my thigh and I had to hold it off with my free hand.

Whatever was in that syringe was going to kill me. My right foot found the edge of the wall and I had the leverage I needed to twist on his neck and it cracked. I could hear more than one vertebrae break in pieces, the sound like pencils snapping in two.

He slumped into a heap, the needle clattering harmless to the floor. I pushed him to the side, fighting to catch my breath. The whole event probably took ten seconds.

I looked closely at her. She was a young sturdy woman in her mid-twenties. Her face was bruised, she was unconscious, breathing lightly.

There was a long clear tube stretching from an IV bag of fluids, hooked into the top of her right hand that was resting on top of the blanket. Wires leading to her chest from a monitor that was blank. It had either not been needed, or had been turned off.

I looked at the chart on the wall next to the bed. Her name was written in bold black letters: Kimberly O'Donnell.

On the wall next to the bed was an open cabinet with bandages and surgical cloth. I grabbed one of each then held the surgical cloth against the needle and pulled the IV tube out of her wrist. The silver needle came out easily. She moaned slightly but stayed asleep. I could tell that she was still breathing. I held the cloth tight against her wrist, then taped a bandage over the small wound.

I looked closely at the IV bag. Maybe there was a small pin hole at the top, I couldn't tell. Maybe he inserted some of the material from the syringe before I caught him in the act. I wasn't going to the take the chance.

Not wanting the nurses to reuse this bag, I pulled it off the ring, then holding it over a trash can pulled the bottom plug and emptied the liquid contents then threw it in.

I searched the fake doctor. The tag on his lapel said he was Dr. Charles Happen, MD. He had a wallet, a phone and a small concealed pistol. I didn't touch the gun. The wallet had cash, credit cards, a Washington DC driver's license and an ID that said he was with the Secret Service. And what do you know, all the ID's in his wallet were different from the one on his lapel.

Kyle Stannish. The face and name on the credit cards, driver's license, and Secret Service ID all matched with the same name and face as the guy on the floor with a broken neck. His home address was an apartment in Washington, DC. I took out my pocket notepad and wrote it down.

Two things stood out.

One: why was a Secret Service agent trying to assassinate an innocent woman.

Two: if you were going to assassinate someone, or commit a heinous crime, you never brought ID with you.

Unless you didn't think you'd get caught.

There was no guarantee that any of his ID's were legit, or that he had any connection with the government, but I had a couple of ways to check.

One was accessing the government database

which I would do later to see if there really was a Kyle Stannish with the Secret Service.

The other way was a little more direct and personal and could help bring some additional opposing players quickly into the game.

I took the phone and left everything else. Every cell phone these days had a GPS tracking device embedded in it, and when someone came looking for it, I wanted to be there waiting.

I looked down at the young woman, wondering if she'd ever be able to see her children again. This was the woman from the newspaper story. A black ink on white paper faceless entity, a story. But here she was in flesh and blood. It was a terrible situation, but at least the children, and she were still alive. I couldn't protect her forever and it was time to leave.

If we could find the device that made her do what she did, maybe there'd be full closure, full healing and she could go back to the simple life she led, feeding and nurturing her kids.

I could stay here and try to explain myself to the authorities, but that might take days. Plus the fact that this whole thing didn't pass the smell test.

Someone was trying desperately to cover something up. I could be in a holding cell, and have an unfortunate accident, like falling from the ceiling onto the top of my head, or have a cardiac arrest for no apparent reason.

She was still breathing slow and steady when I turned and walked towards the door, peered down the hallway to see no one around, then walked quickly out of the room and headed down the stairs.

I stopped at the top landing, pulled out a burner phone, punched in the hospital name into the search bar to find the phone number and dialed.

A young woman's voice answered.

"This is an emergency," I told her. "Send a nurse to room five one oh two immediately. I'm here now and the patient stopped breathing."

I made sure she heard me and understood.

"Five one oh two, yes sir."

I hung up the phone, wiped it down and threw it in a trash can. Alarms were going off at the nurses station and I could hear footsteps running down the hallway.

It was harder going down the stairs than up. The SS agent caught me a good one under my broken ribs and I winced every time I stepped down with my right leg, finally making it to the bottom floor.

The security guard was still reading his newspaper behind his tall desk as I limped towards the front door. I gave him another small salute with my right hand tight over my eyebrow. He acknowledged me with a nod then went right back to reading.

I knew that later in the night, after a full review, every security camera in the hospital would identify me in high definition as entering and leaving in the approximate time frame that either a member of the Secret Service, or an imposter was killed in room five one oh two.

Either way, someone got their neck snapped, and I was in the room when it happened.

8.

I kept to the side of the building and rounded out to the street, into the crosswalk and down a block to where I'd left my car in the no parking zone. It must not have been a very important area, since the car was still there, and there was no boot lock on the wheel.

My watch read seven forty five. I'd only been in the hospital for fifteen minutes. A lot can happen in that amount of time.

As I got in the car and started the engine a tow truck with blinking yellow lights on top of the cab came around the corner and headed straight for me, trying to block me in.

Good luck with that.

A little tap of the accelerator while cranking the wheel and I got out in front of him. He leaned on his horn, probably angry at losing a quick hundred dollar collar.

I sped away and turned right at the first corner and looked for a place to stash the phone.

Wouldn't it be nice to download the contents of it, I thought. Too bad they were all un-hackable. I pushed on the front cover in the off chance that it wasn't locked but was out of luck.

There was a convenience store two blocks down with an empty space out front. Not wanting to let a security camera see the license plate on my rental car, I pulled into the dark alley on the side, got out while palming the phone with my right hand, wiped it down then threw it into the trash can by the entrance to the store.

I backed out of the alley and headed down the street in the other direction, found an open parking space on the opposite side of the street and waited.

It didn't take long.

No more than ten minutes later a black SUV with tinted windows came around a corner up ahead, then drove slowly down the block towards me. I slumped deep down in my seat as it passed by, then raised my head just enough to see the rear end of it in my side view mirror. I got out my mini binoculars and watched it in the mirror. I zoomed in the binoculars and memorized the license plate number.

The SUV stopped in front of the convenience store while staying on the road, a guy dressed all in black jumped out. He had some type of device in his hand and walked straight to the trash can and pointed a flashlight into it, reached down, pulled out the phone, looked around the area then quickly jumped back in the passenger seat and the car sped away.

This guy had short brown hair, military cut. That's all I could make out from this distance.

There was no way my little rent a car could catch up with them, and there was no need to hurry after them. It was dark, the roads were unfamiliar and I was sure to lose them if I tried to follow. I didn't want to catch two small fry. I wanted to catch the whole dirty bunch.

I pulled out my little notepad and wrote down the seven digit license plate number. It was a typical nondescript California license plate with a number, then three letters, and then three more numbers: 5UMB721.

I decided to use one of my burner phones to get a little info.

I had access to every DMV database in the world, and pulled up my secure website, inputting the digits.

The car was licensed to Black Op Security with a mailing address in Washington DC.

I'd heard that name before. Biting my lip and scrolling through the memory banks. They started out in the first Gulf War, army grunts getting their first taste of action and not wanting to go home.

Heading back to the States to run a grocery store or a farm was not an option to these guys, that would be too boring. Being in a battle zone turned them into war junkies. They needed the action, plus the real money was in providing security. Real security in the most dangerous places on the planet, in the middle of an active war zone. The middle east, where the fun never stopped.

A group of Army Rangers, CIA operatives, and Israeli defense force officers along with a few Mossad agents joined forces and formed a little company.

They gathered money, equipment and special employees.

They could go places and do things that wouldn't be reported, wouldn't be advertised. In areas of the world where there were no reporters, no witnesses.

They were off the grid, and there were powers in the world that would pay mightily for certain activities to happen without reciprocity.

They morphed into a paramilitary ready-for-action, armed-to-the-teeth private security firm that could be inserted anywhere needed, no questions asked.

I thought hard. Why are they even here in the United States? All the action is overseas.

The answer was easy.

Sure the action is overseas, but most of the money is in D.C. Most of the money in the world swirling around those marbled buildings.

My dark premonition of being rubbed out in a cellblock while trying to explain how a Secret Service agent broke his neck in a hospital might have come true with these guys on the other end.

It still didn't explain why they would try to hurt an innocent woman who had already gone through so much pain.

If they'd kill that poor woman while she was laying helpless in a hospital bed, what wouldn't they do.

Somebody stole something in Palo Alto.

I knew these bastards were involved.

The SUV had a California license plate. That meant they must have a base of operations somewhere in the state.

I pulled up another database that showed the ownership of real property in the whole golden state.

I punched in Black Op Security. Nothing.

Plugging into another database I searched for the principals of Black Op Security.

There was a John Weston. Retired Army Ranger. He was a Captain in the first Iraq war, earned a Bronze star and a Purple heart.

Conner Larkin. Army Captain retired. Also in the first Iraq war. Also with a Bronze Star and a Purple Heart.

Uri Ambrov. Israeli Civil Defense force. Major, retired. No list of decorations.

Yagiz Kaplan. Turkish Armed Forces. Captain, retired. No list of decorations.

I punched in all four names in the real property ownership database. The results came up in alphabetical order. The names Weston, Larkin, and Kaplan owned hundreds of properties all over the state. But they were common names. Most of the properties were held in trusts. It would take days to filter through them. The name on top though, Ambrov owned just a few dozen properties throughout the state. One in particular was in Kentfield, which was just across the bay, in the southeast corner of Marin county. I looked up the address. It was on Rock road, about twenty miles from here.

How convenient.

I pulled up a satellite map that showed a hillside community rising up from the delta of the bay. At the point of land where the water met the land was San Quentin, and the state prison of the same name.

Then it ran straight north along Corte Madera creek then up into the hills. I zoomed down onto the homes along Rock road. All were large semi-mansions, some were bigger than mansions, what I would call a mansion anyways. Most of them with pools and multiple decks, sprawling walkways through the woods around the structures.

I found the home I was looking for. It was high up on the hill, looked like it had been built into the hillside itself. It was oriented facing south and probably had a view of the bay. If I could judge square footage from a satellite map I would guess it was around ten thousand square feet under roof. About ten normal homes bundled into one.

Tall blue windows on the south side of the home overlooked a large deck with a pool. On the east side of the home was another deck with a spa.

A driveway looped around from the road, under a stone porte-cochere at the entrance to the home then back up to the road.

It looked like it would be a hell of a place to throw a party. I decided to take a drive over there and have a look around.

9.

Uri Ambrov was thirty eight years old but looked much older. Short white hair, thick face with deep wrinkles that started at the top of his hair line, long ridges running horizontally from side to side down to his eyebrows. Furrows etched into his forehead from scrunching his eyes in concentration and worry. More furrows vertical on the side of his mouth from setting his jaw and gritting his teeth on official battlefields from the Golan to Sinai. And on unofficial battlefields from Albania to Morocco, the Sudan. The exterior of his face looked aged. But it was really apparent deep within his eyes.

He looked down at the two pictures in his hand. Wallet sized photos that he took out and gazed at every day. Sometimes for a minute, and other times for hours. One was of a young woman with a bright smile, kind eyes, timid and shy, light brown hair, the sunlight hitting it just right, lighting the errant strands of hair along the edges like a saint.

The other picture was the same woman, a little older with a baby in her arms in a hospital bed. She was looking down at the baby, and amazingly the baby, though just a day old was looking straight back up at her mother with wonder in her eyes. They were connected.

They were the reason that he lived on. They were the reason that he fought on. And even though they were gone five years now he still looked at their faces in the photographs as though they were still alive, because somehow in his heart they were.

Five years ago they were a young happy family. Just starting out in life. He remembered how nervous he was when they left the hospital, and carried the baby to the car, afraid he might trip on a rock, or slip on a grease spot, stumble and drop her. His wife gently and lovingly chided him, a big war hero afraid of a little baby.

She was so small and frail, and seemed only about the size of a loaf of bread. Only when she was safely buckled in her car seat, swaddled with blankets and sound asleep did he relax for a moment. But now he actually had to drive the car through the afternoon traffic, and he could barely walk let alone maneuver an automobile through the narrow streets of Tel Aviv.

They had left the bag with all the baby's supplies of diapers and clothes, along with his wife's small suitcase with her clothes at the reception desk at the entrance to hospital. He made certain that his wife, still weak from childbirth was sitting comfortably in the front seat. He pulled the seat back to give her more leg room, and pushed the back of it so her head would be closer to the baby. Then he turned and sprinted back to the hospital. The little jog did him well and loosened his worry. He was smiling as he walked out of the hospital, beaming actually from ear to ear as he walked towards the car. His wife reached over and turned the key of the ignition so she could roll down the windows. And the car-bomb that was hidden under the chassis exploded into a fireball.

He could still smell the burning metal, plastic, rubber and flesh.

His mind went blank as he remembered that moment.

Five years ago.

No tears came out of his eyes anymore. That well had dried up long ago and would never see a drop of water again for any reason. The deep sands of the Sahara had more moisture on its surface.

It didn't matter if it was five years, or five hundred years. No amount of time would ease the pain.

The cell phone on the desk vibrated. Reluctantly he pulled his eyes from the photographs and looked over at it, then gently put the photos back into his slim wallet, rose from the chair and picked up the phone. It was a familiar number.

"Yes," he said simply.

The voice on the other end was calm, yet it seemed to be a forced calmness. On the edge of the inflection was a tinge of fear.

"We had a problem."

"Can you fix it?"

"It's too late," said the voice on the phone.

They failed somehow. Nothing more needed to be said over the phone.

"Meet at rendezvous one," he said and pressed the red button to end the call.

He turned off the light above the desk and sat in the darkness for a moment, gathering his thoughts. It was time to leave. The mansion was dead quiet. It was always quiet on top of the mountain above Marin County.

He walked through the darkened hallways to the front of the house. It felt comfortable walking in the dark. It was good for his senses, and he liked it. Too much light, food, and creature comforts were bad for a man. Made him soft. He walked out of the front door and locked it behind him.

The air was chilled and refreshing. Fog was rolling in from the bay, filling the air, wafting ghostlike past the lights on the lamp posts lining the road that wound still farther up into the hillside.

He clicked the key in his hand and the black sedan made a chirping noise, the front and rear lights blinking once as the doors unlocked. Then all was quiet again. Far down the road at the bottom of the hill he could hear the faint sound of an engine as a car made its way up along Rock road. With his heightened senses he could almost identify the type of car. It was a small car with a small efficient engine.

He sat in the driver's seat of his car and rolled down the windows so he could feel the fog rolling through, and hear the sound of it for few more moments. Fog actually made a sound if you were alert enough to listen for it. The light water mist mixed in with the air had substance, and when it was moving created a sound barely audible, but it was there.

It was time to leave, but he sat in the darkened car and waited. Waited until the car that was climbing up the road, either pulled into one of the many homes along the way, or passed by. It was a habit he had. A habit born out of necessity in the desert on the other side of the world. In another, less civilized type of world.

When you struck camp, and got ready to move out, late at night, you waited and listened with all your faculties. You made absolutely sure that you were alone, and no-one was approaching that could ambush you.

The little car got closer. It had one more turn and then the straight away past the house. The engine was steady. He could see it now, heading past the driveway.

He tilted his head to the side as it passed to hear the sound of it with as much clarity as possible. Did it slow down, just a tiny bit as it passed? Or was it just the sound change from approaching, to retreating.

From the darkness of his sedan he watched the car pass by. He could barely see a head, but it was facing forward, and did not appear to turn and look at the house as it went by, as the car continued on and up Rock road.

He waited for another moment and then turned on his engine and rolled out of the driveway in a low gear with the lights off. He was all the way down at the hairpin turn before he needed to use his brakes, and then turned on the headlights and disappeared into the night.

10.

The engine of the little rental car hummed steadily up Rock road, winding up and around tall pines trees mixed with mansions that were hidden in their midst.

It had taken a little more than half an hour to drive here from San Francisco, across the Golden Gate Bridge, and through southern Marin County.

The address I was looking for was three quarters of the way up the little mountain. I'd studied it on the satellite map so I'd know the exact location when I came close. One of the rules about surveillance was knowing exactly where you were going and then blending into the environment around you.

This one was tricky. A windy road with no shoulder, nowhere to pull over. All the homes were in the multi-million range and as such would have high tech surveillance systems, so there was no way to park in a driveway or anywhere near an adjacent property and travel the rest of the way by foot. The neighborhood watch system would be full force.

I decided to drive by the home first, get a quick glimpse and then find a place to park and then double back. I kept the engine steady, no slowing down as I maneuvered around the last hairpin turn, then the straightaway that led past the house.

The house was dark, yet there was a car parked out front in the porte-cochere. The windows of the car were down, which was very unusual on a cold foggy night. Moisture would seep into every nook and cranny. My head stayed facing straight ahead as I passed, but in the corner of my left eye I could see a white haired head sitting in the driver's side. It was watching me as I passed.

I continued on, up the road towards a hairpin that turned in the opposite direction, switch backing up the little mountain and past another mansion. From here there was a break in the woods and I had a peek at the road below, and saw the faint blur of red on the hairpin turn down below, the one that was right before the house with the darkened car. It looked like the red color of a tail-light, yet no car had passed by me going down.

I turned the car around, switched off the engine and headlights, put the transmission in low gear and coasted back down the hill, around the hairpin turn to the long straightaway. The black sedan was gone. The house still dark. I had to stop and put the car in park to get the engine started again, then put it in drive and stepped on the accelerator.

Five switch-backs later Rock road met

Goodhill and there were two ways to turn. I'd studied the options before heading up here. A right turn wound farther around the hillside meandering through the home sites. To the left and the road headed down to the college town of Marin and a thoroughfare that led to the freeway. I took the left turn driving as fast as possible without squealing the tires. There were no cars in sight and then down by the college, by the gas and go I caught a glimpse of a black car heading south through the fog.

At the bottom of the hill I turned right and followed it. The traffic was heavier now and I squeezed my way in and around till I was two cars behind. This was the perfect way to follow someone. Except he had different plans. Whether it was by design, or that's just the way this guy drove, he began to weave in and out of traffic passing semi-recklessly at times, and then staying in his lane driving steadily. Then after a short time weaving again, gaining ground on the cars in front of him. As such I needed to do the same, and that was not good. Even though it was dark and semi-foggy I couldn't let him have any inclination that someone might be following him.

He merged onto the 580 freeway then weaved his way into the fast lane and stayed there. We were heading to Oakland. To the right were the lights of San Quentin prison, then we were on the San Raphael bridge, heading over the bay. The bridge was double stacked with the top going north, and the bottom going south. He seemed to be content with staying in the fast lane and I settled in three cars behind. There wasn't much you could do anyways as far as maneuvering since the cars were bunched together like sardines in a can with just a few feet between bumpers and doors. The tires hummed on grooved concrete.

Ten long minutes later we over dry land again and the traffic began to space out, as the options expanded and cars turned both right and left onto different roads. The black car stayed in the fast lane of the 580.

We continued south through Coronado, then past the Mudflats State Park. The fog began to thicken.

There was a maze of roads up ahead like a snake-pit. Seven different lanes going in four different directions and you needed to make up your mind while going seventy miles an hour in the fog.

He weaved to the right as though he was going to take the far right lanes to San Francisco. I stayed in the middle lanes ten car lengths back, ready to change lanes and follow. Then at the last moment he weaved back into the lane I was in that was headed for the next split in the freeway. To the left two lanes split off towards downtown Oakland, while to the right another two lanes split towards San Jose. The picture of a jet airplane indicated an airport was up ahead.

Oakland International.

I was ready to merge to the left, but he stayed in the right lane that branched onto the 880 heading to Alameda, San Jose and the airport.

There was a big sweeping turn to the left and

we passed a small boat harbor on the right, and the Coast Guard island at Alameda, then a few miles later the Oracle Arena went by on the left.

He was in the left lane of the four lane freeway, and I stayed in the middle lane. Up ahead was the turn-off for Hegenberger road and the Oakland airport. We were going seventy miles per hour when he weaved across three lanes, nearly skidding into the exit. I followed, still ten car lengths behind. It was a two lane exit that curved to the right, and then to the left. I stayed in the slow lane on the right.

The exit ended up ahead at a stop light that was red. I did not want to come up behind him and slowed down. Two cars passed me, probably in a hurry to get to the airport and blocked his rear view.

He turned to the right and headed west for a thousand yards, then stopped again at the cross street ahead. Doolittle Drive. There was a hotel on the corner. The cars that had blocked his view of me passed us on the left. He stayed at the corner, and I had no choice but to pull into the hotel parking lot. Then he turned right on Doolittle. I sped through the parking lot.

There was another exit on the other side onto Doolittle, but I could see that he turned left, crossed traffic, went over the curb and into a parking lot in front of a small building. The sign on the building said Civil Air Patrol Squadron 188.

The hotel lot was crowded. One spot was open in front of the restaurant next to the lobby.

I could see clearly through the French double

windows, people having dinner, laughing, happy. More people crowding around the bar.

There was a TV in the corner at the back of the bar. A basketball game was on. There was a break in the action, a time out was called. Across the bottom of the screen was a red banner with NEWS ALERT scrolling from right to left. In the center of the screen was the moving image of a man that looked a lot like me. I was exiting a stairwell and heading straight past the camera.

The image froze with my face in the center of the TV. The news alert banner was replaced by another banner that read: Man wanted for questioning in Hospital murder.

I left the rent-a-car in the parking lot, walked along the road then sprinted across the street.

Using both the bushes and parked cars as a shield I walked silently towards the area where the black sedan parked.

There was another car there. A big black SUV. Two men got out. I pulled out my pocket binoculars for a closer look at the license plate.

5UMB721.

I pulled out the little notepad from my back pocket and checked the number that I'd written down.

Bingo.

It was the same SUV that followed the phone to the trashcan outside the convenience store, which meant these were the same guys from the hospital.

They spoke briefly with the white haired guy, then all three of them walked past the buildings and out towards the airplane parking area.

I followed.

There was a small sleek private jet nearby, white with two engines on either side of the tail, the engines were idling, lights in the cockpit, two pilots going through a checklist.

The curved side door was open, with steps along the inside of it down on the tarmac. The three wasted no time, bounding up the steps into the plane, for a brief moment the man with the white hair paused at the opening, looking back at the parking lot where I crouched next to a car with the binoculars, and the door closed behind them.

It would have been impossible at this distance and with the narrow outline of the top my head that he could have seen me, but it was unnerving in a way.

The engines ramped up, a high piercing whine as the turbine engines spun with jet fuel, then it leveled out as the jet started rolling forward. I was losing my trail. There was no way to follow them now.

Or was there.

It was still foggy, and that meant IFR, instrument flight rules were in effect. If you had a private plane in the United States of America you did not have to file a flight plan, and could fly anywhere you wanted without being tracked, just not during IFR conditions. Every airplane in the country private or not had to file a flight plan when IFR rules were in effect, and there were websites that tracked every single flight.

I pulled out my little notepad and wrote down the tail number.

OE521NX.

Interesting. The first two letters meant that the aircraft was registered in Austria. I tried a public website, but the message said that this aircraft's owner requested that it not be tracked.

I say request denied.

There was another website I had access to that didn't block tracking, and it belonged to the Federal Aviation Administration. The almighty FAA. I never had to use it till now. It was a one shot deal.

With an average of five thousand aircraft in the air at any given time, forty three thousand per day, sixteen million per year, someone needed to be in charge or it'd be anarchy in the skies.

A few years ago, it seemed like it might be a good idea to have access to a couple of secure government websites in case I needed information quickly, without going through any channels of authority.

FBI, FAA, motor vehicle registration, Social Security, and a little known crime database in the U.S. Federal Justice Department that had fingerprints, mugshots, physical descriptions, and the last known whereabouts of every known criminal in the world.

The only secure website that I could not get into so far was the CIA's, yet with my current affiliation with them on this case, it probably wouldn't be long before that was in my tool bag.

I kicked myself, since I should have gotten it before I even left Catalina.

I logged onto the FAA website and punched

in the tail number. The result was instant. Destination Washington D.C. Cruising altitude forty one thousand feet. Estimated flight time five hours, fifteen minutes.

Looked like I was going to be taking a trip back east. But how to get there? I needed a ride.

I pulled out my wallet and took out the two business cards with no names. The one missing the top right corner was the big shot, and the other one was for his assistant in LA. Bob McCade. My contact.

He was all business on the other end of the line. Not abrupt, or anxious, just matter of fact. The phone rang once, and all he said was "Yes?" As though he knew it was me and that I'd be calling.

"McCabe?"

"Yes, how can I help you?"

"This is Badger."

There was a pause on the other end. Maybe he didn't automatically know that it was me calling, and I took him by surprise. His tone changed. He might have tried to hide it, but I could sense unease.

"I'm glad you called. We need you to come in."

"What does that mean? Come in where?"

"To one of our field offices, we need to debrief you."

"Why?"

"We have a bit of a problem."

"Explain."

"Your face Badger, in high definition CCD, is on every news channel in the Bay Area. It seems you were in a local hospital when a man had his neck broken. And before that you were in another nearby hospital when a patient suddenly died. We tried to squelch the story and maneuver it into another angle, but it was no use. It's taken on a life of its own. The local law enforcement wants to talk with you. You're famous."

All of this was old news to me.

I got to the point. "I need a ride."

"We'll come and pick you up, just give us your location."

"Not that kind of a ride."

"We need you to come in."

"I'm not done yet."

"Yes, you are. For now anyways. After we clear this up we can send you back out in the field. We need you to come in for a debriefing, that's all. We'll send a car to you and pick you up. We'll protect you." He paused for a moment while I was silent. Thinking. Then he continued. "What's your location, we'll send someone over right away. Are you in the city?"

Talking to me like a hostage negotiator, trying to lull me into submission, saying the same things over and over with a different angle each time. It was a hypnotical technique. They wanted me to come in. Give myself up.

No way in the world I was going to let anyone get a collar on me now. I might never get out.

This thing, whatever it was I'd gotten myself into, had to be ridden to the end. I hung up the phone, crushed it under my heel, grinding it into the pavement and wedged it under the front of the tire of the car I was standing next to. When it pulled out it would complete the destruction I'd started.

There was no sense looking for help from the CIA any longer.

They got me into this jam, and now I had to get out of it, on my own.

Right now I needed a ride to D.C.

I strolled back across the street, got back into the little rent a car and thought for a moment. I could drive there but it would take days and whatever was about to happen might be too late to stop.

The TV in the bar had the basketball game on again. Everyone in the place talking, laughing, oblivious to their surroundings.

I started the car, drove out of the parking lot and circled the airport to the cargo area till the type of airplane that I was looking for came into view. It was being loaded with forklifts. Big silver cargo containers, rounded on one side and square on the other so they could fit side by side into the fuselage. The logo on the tail rising into the fog said: FEDEX.

If you couldn't jump on a military or a private jet, and you wanted to get somewhere quick, you didn't take a commercial flight. You went FEDEX.

The security for these planes was no less severe, but I knew how to get around it. I came prepared.

I pulled out another burner phone and punched the tail number into the tracking web page. It was headed to the main hub in

Memphis.

Not D.C. but it was a quick start.

Skipper McDougal was my friend from the war who scored a good job with FedEx. He worked out of the main office in Memphis, ran security, gave training seminars across the globe. He was one of those guys that was always on it. Talked a mile a minute. Never seemed to sleep, always one step ahead of everyone else and perfect for a job where you needed to stay ahead of trouble.

We were in the same platoon back in the bad days in the middle east. The days we mostly wanted to forget about.

Maybe he could do me a favor and get me on a jump seat. These cargo planes usually had a couple of extra seats behind the cockpit. I pulled out my list of numbers and ran my finger down it.

The phone on the other end rang twice before he answered. The voice was brisk and to the point.

"This is Skip."

"Mad dog grippa," I whispered. His code name.

When it was middle of the night pitch black dark and you were in a war zone with bullets whizzing past, sticking your head down into mud pits to stay alive, you didn't move an inch unless you knew the person nearby was a friend and not a foe.

Silence at the other end as the words digested, then he replied slow as molasses: "Midnight freaka. What the hell are you doing man? Are you here in town?"

"Oakland."

"That's a crying shame. Sorry to hear it."

"I need a favor."

"Anything."

"I need to a ride to D.C."

"What do you mean, need a ride?"

"I'm at the Oakland airport and there's a plane with your company's logo on it ready to take off."

"Why don't you take a commercial flight."

"It's hard to explain right now."

He didn't argue, or ask for details.

"Okay, maybe I can get you on a jump seat. Let me take a look." The sound of fingers typing on a keyboard then he sighed loud and audible, I thought I heard him whisper the word damn.

Then he came back on the phone asking me clearly. "You see the number on that tail?"

"Yeah."

"Does it say N306FE?"

"Yes."

"You know which plane that is?"

"Is this a trick question? I don't know, it just looks like a normal jet airplane to me."

"That, my old friend, is a McDonnell Douglas DC-10, one of the finest airplanes ever designed and built. It's also one of the most infamous aircraft in our entire system."

I didn't know what to say, so I remained silent.

"You want to know why?" he asked.

"Sure I'll play along."

"April seventh, 1994, flight 704. A FedEx

employee down on his luck gets a ride on a jump seat, no one thinks much about it. But the guy has a death wish and wants to crash the plane and make it look like an accident so his family can collect on his insurance policy. Tries to hijack the plane with a hammer and a spear gun, nearly kills the two pilots and the flight engineer, but they manage to stop him and barely land the plane back here in Memphis. The pilot did loop de loops with that big ass plane to get the high jacker off guard. They were wrestling on the ceiling. And you want me to try to get you on a jump seat on that plane?"

"If it's too much trouble I'll find another way."

"I wouldn't do this for anyone else Badger. I don't think I even *could* do this for anyone else. Okay the ledger says there's three jump seats on that aircraft and two are empty. I'll call the flight crew and tell them you're my trusted assistant and I need you on that plane. I'll make the request, but the decision rests entirely on the captain of that aircraft. He's the boss. If he's having a bad day, or doesn't like the look in your eyes, or the way you combed your hair, you're out of luck. You have ID on you?"

"Yes."

"Okay, get your tail down onto the tarmac and get on that plane, but no luggage and no weapons."

"Yes sir, thank you."

"I'll see you when you get here in about six hours."

Once I got to Memphis it should be easier to

move around. From there I could catch the next transfer to D.C.

I could even drive there in under thirteen hours if it came down to it. Although it was best to get there as fast as possible.

11.

He looked like a beggar in the streets, and no one bothered him. A simple black wool cap covered the top of his head. Three layers of tattered garments covered his upper torso, beginning with what was once pure white cotton but was now a grey sweat stained tunic next to his skin followed by a brown button down shirt, then a black cape draped over his shoulders, ragged and torn on the edges.

His left hand was covered in a make-shift bandage made from cloth torn in strips. Blackened trousers hung loose down the remainder of his gaunt frame, ending in one dirty bare foot, and by the flattened nature of the right side of his pants, it was obvious that he was missing a leg. A fly landed on his cheek, and he slowly waved it away with a wrinkled hand. The eyes under the cap, black and sharp watched the world around him with precision.

He sat near the front door of a small combination hospital and old folks home in District Thirteen on the outskirts of the eastern side of Tehran. It was a quiet area bordering a park and a library, with the steady hum of cars and trucks traveling north and south on the Yasini Highway two blocks away. He looked to be in his late-fifties or early sixties, which meant he would have been in his twenties during the nineteen eighty Iran/Iraq war and might explain the missing leg, giving people more reason to leave him alone.

He tapped his wooden cane on the ground lightly as people passed by, some veering towards him and placing a coin lightly in the upturned cup.

"Moteshakeram," he would say humbly in return while bowing his head in thanks.

He sat in the same spot all day every day for the past week. Waiting for someone.

Someone special.

There was a woman in the old folks portion of the hospital. She was very ill, at the end of her days. She was also the mother of a very important person who might come visiting. That person not only carried a secret, he was in essence *the* secret.

Twenty five years ago, when the United States government began to turn the screws on Tehran to get them to give up uranium enrichment, vast sums of reserves were tied up with the dollar currency. The mullahs decided to pull their currency off the dollar and transfer all holdings into gold reserves.

It was a bold move. The Iranian government purchased five hundred tons of gold from the European Union and transferred it to Tehran.

Not only was it a bold move, it was a smart

one. The value of gold rose in the years until their holdings were worth twice as much.

The gold hoard was in one of the most secure places in the world, because of the simple fact that no one knew for certain where it was located. It was one of the best kept secrets of the twenty first century.

The theory was that they had it hidden in a few different places around the country, maybe some in remote mountain tunnels, and some right in the middle of Tehran or another city. There was no shortage of theories, but also no definitive evidence.

There was however one man who might know the whereabouts of the gold hoard.

Mosef Ahmad. At fifty eight years of age, just about the same age as the beggar on the street who waited for him. He was the head of the agency responsible for the monetary system for the State of Iran.

Educated at Oxford, with a PhD in finance he rose quickly within the hierarchy after the revolution. It was his idea to pull out of the dollar system and go straight to gold.

He was also the son of the mother who currently resided on the top floor of the hospital. Although a very busy man, it was only a matter of time before he paid a visit to his ailing mother.

Intelligence reports indicated that an audit was about to be performed on one of the countries stockpiles of gold reserves. Mosef Ahmad it was rumored, was the overseer of the audit.

The black Mercedes pulled up to the curb. The driver got out and opened the back door.

Mosef was slight of build with round eyeglasses, slightly paunchy in the mid-section wearing neatly pressed slacks and a long sleeved white button down shirt. He was conservative in manner and dress. His black shoes slightly worn yet comfortable. It was obvious that style was not his main concern.

His driver, who was also Mosef's bodyguard, held the door at the top corner, while glancing around the area, focusing on the people walking up and down the street, the cars passing by, and the beggar near the front of the building.

Nothing was alarming. The beggar, although dirty and disturbing in nature, did not appear to be a threat. He stared down at the sidewalk while tapping his cane lightly on the ground.

Mosef began to walk around the beggar, and then feeling pity in his heart, reached into his pocket, counted out some coins in his hand then bent down and placed them in front of the missing leg.

"Moteshakeram," whispered the beggar. He leaned forward bowing down in front of his benefactor, setting his forehead on the sidewalk in front of the shoes in fervent thanksgiving, and placed both hands on Mosef's shoes.

"Now, now, that's not necessary," said Mosef but he was too humbled by the gesture to move away.

The bodyguard, seeing the activity began to walk towards them, but Mosef held up his hand.

Hidden in the bandage of the beggar's left

hand was a two inch long needle with a tracking device on the end of it that was the size of the point of a pencil.

Quickly, without either the bodyguard or Mosef noticing, the beggar inserted the sharp point into the edge of the sole of the shoe, breaking it off the needle then he retreated away, shuffling his back against the wall, hands pressed together in prayer while still singing praises of thanks for the alms.

The beggar remained there for another hour, long after Mosef had come back out from seeing his mother and was whisked away in the black sedan.

He shuffled to his one remaining foot, leaning on the cane wedged under his armpit, and hobbled away.

After struggling for two blocks he pressed his shoulder against the brick wall of a building, turning towards it to shield the small phone he held in his hand under the black cloak. He punched a three digit code, sending the text message and waited. Five minutes passed, then a dark sedan with tinted windows came down the street slowly, stopping next to him, the back door opened and he got in, then closed the door behind him as the car sped off.

12.

CIA headquarters; Langley Virginia. Thirty one year old Justin Marshall sat in front of an array of three computer screens in a small office on the third floor of the East wing. Earlier that day he received the assignment and got straight to work setting up the codes to access the satellite feeds from the other side of the globe.

Pull the feeds and synchronize them into easy to read compartments, exact parameters that followed a specific target.

It was just another day in the life of a former computer nerd from the geek squad in his local high school who got lucky with the right contacts and a top secret security clearance.

Working for the CIA was cool.

As with any other assignment he wasn't informed of the minute details of the mission. Never a name of the target, or the purpose of the tracking.

His job was to track individuals or vehicles, sometimes single targets, and sometimes entire armies. Record the movements, analyze the geographic nature of the surroundings, utilizing all the tools available to the largest, most sophisticated intelligence operation on the planet.

On each HD screen was a different type of satellite map with a grid showing a city with cross streets, buildings, cars, people.

The screen on the left was a color coded cartographic map showing the names of streets, districts, addresses of homes, businesses and buildings.

The screen in the middle was a 3D map generator that pulled data from multiple sources where you could rotate and zoom into any building to see structure layouts, room sizes.

The screen on the right was a real-time live feed from the spy satellite link.

There were somewhere over a thousand satellites circling the globe, all types and purposes. Communications, weather, civilian, military. Launched and operated by dozens of countries, and private companies. While the exact number of spy satellites operated by the U.S government was top secret, it was estimated to be over seven hundred spread out all around the globe.

Tehran, like most cities in the world was monitored twenty four seven three sixty five. When one satellite passed overhead and headed over the horizon out of view, you could bet that another one was right behind it, although usually at a different angle and height and coming from a different direction.

You could take the camera feed that was filming the whole city, the wide angle image, and compress it down to any area that you wanted. Down to the size of the hood of a car weather permitting with high definition, and if the weather did not permit, there was also infrared capacity. Any number of users could take the feed and tailor it to their needs. The beauty of technology. At any given time there were probably dozens of other analysts looking at wide ranges of this same city using the same satellite feed.

Each screen had a small red dot in the center. The target. It was moving slowly through the city. Meandering down streets, crisscrossing, backtracking then moving forward again into the center of the city.

Then finally it stopped.

Justin waited for a few minutes, then zoomed down and in with the center screen just above the street. The 3d screen showed a two story building with a brick wall around it. The red dot was on the street level first floor in the center of the building, and then it went down a floor and stopped. The building schematic showed a basement. The red dot moved further into the center of the building at the basement level and suddenly disappeared. He double checked the other two screens. The red dot had also disappeared from those monitors.

He punched the coordinates of the building into a fourth computer screen and waited while the pdf files loaded onto the hard drive. Hundreds of documents.

He scrolled through them. Building records, architectural plans, photographs, news stories, eyewitness accounts. The records went back to the nineteen thirties. It was originally a Turkish bath house, with a pool on the basement level.

In nineteen seventy one the pool was filled in with soil, re-floored and used as an apartment complex housing the revolutionary guard. In nineteen ninety five the revolutionary guard was re-located and the building was further remodeled, the soil removed, and a concrete re-enforced structure built around the pool. All access was restricted and no building plans were recorded. Yet there were two separate bills, one was for twenty thousand eight inch wide hollow tile cement blocks plus ten thousand feet of steel rebar, and another was a bill that showed fifty five truckloads of concrete were pumped into the building. The components for building solid concrete walls. Stack the hollow tiles over the steel rebar and fill it with cement. Impenetrable.

Justin Marshall nodded his head. Why of course. It was either some type of bomb shelter, a nuclear bunker, or a bank vault. That's why the tracking device went dead. The thick concrete walls were a shield for radio signals, or radiation. They probably saved time and money, using the existing concrete floor of the pool and built around it.

He dug deeper. The company doing the work was based in Germany.

There was an obscure bill from that company with a part number but with no corresponding description of the item that was delivered to the job site. It was an expensive item, two hundred and seventy five thousand dollars. It was from a manufacturer in Switzerland. They built high tech security doors for banks. He pulled up the company website and checked their product inventory. None of the numbers matched. He pulled up their internal accounting system from two years prior to the construction and scanned through all the receipts. Bingo. Here was a receipt for the German company doing the work in Tehran, with a shipping address to Tehran. The bill was for a circular bank vault door seven feet in width. Nuclear bomb shelters and bank vaults used the same type of re-enforced steel doors, except this model had an external combination lock.

You don't lock bomb shelters from the outside. You lock them from the inside. It was a bank vault.

They tried to keep it secret but someone got lazy.

Justin Marshall finished his report quickly and forwarded it on to his superior by internal e-mail.

13.

Montell Davis was looking out the window from his office on the fifth floor in the West wing of the CIA headquarters when his computer went 'ting'. An e-mail had arrived. It could wait for a moment till he finished his train of thought.

Something big was about to happen and he couldn't quite put his finger on it. He'd been in the CIA for twenty five years and if you'd been in this business for that long and paid attention to what went on around you, sometimes your gut feeling was worth more than all the mountains of intelligence that was gathered around you.

Much of their activity was compartmentalized, you completed a task and passed it onto the next in line. It was safer that way. Plus no-one in the world was an expert in every aspect of intelligence gathering. You handled your job, your specific task then moved onto the next. No questions asked.

Two weeks ago he saw a classified document that detailed how a small shipment of gold from a vault in South Africa was audited, and found to have small cavities of tungsten steel inside. The shipment itself was insignificant in size, only half a ton. Forty gold bars, each weighing twenty five pounds. One thousand pounds of gold, and since the price was currently thirteen hundred dollars per ounce, the shipment was only worth twenty million and change.

The shipment went to a jewelry company in Morocco who had been doing business with the company in South Africa the same way for decades.

They melted the gold and manufactured all types of expensive jewelry from necklaces to specialty gold coins. In the smelting pot, however, something was wrong.

They drilled small holes in the bars to assay the purity, and discovered nearly one third of the bars were filled with steel. Someone had drilled holes lengthwise along the bars, inserted tungsten steel rods in the vacant holes, then covered up the ends with caps of pure gold, hoping to elude discovery.

Twenty million in gold was now worth fourteen. The story was quickly hushed up, the shipment was switched for another batch of gold that proved to be ninety nine point nine percent pure, as good as you could get and promises were made to keep it quiet. After all it was a private transaction, and there was no reason to get people worried about their gold reserves coming from this particular vault.

Keep it secret.

It was highly possible that this particular batch of gold bars was never meant to be used in jewelry, only to be utilized as gold reserves. Perhaps someone had made a mistake.

One week ago the request was made to let the story slip out into the foreign intelligence community, source unknown.

Immediately after came the request to tag a high ranking finance minister of Iran. Tag him and track him. Not an easy feat to accomplish. It would have to be a quick tag, a one and done, one day procedure. An article of clothing that the target was wearing. It needed to done while he was in Iran. The timing would have to be precise.

Research showed that he was in Brussels for a conference when the gold story was released. He travelled to the conference on a private government aircraft and it was assumed that he would return on it as well, making physical contact nearly impossible.

Somehow they needed to get him to some unsecure place where the tag could be inserted.

Research showed that the only member of his family that he was close to was his mother and she moved around quite a bit. Somehow she needed to be slowed down and sequestered. Further research showed that he was not only close to his mother, he doted on her. The decision was made to poison her, not kill her, just enough of a dose to send her to a hospital for the dual purpose of keeping her in one place, and making it necessary for her adoring son to visit her.

Two critical assets were utilized to accomplish the poisoning and tagging. Two critical assets as in spies. This was one of the reasons that Montell began to suspect that something big was on the horizon. Spies were not easy to maintain in Iran, the consequences of being caught were more severe than in most other countries.

It was his understanding that the assets being used were some of the best that they had in the country. The tactical importance ranking was high for the mission.

He tried to imagine the logistics and the people involved. Getting close enough to an old woman to poison her without being detected might be easy enough. A tiny discreet spray onto her skin in passing, or an undetectable gas in her general direction.

Putting a tag on an upper echelon official with a bodyguard was another story altogether. This wasn't like being in grade school and slapping a friend on the back with a makeshift sign that said 'Kick Me'.

Get caught putting a tracking device on the wrong person would get you put into the morgue, or worse. They might do things to you that would make you *want* them to put you in the morgue as a more pleasant alternative.

Another problem was that tracking devices could be found with a signal detector. Putting a bug on someone was only part of the equation. Keeping it on them long enough to be effective was the key.

The good news was that the agency had a new generation bug that did not give off a trackable signal, and it was put into play.

14.

Mosef Ahmad was a simple man with simple tastes. He lived in the same small apartment for the past ten years, married with one child and another one on the way.

He had a degree from Cambridge in chemical engineering, and a masters in finance from Oxford.

Education and stability were at the core of his beliefs. Particularly stability.

What he didn't like was surprises.

Last week during an audit of the gold reserves of South Africa, some of the four hundred ounce bars, the standard bearer of the class were found to be filled with pockets of tungsten.

It was an old trick, as old as the world in some ways if you considered the world as we know it being filled with men and women trying to gain an unfair advantage by cheating and stealing from their fellow human.

Tungsten steel and gold weighed roughly the same, whereas gold was five times as expensive. It was easy to hide tungsten inside of gold. The thieves would take a lump of tungsten and pour the molten gold around it, stamp it and sell it on the black market. They even forged the letters of authenticity that went with the gold bars.

X-rays couldn't detect it. Only by drilling holes into the gold bars and analyzing the metal would work.

The vault in South Africa is where much of the tonnage belonging to Iran was stored during the embargo. One out of fifty bars was tested when it was shipped back to Tehran many years ago. One in fifty wasn't enough. Now it all needed to be tested.

It was under Mosef's advice that the Iranian government consider purchasing heavily from the international gold market. Gold was stable. It was immune from the irrational ups and down of individual countries currency, especially that of the U.S. dollar. When they bought three hundred tons in the year two thousand nine, the price of gold was six hundred and fifty dollars per ounce. Now it had tripled and was nearly two thousand dollars per ounce. But if it turned out that some of the gold that they had in storage was salted with tungsten, there would be a problem.

Near the center of the city was a building that had been retrofitted many years ago and served as a secret underground storage vault for fifty tons of that gold.

It was a small percentage of the total reserve of nine hundred tons. They bunkered the gold reserves purposely in different areas of the country in case of disaster. There were ten bunkers scattered around the country, some in Tehran, and others in underground tunnels deep in the surrounding mountains.

This particular vault held fifty tons of gold. One hundred thousand pounds. Each gold bar weighing a standard four hundred ounces, or twenty five pounds. Measuring nearly exactly 7 x 3 5/8 x 1 3/4 inches in dimension. Ninety nine point nine percent pure. One hundred thousand pounds of gold, with each bar weighing twenty five pounds, meant there were four thousand bars in the vault. Each and every one would need to be counted, weighed, and assayed. A pinpoint hole would be drilled in both ends, the metal analyzed and pray with his head on the end of a spear that no tungsten would be found.

He had a ten man team set up. All the equipment was in place. They would meet at the bunker, and methodically weigh and test each bar. If each man could test ten bars per hour, it would take forty hours to complete the job. They would live in the vault until they were done.

His trusted bodyguard Kamel, drove carefully through the city streets. He'd been with Mosef for the past five years, ever since an attempt was made on his life when travelling to an economic conference in London. It was unfortunate since he went to school all those years in England, ten wonderful years in fact, never having a problem, yet now since he was connected to a government that some people viewed as hostile, he became a target.

Kamel stood six foot two weighing in at nearly two hundred pounds and could break an arm in half if it got in his way. He was trained in all the martial arts and carried all the usual weapons. His most important talent however was spotting danger well ahead of time.

"Avoiding trouble is the best defense," he would always say.

Kamel parked the car two blocks away. They would walk the rest of the way, zig zagging down alleyways and across side streets before reaching the vault. Mosef thought it was an unnecessary precaution, but Kamel insisted. Mosef was the head of finance, and there could be spies anywhere, following him through the city. The last thing they needed was to pull up in front of the secret vault and have someone comfortably following them. Might as well make them work for it.

It was an old two story building, dusty orange in color with a gun metal roof. Built out of brick and steel at the turn of the last century. In a city where most of the buildings were hedged in close, this building was set back from its neighbors, with wide avenues on each side. A ten foot high cement wall topped with razor wire surrounded the property.

The rumor in the neighborhood, nurtured by the regime, was that the building housed an interrogation center, with a torture chamber deep in its center. No one in their right mind would try to break into this property. No cars were parked out front, or on either side. An eight foot tall metal barred gate served as the main entrance. It was closed.

There were two black sedans parked inside the compound. They bypassed the gate and walked around the corner. Halfway down the street was a metal door cut into the concrete wall with a security camera positioned above it. As soon as they were in front of the door, it opened and without a word they entered the compound. The door clanged shut behind them.

Two men in military gear stood to the side with automatic machine guns in a ready position, fingers on the triggers, safeties off. A third dressed like a doctor with a white lab coat nodded to the visitors in acknowledgement. He was holding what looked like a large flat faced black camera with three lenses stacked one above the other. It was in fact a biometric scanning device. He stood first in front of Kamel who obliged by placing his fingertips on his eyelids to open them wide. The man held the camera inches from Kamel's face, scanning the iris in the center of the eyeball for a few moments, then he moved over in front of Mosef and did the same.

"Welcome," said the man in the lab coat. "We are all set up and can begin when you're ready.

"Then let's get to work," said Mosef.

15.

It was half past two in the morning when the jet touched down in Memphis. My seat mate woke up when the wheels met the tarmac with a loud bang, rubber skidding, reverse thrusters roaring throughout the fuselage, pushing us violently forward against our seatbelts with the sudden deceleration. He looked at me with stunned bloodshot eyes then turned his head and went back to sleep as we taxied to the terminal.

Skipper was waiting. He was wearing a light tan jacket over a white t-shirt, blue jeans and tennis shoes, and from a distance looked more like a kid getting ready for his paper route, than the head of security for a major company. But as he got closer the hardened edges of his chin and cheekbones gave the impression of a man you wouldn't want to cross. With the sharp angles of that face, you knew the rest of him was probably just as sharp and cruel.

He went forward and thanked the pilot for giving me a ride then motioned for me to follow him.

The pit crew wasted no time. The turbines hadn't completely stopped whirling when the cargo doors were open, ramps wedged into place and the unloading was underway. Shouts and directions as the silver containers wheeled out of the plane. They were on a mission for speed.

I followed Skipper through the terminal. Two in the morning and there must have been over three hundred people working in this section of the giant building, moving silver metal crates from one end to the other.

"This is the busiest time of the day for us. We have one hundred and forty planes from all over the country landing from ten at night till one in the morning. Seven thousand employees sorting one and a half million packages. They sort 'em and load them back onto those planes to head out to every city in the country."

He bobbed and weaved through the traffic then down a hallway to a door that opened into a small office. The door closed and it was suddenly quiet. He motioned to a pair of chairs in front of desk.

"I'd rather stand if you don't mind," I said. "It was a long flight."

He shrugged as he sat in a big leather chair, picked up the phone, punched in a set of numbers. "Yeah," he said into the mouthpiece. "How soon before you're ready? Alright ten minutes."

I was looking at the pictures on the wall. Dozens of corporate type outings. Golf, hunting, rodeos, judo matches, marlin fishing, zip lining over canyons. Company bonding adventures.

Group photos with Skipper right in the middle of each one, smiling, happy times.

"Last time I saw you..." I hesitated, pulling up the jarring memories. "You were face down in the dirt with shrapnel in your back outside of Baghdad and I was cover firing as they loaded you onto a gurney for a ride on a helicopter."

"Times change."

"Boy I'll say. This looks like a pretty good gig you have here. Nice and plush. All you need to round this place out is a couple of broads in bikinis, a hot tub and a bar."

"Yeah wouldn't that be something. It has its perks. This is a busy company and they want to keep it running smooth. They pay good money, give me all the tools I need to keep ahead of the crime wave, and if we're good boys and girls we get to go on those cute little adventures you see in the pictures every now and then." His tone turned back to serious. "Listen Badger, I'm sorry I had to leave you guys back there. All I can remember is that I was walking down the side of the road with the platoon, and the next thing I know, I'm waking up in a hospital in Germany hooked up to a bunch of tubes and machines."

"You didn't miss much."

"A year of rehab till I could walk again, then my time was up. I got an honorable discharge and never looked back. Got a job in security at the bottom rung of the ladder and worked my way up."

"I know. I've been keeping tabs on everyone from the platoon, the ones that are still alive that is. I'm in security too. Sort of."

"Yeah, I checked you out too, after you called. While you were in the air. You've been a busy little bee. Saving rock stars. Zapping Chinese hit men. Recruited by the CIA."

"Not sure how you know about that last part, but it doesn't matter. So tell me what kind of tools did they give you here?"

"I've got access to every database known to man. They're looking for you in San Francisco. The CIA."

"Yeah."

"And soon they'll know you're here."

"How so?"

"They *run* the database. And they have cameras everywhere. Even here in this warehouse. There's nothing I could do about that. By now with facial recognition software, an alarm has gone off somewhere and they're sending a crew."

"So why am I still sitting here?"

"Thousands of people running around this little area. There's probably a few close matches to your face. Ten minutes from now a small plane will take off bound for Miami and you're going to be on it."

"I don't want to go to Miami."

"Sixty miles into the flight it'll drop down under the radar and change course north to DC. You did as I asked and brought no weapons?"

I held out my hands, palms facing up.

"As ordered sir. I was hoping you'd have a bag of tricks."

He nodded.

"I always have a few extras lying around."

He opened up the drawer in front of him and took out a small leather bag, set it on the desk, and began pulling out the contents. Two matching .45's, two spare packs of bullets, a hand-held Taser, binoculars, burner phones, and a can of the all-around useful pepper spray.

"You might need some these."

I picked up the Taser and looked it over. It was small as ball point pen, but I knew what it was from the metal prongs. I pressed the activating button listened to the crackling sound of electricity and watched the blue spark sizzle between the prongs.

"Impressive. Where'd you get it?"

"I know a guy."

I picked up one of the handguns, feeling the weight of it, then checked the clip. It was loaded.

"Careful," said Skipper.

I popped the clip out of the bottom, checked the barrel to make sure it was empty and pulled the trigger a few times to get a feel of the tension. Then I sighted straight down the barrel, then tilted it back with the barrel in the air, then back on line as though ready to fire, testing the swivel weight. Then I unloaded the second gun and did the same. Set the triggers to safety and loaded the clips back. I picked up the pepper spray, it was a new canister. Still, it was always best to test these things, last thing you wanted was to rely on something at a critical moment that was out of juice. I held it at arm's length away from us, pushed down the safety button and gave it a quick burst towards the door. It was loaded.

"Remember that bar in Reno?" asked

Skipper.

"Which one?" But I knew where this was heading.

"The cowgirl bar. We went there after we graduated from basic training, drove all day to get there since we heard what a hot spot it was. Once inside we split up and I was sitting at the bar talking to a little honey. I was making a little bit of headway. Only problem was that I didn't know she had a jealous boyfriend the size of a car. He came up behind me, put me in a headlock and was about to bash my head on the counter when you dropped out of the sky and gave him a karate chop to the side of his neck, he went flopping on the ground like a fish out of water, then we got surrounded by a dozen of his friends and had to fight our way out?"

"Fun times."

"And what about the time in Mosul, when that guy came running at us with the rocket propelled grenade launcher and you pushed me out of the way just as the grenade flew right by my skull?"

"That was a close one."

"I still wake up sometimes at night in a cold sweat and see that missile go past my nose. Feel the heat of it singe my eyebrows. See the explosion that was meant for me. Sometimes it doesn't happen for weeks, or months, then out of the blue I'm right back in it. This right here, getting you on these fun little plane rides? Doesn't come close to paying you back for those times, I still owe you."

"You don't owe me squat. But I appreciate the

ride and the hardware."

He looked quickly at his watch then leaned over the desk.

"So what happened," he asked. "Why is the CIA hot on your tail?"

I shook my head. This wasn't for him.

"I don't know yet. Maybe I never will. They hired me for a job out of the blue. Came out to Catalina while I was sitting on my boat minding my own business, and sweet talked me into joining their club. I'm supposed to be on their side. Somebody stole something and I was supposed to find it. Things got a little rough and a couple of people died. Somehow it got pinned on me and now they want me to come out of the cold so to speak, so they can wrap their loving arms around me, and take care of me. Read me a bedtime story, and tuck me into bed for a long nap."

"Put you in a headlock and bash it against the counter. So what's in DC?"

"There's a guy I'm looking for."

"What's his name? I'll look him up on the database."

He hovered his fingers over the keyboard.

I shook my head. "I know everything I need for now about him and I don't want you getting involved."

"You don't think I'm already involved? By the time this day is out I'm going to get interrogated by a couple of suits from the CIA."

"That's why it's better you don't know anything, other than I was here, and I'm gone, whereabouts unknown."

"I'll go with you. You know the old saying where two heads are better than one?"

"Sorry Skip, not this time."

He grimaced, then reached behind his chair, put a folded blue jumpsuit and lime green vest with silver reflecting stripes with a matching colored hat on the desk. They were dirty and covered in streaks of grease. "Put these on and pull the cap down over your eyes when we go out of this office. You're part of ground support now. Follow behind me but not too close."

16.

We left the paneled office, went down a hallway to an emergency exit door. WARNING, the sign over the door read, ALARM WILL SOUND IF OPENED.

Skipper pulled out a wad of keys, put one in the silver lock on the handle, turned it clockwise and pushed it open. No alarm. Lights washed the outside of the building. It was dark out on the perimeter. A jet was landing nearby, we could hear the screech of the tires as it set down on the tarmac and the roar of the afterburners. I looked at my watch. It was half an hour past one. Four hours to sunrise. We walked away from the building out of the harsh lights.

Skipper was looking down and across the tarmac, half a mile away sat a parking lot for small planes. There were about a dozen, mostly one engine models.

"Head over there as fast as you can. Walk, don't run. There's no need to call attention to yourself, even though someone will see you on a video feed eventually. Hopefully not until you're long gone and safe as you can be at your next destination."

"Which plane is it?"

"You can't miss it, looks like a big green bug. Like a wasp with a propeller. The pilot's name is Devon, you don't need to know his last name, you won't be together long enough to become friends. He'll take you to a little airfield well outside of DC and I'll have a car waiting that will take you to the outskirts of the city limits. You can get dropped off anywhere you want, a library, car wash, liquor store, public park, you name it. And then you're on your own. And I don't want to hear about you in the news, okay? Don't accidently shoot yourself in the head, or fall off a bridge into a river in the middle of the night."

"I'll try my best."

I walked smooth and fast with my leather handbag next to the fence line towards the small planes, wary of everything around me. Aircraft support vehicles, fuel tankers, the odd security car with the yellow lights on top drove in the area with me. No one bothered me.

A short four foot chain link fence separated the small planes from the tarmac, more for delineation than any type of security. Thought about hopping right over it, then thought twice and walked the extra twenty yards to the little gate. No need for any extra added attention. Skipper would be proud of me.

All around the airport was thriving, with planes taxiing, taking off, and landing. One sound nearby stood out, a loud single-engine turboprop aircraft idling. I headed towards it, and there it was, at the same time one of the ugliest and most beautifully unusual aircraft I'd ever seen.

It did in fact look like the curved thorax of a giant green wasp with a four bladed black propeller sticking out front, long straight wings perpendicular from the body of the insect, coiled on the edges sitting gently on two giant round soft rubber wheels that looked like they belonged on a kid's bouncy castle.

He was a tough looking guy with a big soft face and round smile watching me walk towards the airplane. He smiled bigger when he realized I was the guy he was waiting for and waved me to hurry up.

My fast steady walk became a jog. He motioned to the passenger side. The gull wing door hinged on the top was open, the deck five feet off the ground. How in the heck I'm supposed to get up there was my initial thought, then saw the straight metal pipe with the flat footstep and I was up and in.

It was a bare bones interior, no insulation, just sheet metal, instrument panels and plexiglass.

"Here put these on," said a meaty voice as I settled into the firm seat. "We gotta get going." He didn't ask my name, just handed me a headset and I nestled them over my ears, adjusting the microphone till it was in front of my mouth. "Test, test," he said while looking straight at me.

"Yes, I hear you," I said into the mic.

He nodded, pushed a mic button on the

control stick and transmitted: "Memphis Ground, November Seven Zero One Two Whisky Sierra VFR to Miami with information Alpha requesting taxi."

A few seconds went by and a metallic voice came over the line.

"November Seven Zero One Two Whisky Sierra taxi runway Zero Nine. Altimeter 29.92. Wind One Zero Zero at Ten Knots."

Devon looked all around the aircraft, then satisfied that it was clear, released the parking brake, and eased the throttle slightly forward and we began to move. It was like we were sitting right on top of the turbine engine itself. Even with the ear protection the noise was nearly deafening, the plane shaking with power. It wasn't a plane, it was a hot rod, a dragster with wings and we were waiting for the green light on the tree.

I could see and hear him laughing in joy at the sound of the engine. I was trying not to be terrified. I hated to fly on buttery smooth commercial jet airliners, and this was a bush plane straight from the outback.

He released the parking brake, and we began to move. With smooth applications of differential braking with the rudder control pedals we left the small plane parking area, rolling straight along a double yellow line for a few hundred yards, then circling around and stopping at a crossing with a double yellow line and two dotted lines demarcating a wait area perpendicular to a runway where he switched radio frequencies in preparation for take-off.

"Memphis tower, November Seven Zero One Two Whisky Sierra ready for take-off."

"November Seven Zero One Two Whisky Sierra cleared for takeoff runway 09. After take-off, turn right to a heading of One Five Zero. Climb and maintain Five Thousand Five Hundred. Contact Departure Control on One Thirty Five Point Nine for flight following. Squawk On Two Zero Zero."

Devon read back the instructions and insured the aircraft was configured correctly for take-off.

The plane moved forward onto the wide runway, made a sharp turn to the left till we were pointed straight down the center line. Devon set the parking brake, and advanced the throttle lever all the way forward; the plane was sitting there shaking as the propeller strained to accommodate full throttle. I thought the engine was going to bust right out of the cowling. Then he released the parking brake and we shot forward as though from a slingshot, and it seemed as though we only rolled a few feet before we were airborne. The shaking stopped as we were free from the ground, rising steadily he banked slowly to the right to a heading of 150 degrees and up we went at a steep angle, the lights from the airport fading away.

At five thousand five hundred feet we leveled off, the engine humming now. The sky above and surrounding us was pitch black, down below dotting the dim landscape pinpoint lights along roads and houses with giant swathes of uninhabited wilderness, and farmland. The plane flying steady and smooth, I relaxed and unclenched my fists.

There was a computer screen in the center of the dashboard, on-board radar that showed the terrain below and in front of us, the shape of the airplane steady marching forward. Airspeed two hundred knots, heading 150 degrees south east.

Devon clicked the mic and spoke into the headset.

"We'll head on this course for the next sixty miles or so, until we're out of the reach of the airport's radar, then we'll dip down to about five hundred feet in elevation and head north towards DC."

I just nodded, and he continued.

"Even though we're flying VFR, we have a transponder device in our tail section, a little electronic beacon, so the air traffic control can see where we're at all times, but when we get about sixty miles southeast of the airport I'll turn off the transponder and we'll drop off their screen. We'll be invisible."

"Won't they think something's wrong?"

"Naw, I'll make up a good excuse. And besides, we're small fish. We're a private plane under Visual Flight Rules, so as far as they're concerned we're on our own. Sure they'd like to keep track of us but it's not required. There's still a little bit of freedom when you fly a small plane in this country."

We flew in silence for a few minutes, then over the headset came instructions from Air Traffic Control.

"November Seven Zero One Two Whisky

Sierra over."

Devon responded. "November Seven Zero One Two Whisky Sierra, go ahead."

Air Traffic Control continued. "We are relaying instructions from your company for you to return immediately to the airport. Please turn to heading Three Zero Zero. Descend and maintain four thousand five hundred feet. Local altimeter setting is 29.96."

"Please kiss my ass," said Devon who looked over at me and shook his head. He keyed the mic. "November Seven Zero One Two Whisky Sierra, what is the reason for this request? Over."

"November Seven Zero One Two Whisky Sierra, your company advises that the service records for your aircraft are out of date, and an immediate maintenance inspection is required."

"Negative tower, my service records are up to date and accurate, we're continuing on to our destination, Miami International Airport, over."

"November Seven Zero One Two Whisky Sierra, your company advises that you are in violation of Federal Aviation Regulations and that your immediate return is directed."

Devon turned to me, and clicked the intercom button. "Bullshit." He pointed to the screen. "Ten miles to go to the sixty mile mark."

We flew in radio silence for a few minutes, I was just starting to feel comfortable till all hell broke loose.

The plane shook violently as a military jet shot past, off the right side almost close enough for me to reach out and touch the flames coming from its engines as the afterburners kicked in and the sharp edged plane slipped out of sight banking up and away.

"Son of a bitch," shouted Devon as he fought to maintain control of our little plane in the turbulent jet wash. Then he turned to me and smiled. "Friends of yours?"

We both leaned forward to look up and out of the front of the windshield, where we could see the interceptor jet's running lights as it was circling around and heading back for another visual pass.

"The problem," said Devon. "With a plane going five hundred miles an hour is that it takes a couple of miles to turn around. Change of plan." He flipped some switches and retarded the throttle. "Transponder off. Lights off. Engine off. Watch this!"

It was the engine off that concerned me, my fists tightened into balls, fingernails digging into my palms.

We banked sharply to the left and started descending, the engine silent, the only noise now was the two hundred mile an hour wind against the fuselage and the pounding sound of my heart trying to beat out of my chest and the inside of my eardrums.

Devon was calm as we descended in a controlled bank.

"This plane is built with a combination carbon fiber, fiberglass, and Kevlar which are all basically plastics, and virtually radar signature free. Besides the metal lug nuts holding the wheels on, the only significant metal part on the exterior of this aircraft is the propeller and it is now faced down and away from our pursuer, shielded by our invisible armor." He laughed crazily at the top of his lungs and shouted. "Try to find us now you bastard!" Little flecks of spittle flew out with his gesture.

I forced a breath of air into my lungs hissing it past my teeth so I could speak. "But... why'd... you have... to turn off... the engine?"

Devon chuckled.

"Heat signature. Those fighter jets have top of the line infrared radar to combat enemy stealth jet powered aircraft. What we have here in our little plane is a bad-ass turbine engine that gives off a lot of heat both on the cowling surface and out the exhaust pipes, but at five thousand feet that heat cools very fast. It's bad for the engine, but good for us in our current predicament. Don't worry, I practice dead stick landings all the time, just in case the engine goes out when I least expect it."

Dead stick landing, I didn't like the sound of it. Especially the dead part.

He banked to the right, then to the left. There was nothing for me to get my bearings on, no lights, no horizon, just darkness and somewhere down below invisible and coming fast towards us was the hard surface of the earth.

Devon swiveled his head forward and backwards trying to find the orange glow of the jet's dual-engine exhausts.

"There you are you bastard," he finally said while looking up to the right out of the windshield. Two pinpoints of orange from the fighter jet far up in the sky circling around to the right again, zigzagging, searching for us.

Devon banked further to the left to put some more distance between us, the altimeter read three thousand five hundred feet and was steadily winding down.

"With the lightweight construction of this aircraft I have a ten to one glide ratio." He turned to me nonchalantly. "Most small planes only have a nine to one glide ratio."

Imagine that. A bead of sweat rolled off my forehead and down the ridge of my nose while I struggled to catch my breath. We were going to die.

"Since there's five thousand two hundred and eighty feet to the mile, and at three thousand feet I can glide for thirty thousand feet give or take, that means..." He did some quick calculation in his mind. "That means we can glide for about five and a half miles." He continued on with the most important part as far as I was concerned. "We're losing five hundred feet of elevation per minute and we have about six minutes to find a place to either land, or get this engine started again." He looked over at me again and nodded for emphasis.

My voice was surprisingly small and timid and I could barely get the words to come out. It was more like a whisper. "I vote for starting the engine."

He laughed like a crazy person.

"There." He pointed down. A long straight road cutting through the countryside below and to the left of us. You could tell it was a road with the intermittent cars with their headlights stretched along its length.

"I have an idea," said Devon. "We'll put this plane right down on the deck, get it down to maybe a hundred, two hundred feet and see if we can fire up the engine. If our little free fall locked up the fuel line, or messed with the engine in some way so that we can't get it started, we'll just land it. Otherwise if we get the engine going we fly right above the road and if they're still looking for us with their infrared radar, we'll have about the same heat signature as one of those cars." He looked over at me for confirmation. "Sound good?"

I however was staring intently at the altimeter which read one thousand feet, nine hundred, eight hundred, seven hundred. "Start the engine," I whispered. "Start the engine."

"Right, here we go." He banked again to the left then leveled out.

Five hundred feet, four hundred, three hundred.

He flipped two switches then pushed a button and the engine struggled to start, chugging over and over like an old car.

"C'mon baby," he coaxed it, pushed the button again and the engine roared to life.

Two hundred feet, one hundred. My eyes were still glued to the altimeter, but on the edges of my vision, the perimeter of my sight line I could see telephone poles, wires, farm houses, trees, cars, the road ahead, perpendicular to our angle coming straight up at us.

At this point with the propeller fully engaged,

and the unmistakable full throttle whop of sharp metal propeller against air, the plane surging forward and for the first time in the last ten minutes I could feel the pressure on my seat as we leveled out and felt the pull of gravity denied again, and knew that we were pushing against it rather than falling straight down at it.

Leveling out at fifty feet, the height of a four story house, Devon brought us up to a hundred feet as we flew straight along the top of the highway.

"We'll be okay as long as no one complains, and calls the police," he said. "The minimum flight altitude for a private plane is five hundred feet you know."

He searched the sky above and around us then looked over at me. "It didn't take them long to scramble those jets did it? You know it costs about thirty five thousand dollars an hour to fly those things? They're not cheap."

"You seem to know a lot about them."

"Of course I do. I used to fly 'em. Those and just about every other aircraft in the US military arsenal. Troop transports, helicopters, gliders. But those F-15 Eagles were the best rides I ever had, speed on a dime."

Now that we were actually flying steady again, my nerves calmed down. "So what happened?"

"I made one little mistake."

"One mistake huh?"

"Yeah." He turned towards me and shrugged his shoulders. "The General's daughter. Of all things."

I whistled.

"Yeah, she told me she was over twenty one. But she was really two weeks away from her eighteenth birthday. Fourteen days to be exact. Little details you know? Some people take offense when it comes to little details. Two weeks later I would have been okay, maybe. I still would have been in trouble, but not as bad as it got. When it comes to the military they take little details pretty serious. Especially when it involves the General's daughter. It was my mistake, I should have physically checked her ID."

"So they kicked you out."

"Dishonorable discharge, loss of any and all retirement benefits, plus one year of hard labor at the world famous United States disciplinary barracks at Fort Leavenworth." He turned to look at me. "That's in Kansas you know. A real shit-hole of a place if you ask me. But maybe I'm just bitter, what do you think?"

"I've never been to Kansas."

"Well you're really missing out. So what about you?" he asked. "What in the heck did you do to make them scramble top of the line military hardware after your ass?"

I was silent.

"Never mind," he said. "I don't want to know. Skip asked me to deliver a package because he knew I could get the job done, no matter what. I was in the military for ten years and then they took away everything I'd worked for. I had to start from scratch and make up for lost time. I run a special type of package delivery system."

"You could probably get across just about any border the world with an airplane like this."

"Oh I do, quite often." He looked at me with serious eyes. "But I never transport illegal drugs. Ever. I only transport people. This is a highly modified bush plane and I can go places not may other people can. Sure you can helicopter in and out of just about anywhere, but helicopters can't glide now can they?"

He had a point. Having a helicopter wouldn't have helped us with the fighter jets.

Devon flipped the dial on a police scanner mounted just below the instrument panel. "Let's listen in on the police scanner."

I looked at my watch. It was four fifteen, we'd been in the air for close to an hour and it seemed like a week.

The police scanner was quiet, then someone came on. It was a woman's voice. Dispatch. Asking if anyone has seen or heard of a low flying plane over highway fifty five.

Devon looked over at me. "What do you think the chances are that we're flying over highway fifty five right about now?"

"Pretty good I'd say."

"Time to veer off."

Devon banked to the right and climbed up to two hundred feet flying at a right angle away from the highway, and soon it was out of sight.

Dispatch was still trying to find out if any patrol cars had seen or heard a low flying plane. One patrol radioed back to ask in between a yawn if the person doing the reporting had mentioned a mile marker. Dispatch radioed back that they did not. The patrol radioed back that highway fifty five was nearly eighty miles long so how in the heck could they investigate the complaint. Dispatch radioed back to disregard the complaint, and they'd mark it as not enough information to proceed.

The sky to the east was lightening to a dull grey.

I decided to continue our conversation, at the very least to keep my pilot attentive.

"So you fly people in this plane?"

"You'd be surprised how many people love to fly in and out of foreign countries without going through customs. Little rendezvous with their special secret friends. I'm talking legitimate, bonified citizens who want to travel without restrictions, without the messy little paperwork and red tape that comes with government intervention. Sometimes they don't want their business partners to know what they're up to. Or their spouses. Imagine that."

Unfortunately I could. I remembered the bar waitress on Catalina, the man-eater cop's wife. Some people had no morals.

We flew straight east.

"See that city up ahead? That's Chattanooga, we'll stay just north of it and keep on our heading, then in about twenty minutes when we see Charlotte we'll head north east and run along the left side of the Blue Ridge Mountains."

He put the aircraft on auto-pilot, then pulled out a map from the back seat and unrolled it in his lap, studying it. There were purple lines denoting some type of areas, Washington DC was right in the middle and surrounding it was a blue round line highlighted with white and notched with blue squares like barbed wire.

"This is an aviation map," he explained. He pointed at the circle surrounding DC. "This is a highly restricted area. Seven hundred foot floor, no exceptions. And this right here," as he pointed to the bottom of the circle. "Is the Dahlgren Naval Surface Warfare Center. They'll shoot you down. This little white line surrounding the whole area is the DCA VOR sixty nautical radius. After 911 the powers that be decided to make a buffer zone. You've got a sixty mile radius where you need special permission and a flight plan, and a thirty mile zone where you need an air marshal on board. If you somehow squeak your way into the sixty mile radius without being noticed and make the mistake of entering the thirty mile zone without permission, do you know what could happen?"

"They'll shoot you down?"

"I don't know if it's ever happened, but we ain't taking that chance. We're not even coming close to the sixty mile radius. Why poke a bear in the nose, know what I mean?"

He followed his finger along the map.

"Somewhere right over here in between Harrisonburg and Lynnwood, at the foot of the Shenandoah National Park is a big sand pit sticking out like a sore thumb. That's our land mark. It's a sand quarry, and supposedly there's a little dirt road just a hundred yards to the north of it that we can land on. If we're lucky your next ride will be there."

I had no doubt it would, knowing Skip.

We hugged the shoulder of the aptly named mountains. They did look blue juxtaposed against the ruby red sky, somewhere over the ridges the sun was rising on the eastern seaboard.

Our altitude was five hundred feet, and our airspeed two hundred fifty knots per hour. We'd been in the air for three and a half hours and it seemed almost lethargic after the excitement at the beginning. In the dark, plunging to earth with no engine while pursued by a fighter jet.

The engine hummed along and we alternately monitored the police scanner and the Air Traffic Control. No mention was made of a lost bush plane. We were nearly a thousand miles away from that event.

"There it is," said Devon pointing straight ahead. Groomed farmlands, both freshly plowed dirt and green pastures ready for harvest spread out below stretching far to the west and nestling against the blue green mountain range. Sticking out like the proverbial sore thumb at the foot of the range was the sand quarry.

Devon decreased the airspeed by pulling back on the throttle, then engaged partial flaps to slow the plane down further. We circled the quarry and looked for the landing area, a dirt road running from the quarry out into the farmlands. We could see a little blue car parked on the side.

Devon looked over at me with mischief. "I could do a dead stick landing if you want."

My answer was swift. "No thanks."

"Okay but you're missing out."

My sweat covered fists balled up as the plane banked sharply around bumping and grinding on the sudden turbulence. Devon increased the flap settings in increments, reducing airspeed even further as we slowly fell out of the sky towards the road.

It seemed as though he was playing some sort of game, teasing the aircraft in the wind, nearly stalling while keeping the bare minimum forward airspeed necessary to stay aloft, all with deft touches on the control stick.

Right at the end when there was about twenty feet of altitude left and it seemed certain that we would be crash landing, and I was bracing myself and pulling in my last breath through my clenched teeth, he goosed the throttle ever so slightly to give the plane just enough forward momentum to stay in the air and then we gently settled on the dirt road, dust and rocks flying behind us as he braked gently and we mercifully stopped. The plane rocked gently on the struts, while he powered the engine down and shut it off, the prop slowly coasting to a stop.

My ears were ringing. Sweet mother earth, it was great to be back on the ground again. I took off my headset while Devon did the same. He turned to me with a wry smile.

"Thank you for flying Devon airlines." Then his face turned serious. "Look Badger, you know what I told you back there about the General's daughter?"

I shrugged my shoulders. "Yeah?"

"Well, nothing happened. I didn't even kiss

her. But they had photos that looked like we were hugging, and we actually were on a date so that was enough to convict me."

"It's in the past. They got their pound of flesh out of you. Don't let it eat anymore from the inside."

He shook his head. "My point is, whatever it is you're going to do up there in DC, remember it doesn't take much for the people in power to take what they want from you. They can take everything."

I nodded. "I know. But they'll have to catch me first."

It was time to arm myself.

I grabbed the leather bag and set it my lap, unzipped it, pulled out the Taser and put it in one pocket, then picked out one of the pistols, checked the clip and put it in my coat pocket, then let myself out of the plane, stepping gingerly on the metal pad then jumping the rest of the way to the dirt road. Digging down with the toes of my shoes, terra firma.

The little blue car was parked next to a row of dirty bushes, caked with brown dust from sand laden trucks traveling up and down this road to and from the quarry.

A tall skinny guy with short cropped dark hair and a red baseball cap was standing next to the driver's side, leaning his elbows against the top of the car, watching me walk towards him. Then he got in the car, shut the driver's door and started the engine.

The passenger side window was down. I bent over and looked in. He had brown hair and sad dark eyes.

"I guess you're my ride," I said.

"Skip called a couple of hours ago, and here I am." He motioned to the door. "Get in, let's get going."

I obliged, settling in with the handgun tucked tight and secret in my coat pocket and the leather bag on the floorboards between my feet. He pressed a button to roll up the windows, put the car in gear and slowly moved off down the gravel road, rocks crunching under the tires.

After about a mile the gravel road turned onto a paved highway and he pressed on the gas merging quickly into traffic. I glanced over at the speedometer, fifty five. The sun was still down below the mountains but the sky was a bright blue as we passed by houses and farms, then merged onto a larger highway heading through a pass in the mountains then onto a plain with DC visible in the distance.

He still hadn't said a word since I got in the car, and neither had I.

We merged onto a larger highway, more like a small freeway, four lanes in either direction, now going like sixty five, cars packed in all around us like sardines. America's workforce heading to the center of the universe at seven o'clock in the morning. The sun high on the horizon now, blazing through the windshield. He put down the visor and drove.

The traffic began to bottleneck as we got closer to the city.

He opened up the center console in between the seats, pulled out a baseball cap and sunglasses and handed them to me.

"Put these on."

"Okay, but why?"

"Skip told me to take care of you. Make sure you got to the city with no problems. No problems means no one knows you're here. See the light poles lining the road up ahead?"

"Yeah."

"Notice anything different from the ones right next to us?"

I looked at the light poles to the right of us, then compared them to the ones up ahead. We were crawling along now in the traffic so I had plenty of time to focus my eyes.

"The light poles ahead have little round balls on them."

"Welcome to the surveillance state. We're ten miles from the center of the city and this is where it starts. Every street, every sidewalk, every trail or waterway has cameras. Every corner of every building. Anything and everything that is walking, riding or crawling gets photographed and scanned. Every car, person, bird that's flying, or bug that's crawling on the ground gets a look. The bad guys think they can ride in a metal car with tinted windows and get in without anyone knowing, but they're wrong. Some of the cameras are digital, and some are infrared that can see through metal and glass, but all those images go through spatial software. Facial recognition software."

"How do you know all this?"

"It's my job. I work for the state. Those are my cameras."

"How do you know I'm not a bad guy?"

"Because Skip said you're not, and Skip's my older brother. He said to get you in here safe and sound and that's what I'm doing. That's all I'm doing. I don't know why you're here, and I don't want to know."

17.

The little blue car stopped in front of the dry cleaner and I got out without another word. I barely had the passenger door closed when the car sped off.

I stood there for a moment, lost. Two words bounced around in my thoughts: "Now what?"

Checked my watch. Nine thirty. I was on the outskirts of Washington DC, a city I'd only been to once briefly in the past, looking for a man I'd never seen for a reason that was still unclear.

Someone stole something from Palo Alto and it was suddenly important enough for them to stop me from finding it that they'd scramble a half billion dollar jet fighter to try to knock me out of the sky.

They hired me for a job, then tried to kill me.

I pulled the baseball cap tighter over my brow, adjusted the silver metal framed sunglasses over my eyes and looked at my reflection in the store window.

Silver framed and silver coated aviator style reflecting glasses that covered most of the eye sockets, eyebrows, and nestled down over the tops of the cheeks.

My reflection looked like either a cop or a killer.

Or a bum.

I needed to tone it down a bit. Tilted the cap a little to the side and smiled. That's better.

I was in the most heavily fortified city in the world, with millions of cameras on every street corner hooked into a network of facial recognizing software system arrays, somewhere in the CIA, or NSA headquarters, probably both of them and another one that no one even knew about, or had ever heard of.

If they found me I'd probably never even know it. I'd be alive and kicking one moment, and the next split second blackness.

I needed a car, so that's why I had my ride drop me close to the airport, because that's where all the rental cars were.

I started walking down the sidewalk next to fences topped with barbed wire, fences to keep unauthorized people out of the airport, fences with bits and pieces of paper and trash, flotsam and jetsam trapped in the mesh wire at the bottom near the concrete, trash from the great society, the capitol of the greatest country in the world. White paper and trash, like snowflakes from a great blizzard caught up in the fence, but never melting. It reminded me of a story I'd heard long ago.

There were thousands of Indian tribes in the north American continent, even though the US government only recognized about five hundred seventy five.

Some of the tribes were tens of thousands strong, while others had only a few hundred, and were scattered everywhere throughout the continent.

Every tribe had its own legends, spoken and written with pictographs and paintings on the walls of caves, or stretched on canvas from the skin of bison and wolves.

Most of the legends revolved around animals with magical powers, beasts that transformed themselves into powerful and crazy demons that terrorized the human tribes.

Legends designed to keep you on your toes when you were out in the wilderness, keep you on your toes so you'd never be complacent or lazy. Keep your knives sharp and your bow and arrows ready.

One particular legend that I remembered my Grandmother telling me when she'd rock me on her knees was the animal that I was named after.

A tribe was stuck in the mountains in the middle of winter with no food. For many days none of the warriors was able to track down any animal in the blizzards, and they always came back empty handed. Day after day. Night after night. Time was running out for the tribe and they were getting desperate. They were starving.

In the middle of a heated powwow while women and children were crying in hunger, a little boy raised his hand and said that he would try. All the braves surrounded and scoffed at him, shoving him to the ground for trying to humiliate them. How could a small boy prevail when the strongest of the braves had failed. The chief raised his hand for quiet. Send the boy he commanded.

Sure enough the young boy, inexperienced, small and frail went out into the blizzard alone, tracked down a deer and brought it back to the tribe to everyone's amazement.

Again they sent the boy out alone into the blizzard and again he brought back a deer. Over and over, every time he went out he came back with a deer.

So now, the strong brave warriors were thoroughly humiliated and curious as to how this small boy could prevail, so they set out to find his technique and steal it for themselves.

They hid in a densely wooded area outside the camp.

When the small boy left his teepee and walked into the forest he magically transformed into a fierce and unrelenting badger bear and ran off into the woods to track down the deer.

The largest and meanest of the braves ran after the badger so that he could be the one to bring back the deer and reap the praise from the tribe. He tried to wrestle the deer away from the badger, but the badger killed the brave, and brought the deer back nonetheless, and this time the chief announced that the little boy was the bravest of the brave, and would be next in line to be the chief.

Then as the story ended, his grandmother would dip her forefinger into the ashes at the edge of the fire pit, draw a symbol on his forehead and proclaim that he was the little boy from the story. The champion tracker that saved the tribe.

If only that were true.

I kept walking along the barbed wire fence towards the rental car center. A transport bus pulled up to the middle, spilling out passengers, some with luggage, most carrying only a briefcase, day travelers in suits and ties, heading to a power meeting in the city. I blended into the pack and waited in line with everyone else hat and sunglasses tight.

When it was my turn, I pulled out my alter ego from my wallet. Stanley Carpenter from Seattle.

Twenty minutes later I was settling into a little white compact car, unobtrusive, heading for the exit, out the gate and over the sharp metal tire spikes that were pointed outward, heading to the city.

Black Op Security. I needed to see the front door of the operation, the spatial position, not just on a map, but in real life. It was located on the north eastern portion of the center of the city next to a doggy day care. One mile from the capitol rotunda.

D.C. was a funny place. A true cosmopolitan town with a diverse occupancy on any city block. You could have a pizza shop and oyster bar on one corner, and the Peruvian Embassy on the opposite corner. The Church of the Holy City on one block, and the Barber of Hells Bottom on the next. The J. Edgar Hoover FBI building on one side of the street and the Hard Rock Café on the other. Stoned faced agents and stoners facing off.

The city was set up to take care of a wide range of clientele with sophisticated needs.

Power brokers and wanna be's from all over the globe came waltzing into this town to rub elbows, both seeking influence, or conveying it all the while with favors both extended and received. Everything was tit for tat, quid pro quo, and anyone who denied it was either incompetent and naïve, or a flat out liar. The city was built out of blood, sweat, tears and back scratching.

Oh yeah, and money.

There was more quid pro quo money to be made per square inch in DC than any other capitol in the world. It has the highest per capita income ratio in the United States, but that's only what you see on the surface. Like a thin layer of ice on a lake thousands of feet deep and hundreds of miles wide.

I was here to drill a hole in that ice and do a little fishing, see what I could pull up.

Black Op Security.

Traffic was heavy in the late afternoon, and I was patient. Following all the rules, staying in my lane, using the turn signals, well under the speed limit, watching for distracted pedestrians gazing into their phones while walking, and drivers doing the same.

Less than an hour of driving later I was there. Old brick buildings on one side of the street and a gleaming steel and glass structure half a block wide on the other.

On the old brick building side of the street sat a pink marble statue of a proud poodle in front of a lime green door. The doggie day care. Next to that building was an unobtrusive non-descript ordinary plain red brick two story building with a double hung white door at the front and on the head beam over the door way three small black letters: B.O.S.

I circled around at the end of the block and parked across the street over a hundred feet away, but close enough to see the door and waited.

It had been a long day. I wanted to lean the seat back and take a nap, but instead got out of the car, walked around the front bumper and looked down at the meter, nonchalantly tapping the top of it, putting my face close to read the numbers while keeping the corner of my eye on the white door. It was two dollars and thirty cents per hour. Now, whoever came up with that number must definitely work for the government. Nine quarters and a nickel. No one carries that kind of change. But of course you have the option of using a credit or debit card. I inserted the plastic and chose the one hour option.

Long shadows painted the walls of the buildings up and down the street. Car after car stopped in front of the pink poodle statue and dog after dog was led by leash and placed as carefully in the vehicles as though they were the heads of state.

I walked around the back bumper this time to mix it up and sat in the driver's side pulling down the visor and clicking the seat back a notch.

The shadows got longer until they were one big shadow that merged and covered the entire city, the warm glow of sunlight had left, a dull grey taking its place, yet still the plain white door remained closed and uninterrupted.

A meter maid vehicle was making its way down my side of the street. I could see it in the rear view mirror. A green and white two seater with a bar of red and white lights over the windshield. I couldn't see whether it was a man or a woman driving it. I looked over at my meter. My hour was up. I either needed to pony up dough in the next couple of seconds or move on.

No sense in waiting, and I really didn't want to cause any commotion or bring any attention my way so I eased out of the driver's side door, nonchalantly strolled around the front bumper, put the plastic card back in the slot and selected one hour.

As with most other things in life, when you wanted the phone to ring just go to the bathroom, or if you wanted to have a guest stop by unannounced lay your head on the couch for a quick nap.

In this case as soon as I retrieved the card from the meter, out of the corner of my left eye there was a movement across the street. The door to Black Op opened. My head stayed still, studying the parking meter with one eye while keeping the other sideways at the door with my peripheral vision.

It was a woman in a grey pant suit. Long black hair cascaded down her backside as she closed the door behind her, steadied the bundle of files in her arms and made her way down the stairs. She turned at the bottom and walked up the street away from my location.

The meter maid passed by, driven by a sharp featured woman. As it slowly passed and blocked my view of Black Op and the woman who'd left the building, I went around the rear of my car to the driver's side and got back behind the wheel.

I'd been there for an hour, had seen no movement in or out of the building, and needed to make a decision. Wait to see if anyone else was there? Or follow the dark haired woman.

She got into a two seater late model BMW sports car, dark blue with a black convertible top, pulled onto the street and sped past me. I could hear the engine RPM's whirring high pitched between shifts.

Where were the cops when you needed one?

She was a speeder. This would be a problem. How to follow a speeder without getting tagged myself, since it was usually the tail guy who got nabbed by the police. If they had two people speeding, they would always go for the one in the back.

I turned the ignition, pulled out of the parking space, into a tight U-turn. She was already a city block ahead when I got up to speed. Using all three mirrors and jacking my eyes around, looking for the cops while keeping an eye on the little car.

Why did she have to drive such a small car? It disappeared into the traffic ahead of me, swallowed up by delivery trucks and normal sized vehicles that blocked my view of the sportster.

There now, two blocks ahead of me, it turned left. She was getting away. I was hemmed in by a long line of cars and there was no way that I could pass anyone.

After a three minute eternity I made it to the cross street through the traffic light and turned left onto a two lane street with a hundred other cars going each way. It was quitting time in the capital.

I'd lost her. I could always go back to Black Op and wait till dark and have a look around inside.

The traffic slowed to a crawl. Up ahead on the right side, blue lights flashing, capitol police had pulled someone over. Parked in front of the cop car was a little blue sports car with a black convertible top. The dark haired woman was handing the patrolman a card. The traffic in front of me slowed even more as people craned to get a look.

Someone was getting a ticket and people always liked to see who it was, and shake their heads in shame at the poor dumb bastard, or laugh and give thanks that it wasn't them in that position.

I kept my eyes steadily forward as I passed them. One of the patrolmen was looking down at the plastic card which looked like a driver's license, while the other was trying to get the traffic to move along, waving his arm in a circular motion.

Amazingly he handed the card back to her

and walked to the patrol car followed by his partner.

I wonder what it said on that license? Some special mark or designation. Diplomatic immunity or some sort of professional cooperation.

Either way it didn't matter, she was behind me now and with the traffic still at a slow pace would be easier to keep track of her, unless she pulled into a cross street and I wasn't able to back track in time.

With my right mirror I could see her pull into traffic five cars behind me. We travelled for three city blocks, then I saw the turn signal on the front right side above her bumper flashing orange. She wasn't turning onto a side street, she was turning into a parking space, the car that currently occupied the space had its left turn signal on as it attempted to merge into traffic, and they came to a silent mutual diplomatic agreement, as that car left the space and she pulled into it.

I could see no such luck in my immediate future, every space far into the distance was occupied by a car. In my rear view mirror I could see her get out of the little car, walk around the front bumper and head back towards a row of small restaurants.

This particular stretch of city block had a varied array of original red-colored brick buildings mixed in with painted brick buildings, two to four stories high, square, solid, but all made of bricks. The sidewalks were made out of bricks, even the gutters were brick.

There were coffee shops, art galleries, boutique clothing stores with everything seventy percent off, while I just needed a sudden place to park.

A woman walking down the sidewalk stopped in front of a car two doors up and looked at the meter. I could see a smile on her the edges of her face. She looked triumphant, as though she'd won the game and taken the time down to the last minute. I slowed down. The car behind me gave a gentle toot on its horn. I rolled down my window and waved it around me, I could see the driver in my rear view mirror throw his hands up in dismay. There was nowhere for him to go, impossible to go around me with the steady traffic on the other side coming towards us.

I stopped and waited as the woman took her sweet time fumbling with her keys, finally opening the driver's side door, she looked back at me, could see that I was waiting for her and smiled as more cars started beeping their horns. Impatience in the city did not bother this woman and she slowly and methodically got into the car, adjusted her seat then started it up and crawled out of the space into the open lane in front of her.

Lucky for the people behind me there was enough room to angle my car right into the space without having to parallel park.

The first car passed me, I could see an angry face look at me as it went by. Not wanting to wait for an opening in traffic I slid across the seats and exited the passenger side.

The clock in my mind said that it'd been

around two and a half minutes since the woman in the little blue sports car went into one of the restaurants.

I walked quickly, then stopped near the back bumper of the little blue car, pulled out the tiny GPS tracker the size of a breath mint out of my pocket, peeled the backing off, pretended to drop my hat on the ground, and placed the tracker up under the bumper. No sense in getting cute and trying to put it somewhere where it could never be found, if she was suspicious and electronically scanned the vehicle, she'd find the tracker. It was a basic bug that emitted a constant low frequency signal and would be easy to find no matter where it was stashed.

There were now three choices to make, three establishments nestled right next to each other. A Chinese take-out restaurant, a rib and fries sports bar, and a mixture bar/fine dining restaurant with a cutsie name: The Watering Hole.

Hanging on a beam out in front of the Watering Hole was an etched wooden sign with a scene out of Africa. A watering hole, a green oasis in the middle of a brown desert.

Surrounding the blue water was a pack of lions and leopards lounging in the grass, while elephants and zebras that looked like donkeys drank from the water. All the animals wore either suits and ties, pantsuits or dresses.

It was a metaphor for this town.

I made a quick choice and headed for the door.

18.

Always look for the exit. That's what my Dad told me from the time I was born it seemed.

Every single time I went somewhere, from my youngest memories, he always said to look for the exits. He told it to me so often that I started trying to beat him to the punch and say it before he could get it out.

"The first thing you do," he'd say. "Whenever you go somewhere, no matter what. I'm telling you right now. Doesn't matter if it's a restaurant, or a movie theatre, a playground next to your school, or your buddies house down the street, always..." Then he'd emphasize the word 'always' accompanied with a scrunched-up combined exasperated worried face then a silent pause before he continued:

"Always look for a way out, or preferably multiple exits, escapes, identify them, know where they are and how you're going to get to them, what obstacles are in your way out. Then, *and only then* you can have your fun, let your guard down a bit, but only a bit."

The Watering Hole bar and grill was in a brick and mortar building that had probably been constructed before the Civil War. There was one entrance at the front, and one at the back probably at a back street or alley way where they delivered the food and booze, threw the trash. So even though there was a front door and large pane glass windows that I could throw a chair through, there most likely were in essence only two exits, one in front and one in back.

The double sided front door was wide open, the thick wooden slabs that looked like they were picked up from a monastery in Tibet propped open by two metal pails filled with rocks.

It was bustling inside. You could hear the commotion from the sidewalk before you even got in front of the doors. A popular place. It seemed that the neighbors might be jealous of all the action it was getting. They were quiet and tame compared the jungle scene at the Hole.

Three men in suits walked out of the doors, red faced alcohol blushed cheeks, then another group of men and women went in through the doors. They were also wearing suits, although some had loosened their ties.

I looked like a bum in comparison, then to my delight a pair of normal looking people, tourists probably dressed as I was in slacks and t-shirts came around the corner and entered the bar.

I took the cap off my head, folded the bill and shoved it in my back pocket but kept the mirrored sunglasses tight to my cheeks and went inside.

The bar was straight ahead and stretched along the left side for twenty feet, while the dining room filled the right side, and went all the way to the back of the building. The entire room was about sixty feet wide with thick roughhewn beams stretching the whole way across the ceiling, held in place by columns that looked like telephone poles.

Out of habit I glanced at the occupancy limit sign framed and tacked to the wall next to the entrance. The limit was two hundred and twenty five patrons, and by the sound of it they were nearly all here.

The brick walls and the wooden beams all seemed to magnify the sounds, it was like being at a mini raucous convention.

Never pause at the entrance to an event, or place where there's action. That will bring attention your way. A pause in the doorway will get you eyeballs faster than greased lightning. Get through the door and head to an open spot in the middle of a crowd, assess the situation as you go.

The open spot in the middle of the crowd was towards the end of the bar. One open seat in between a burly guy and his wife by the looks of it, and two male lawyer types with their coats draped over the bar stools, crisp long sleeve shirts rolled up at the elbows meticulously discussing the case of the day.

I sat down and made myself comfortable, back to the crowd for now, settling into an anonymous role. Just another guy in town, looking for a drink to slate my thirst after a long day. The bartender caught my eye and motioned for me to wait a moment. He was mixing ten drinks at the same time, no wasted motion trying to keep pace with the animals at the watering hole. He'd flip two glasses at a time off the rack with one hand while the other crunched the metal scoop in the ice, one fluid motion filled the glasses then flip two more. Lined up in front of him on the bar rack bottles flew out of the caddy at waist level. Shots of bourbon, then scotch, vodka, rum. On down the line, then topped with sodas, juices and the odd slice of lime. He retrieved spent drinks from the patrons in front of him on down the line, replacing with the drinks he'd just made, then hustled down the counter to stand in front of me, still with time for a smile.

"How're you doing Duke, what can I get for you?"

He called me Duke. Probably a nickname he gave to most people he'd never seen before, like some people would call you Buddy, or Sport, or Dude if you were on the west coast. Duke was more refined and probably got the patron feeling pretty good about themselves and would lead to a bigger tip. Like you were suddenly Duke Kahanamoku, or John Wayne come to life.

"I'll just take a club soda with lime," I said politely. Then added: "Thank you."

He seemed taken aback, squinted at me with a quizzical look on his face. As though he'd never heard that particular drink order in his life.

"So what gives, you on the wagon?"

Damned nosy bartender. The hackles rose up on the back of my neck. I kept my face slack, my features unchanged, breathing out slowly, drooping my eyelids to maintain an inner calm while at the same time wanting to reach over the bar and throttle him. He was waiting for an answer, the quizzical look still on his face.

"I just feel like having plain soda today." Then I added. "If that's okay."

He put the palms of his hands up in surrender. "Hey fine with me Duke, I'll be right back."

I hunched my shoulders getting ready to slowly turn in the barstool and survey the surroundings, find the black haired woman from Black Op. The bartender came back down with the soda topped with a slice of green lime, put a napkin down then the glass and said simply: "Enjoy." Leaving me in peace.

I took a sip of the cold drink. Neither of the people on either side of my were acknowledging my presence which was fine with me.

Mr. anonymous.

Then from a table nearby a loud voice shouted out. "DUKE, hey DUKE over here!"

The voice was so loud and overwhelming that half the crowd in the restaurant stopped talking and turned to see who this Duke fellow was.

My eyes met the bartenders who was down at the pour well loading more glasses with ice. His eyes narrowed and he motioned with his head towards the sound of the obnoxious voice behind me in the crowd. The patrons to my right and left hadn't noticed me when I came in, sat down and ordered my drink, and even they were now turned in their barstools, watching me.

My anonymous time was over. I turned in my

barstool with my drink in my right hand just in case I needed something to throw in defense.

Two people in this establishment thought that I was someone named Duke, and that might be a bad thing if someone was out to get the guy.

The loudmouth was sitting at a table near the window, wearing a bright red aloha shirt. The shirt was plastered with green palm trees and yellow hibiscus flowers, while the person wearing it just looked plastered. He had short cropped hair, standard issue for a Marine, and had the air of someone used to both giving orders and taking them without question. There was a half empty pitcher of beer in front of him and he was flanked by two good looking bimbos, one blonde and one redhead. Both with wide grins and hoop earrings. The blonde had her elbow on the table and was wiggling her long fingernails in greeting.

The loudmouth meanwhile was beaming from ear to ear vigorously waving me over. He'd stopped shouting and was now trying to reel me in like a fish on a line.

Half the establishment seemed to be looking at me, and I'll be damned if one of them to the left of my vision in a dark corner of the restaurant farthest from the door was the woman from Black Op.

There was no getting around it. I played along and swiveled out of the bar stool and walked over to the table. The show was over now and everyone went back to their personal conversations, the room started buzzing as before.

I stopped at the table, there were three empty seats facing the back of the restaurant. I stood in front of the one in the middle and nodded at my new found friends.

"How are you all doing today?" I asked.

Mr. Aloha took a big breath, got out of his chair, walked around the red head, stuck out his meaty hand then thought better of it and put me in a bear hug, patting my back for a few happy beer filled moments before letting me free. He stood back to admire me.

"How are we doing you ask? Damn son, how the hell are you doing? When did you get out?" He quickly thought better, and pulled out a chair next to the redhead for me, and patted the cushion. "You better sit down, after everything you've been through. C'mon now." He gently guided me into the chair. I relented. Now I had a good view of the black haired woman at the back of the restaurant. I could play along for a few moments and let the boisterous one down slowly.

He went back around, sat in his seat, took a hearty gulp of the remaining beer in the mug, wiped the froth from his lips then gestured magnanimously across the table.

"Girls I'd like you to meet the one and only Duke Cranelly, friend to all and foe to none if you're enough lucky that is. Because you don't want this guy on your bad side, believe me. Sergeant of arms at Quantico, protector of Camp David, felled by an errant mortar blast at the training range two weeks ago, put back together nicely by the looks of it, and ready for action again."

He poured more beer into his mug thirsty as he was from all the talking. He leaned across the table conspiratorially. "How's the toe, were they able to re-attach it?"

"The toe's fine. Not a problem." I also leaned over the table to meet him halfway and spoke softly. "You got the wrong guy, you see my name isn't Duke, but apparently I must look exactly like him since both you and the bartender over there think that I'm him."

The girls giggled, the blonde holding her hand against her mouth.

He shook his head, rubbed his eyes with both hands, blinked twice and looked carefully at me.

"C'mon you're pulling my leg."

I shook my head. "I wouldn't do that to you."

"You're bullshittin' me."

"Nope."

"Who are you really?" He said, looking at me closely through blood shot eyes.

"No one special."

He scowled.

"Hold out your right hand, the one with the scar."

I obliged holding it across the table and turning it over top to bottom. He reached over and grabbed it, leaning over with intense eyes, tracing the back of my hand with his index finger.

"You got a four inch scar across the top of your hand from thumb to little finger. Courtesy of a prisoner at Quantico trying to escape and get by you with a homemade shank two years ago, may he rest in peace the poor bastard."

He finally sank back in his chair, finding no such scar.

"Well I'll be damned," he said. "I knew it when I asked you who you really were. Duke would of said he's just a meatball."

"Duke sounds like quite a guy."

"He is. Best damn brig guard in the Corps. Ex-brig guard I should say. Now he works the training ranges. And I'll be damned to find out he has a doppelganger, a virtual double. Here check it out."

He reached into his pocket, pulled out his cell phone and scrolled through the picture tab.

"Here," he said. "See I'm not crazy."

He held the phone in front of the girls first, and then reached it across the table towards me.

It was Mr. Aloha and Duke standing at attention on a stage during a military award presentation. Both were stone faced, ram rod straight backed with a General standing in front of them with some sort of ribbon ready to be pinned on one of them.

He scrolled through the pictures again and found one where they were seated at a table scattered with beer bottles and plates of food, each with a big grin.

It was me sitting there, and even though it was somewhat unnerving to find out someone in the world looked exactly like me, in a way it was a relief. I was a fugitive of sorts in the middle of a city under surveillance, and my double was a respected trainer at one of the most secure military bases in the country.

My eyes drifted over the blonde's head to the back of the restaurant. The blonde thought I was looking at her, she smiled coyly twirling one of the locks of hair next to her eyes.

The woman from Black Op was chatting with a man in a suit to her right. The waitress brought her a small clipboard with a check on top and a credit card sticking straight up from the top. She studied it for a moment, then wrote with a pen and signed with a flourish. The man at her right got out of his chair then helped her out of hers, pulling the back and offering his hand.

Time to go.

"So," I said to my new friends as I gently slapped my hands on the table and also got ready to leave. "Duke Cranelly huh? Well tell him Joe Thomas from Texas was here in town, and maybe we can get together sometime. I'll buy the two of you a drink, how's that? I'm here for another couple of days."

"Sure," said Mr. Aloha. "I'm Josh Hailey, and this is Trish and Patti. What's your number Joe, I'll put you two in touch."

"Yeah well," I said stalling as I thought about the options and potential danger. "I got this new phone here, lost my old one on the plane ride over, and had to get a burner. Why don't I get your number and I'll send you a text."

Then I had a better idea. Why not try to get connected with this Duke fellow in case I ever needed an alibi. For that I needed his phone number to trace it.

"Tell you what," I said. "Why don't you take a picture of me as proof, and send it to both me and him at the same time, then we'll both be connected. Who knows, we might be long lost cousins, or twin brothers separated at birth."

He had his phone ready, pointing across the table. I kept my face stoic until he put the camera down.

I got my phone ready. "Okay what's your number."

His face flushed. "Holy cow what is my number?"

How many beers had this guy had. He punched the contact list and pressed on his face then slid the phone across the table. I punched his number into my cell phone, pushed the send button, then got out of my seat.

I reached over and shook their hands in turn, the blonde tried to linger hers against mine, I gently pried it away, then walked back to the bar to pay my tab, keeping my back to the woman from Black Op and her friend who walked behind me towards the exit.

19.

When Uri Ambrov's plane landed in D.C., the rear wheels touched down at exactly seven forty one in the morning. They'd been in the air for exactly five hours and fifty one minutes since the rear wheels had left the oil blackened tarmac at Oakland International Airport. Five hours and fifty one minutes from coast to coast.

Uri knew this because he monitored every detail around him. Every miniscule piece of information that touched everything that had anything to do with his life was catalogued and frozen in his cold machine-like memory banks for retrieval at any time he desired.

Through calculated pre-meditation and precise training over many years he'd learned to combine three types of photographic memory into a highly functional aspect of his being.

No one on earth had ever been proved to have complete photographic memory where you could look at pages of books in a library all day long and remember every word on every page forever. That would clutter a mind and prevent you from free thinking and problem solving.

There were three types of photographic memory, visual, auditory and kinetic.

Just about every person on the planet had kinetic eidetic memory where you remembered a feeling for a long period of time. It's how you remember how to ride a bike, or get up and walk without having to think about the mechanics of how to do it.

There was auditory eidetic memory where you could remember everything you ever heard, every song, or conversation.

And there was photographic eidetic memory where you could remember everything you saw. This phenomenon was more common in a small percentage of children where they continue to see a vivid afterimage lingering in their mind's eye many minutes after it's disappeared, as though it was still there.

Uri had trained himself to see certain aspects of life around him, time, distances, people's traits, voices. He could tell what number was being dialed on a phone just by the sound of it.

Or what type of engine was in a car, or plane. Anything and everything to distract him from the one memory that he could not erase, because there was a fourth type of eidetic memory.

Smell.

And there was one combined eidetic memory that he could not escape. The visual, auditory, kinetic, and odor of the exploding car with his wife and newborn child inside.

Everything from that moment forward was an attempt to right that wrong. To erase it from the fabric of the universe and from his soul.

The jet rolled along the tarmac towards a private area with a portable ramp, he could see it just a few hundred yards away.

Two large square black SUV's waited nearby, the drivers standing by the doors, burly, bald headed square jawed and ready. Ex-military, Black Op security drivers.

The man in the seat opposite Uri was waking up from his long nap, blinking his eyes, yawning while rubbing his face to get the blood circulating upwards into his brain. He was one of the foremost experts in the world in software development for psychiatric manipulation of humans.

"We've landed," he mumbled.

"Yes," said Uri. "Tell me Dmitri, what is the square root of fifteen."

The man scrunched his face, then took a deep breath. "Three point eight seven two nine eight three..."

"That's enough," admonished Uri. "You're awake. That's good. I wanted you to sleep on the trip across the country because we have much left to do. What do we need to accomplish to fine tune our device before we get it into the right hands?"

"I'm hoping it's just a minor coding issue."

"Hope won't help us."

"Yes, that was the wrong use of a word," said Dmitri, now completely awake. "It's incredible actually how the device works since it starts with the first two words, quick read. Sort of a tongue twister that sets up the brain in a unique way for the insertion of the code. You see the left side of the brain controls reading, speaking, sequential thinking, while the right side controls abstract meaning and context. Somehow those two words merge the two sides in a unique way, it may have been an accidental stroke of genius, or calculated, but it confuses the sequential thinking with the abstract for just a fraction of a moment to make the brain more receptive for manipulation. I'm anticipating that with a slight adjustment of the coding that follows, the impulse that's injected into the subjects' mind after reading the title will be inescapable. They will believe that whatever we tell them to do is without a doubt the right thing to do. Every human brain has a general receptor value that tells them what is right from wrong and we have to in a way bend our instructions around that receptor value. It's the same concept as what happens during a successful hypnotic trance. We are in essence inducing a hypnotic state of being without the inherent nuances and outward projection of someone who is under hypnosis."

"Continue."

"The woman who disobeyed the command to throw her children into San Francisco Bay did so because the curve around her receptor values were not severe enough. I think it's a software coding issue we can fix."

"And if not?"

He ever so slightly shrugged his shoulders, not wanting to show offense. "The receptor value for a woman to destroy her children may be too high a curve to surpass, it may in fact be an inherent trait permeating every single molecule of her entire body that cannot be gone around so to speak. In other words it's controlled by more than only her mind."

Uri's eyes hardened as he stared at the scientist across from him.

"However," continued Dmitri. "The receptor value for a man in power to destroy an entire city that he considers an enemy may be very easy to overcome. The curve will be low. The desire will be there intrinsically even though hidden by a facade. We're talking about two entirely different psychological species of humans if you will."

"We're running out time," said Yuri. "We have two days until all the pieces will be in place. When all the key actors will be accessible at the same time for me and our team to deliver the device."

Uri turned to look out the window, silent with his own thoughts. There was no need for Dmitri to know all the details of who what why and where. All he needed to do was deliver a workable device within two days.

The plane stopped rolling and the stairway bumped slightly against the fuselage, and yet Uri's mind still revolved around near future events.

Two days until the meeting with the Secretary of Defense and the President at Quantico at two thirty in the afternoon.

Exactly fifty four hours and forty five minutes from now. And counting.

20.

Connect the dots. That's the game I was playing. Just like when you get the piece of paper with the random black dots all over the page, each one with a number, and you connect one to the other and soon you have a scene or a face. It's easy. Only in this case at the present time I only had a couple of dots with no corresponding numbers to tell me how to connect them.

I needed more dots. And I needed to find Yuri Ambrov. Where was he? Who was he?

I wasn't very concerned about the woman anymore. I'd track her car and find out where she was going next. If she found the tracker device, I could research her car license plate and find out where she lived.

Right now there was another fish to fry, I needed to track the guy she had the quick dinner with. He was tall and lean with slick black hair and a smooth grey suit. They walked together down the street, slowly, still chatting. When they got to her little blue convertible, she turned to him, he leaned over at the waist, graciously taking her hand, kissing it lightly, raising back up again, nodding smartly, and it seemed as if his heels clicked together as he did it.

He was a foreigner. Americans didn't act like that way with women. Maybe he was French, or Russian. Whatever he was I suddenly didn't like him. It was annoying seeing people act that way, the word pompous came to mind, or smarmy. Maybe it was sincere but it always came off as disingenuous. The kissing of a hand and clicking of the heels.

It was aristocratic, elite. Officer's corps chic manipulation strategy.

But in a way maybe it was better than how some of the inner city blokes treated their women ordering them around while wearing wife beater undershirts. Still it irritated me for some reason.

I needed to find out who this guy was. He was my next lead.

She walked around the back bumper of her sports car, got into the driver's side and sped off. Unless she had an on-board electronic detection device, she'd be easy to find.

I leaned against the cool brick wall in between the Watering Hole and the Chinese restaurant and pretended to look at my phone.

After the sports car sped off, the smooth foreigner looked down the sidewalk in both directions, I know that his sight lingered on me for a longer moment than necessary. He must have recognized me as the person hailed loudly as Duke in the restaurant. He might even be wondering what I was doing outside of the restaurant at that particular moment in time.

He stepped to the curb and hailed a cab, got hastily in the back passenger seat and sped away.

It was going to be a heck of a lot harder to track a cab in this city.

The cars parked on the side of the road hid the cab as it sped away. I hustled down the sidewalk, smiling as though enjoying a jog to avoid attracting attention, jumped into the little white rental car and gave chase.

Now as the sun was nearly setting and darkness settling in I could give this little pursuit my full attention.

For some reason the traffic was lighter at this time of evening, most everyone must be at their destination for the moment. I caught up to the cab quickly. It went two blocks west, then took a left turn, went another four blocks, a quick right then merged onto the Francis Scott Key Bridge heading south over the Potomac, three lanes in either direction, my tires hummed on the grooved concrete.

The bridge rounded as though a hill, at the apex in the middle I could see all the way down the grey green Potomac as it curved around to the right, the banks on both sides heavily shrouded by trees and foliage, not a single dwelling in sight.

We came down on the other side, the cab merged onto Fort Meyer Drive a one lane road leading south through Arlington.

I've been here before. Long ago, after being discharged from the Army, I took a quick trip to the outskirts of D.C. to see what I went overseas to protect. In some ways I felt it was the memory of soldiers that passed before me. The ones who didn't make it.

To the east was Arlington National Cemetery, a sprawling somber grass filled tree lined park with all that it entailed. John F. Kennedy's gravesite, the Tomb of the Unknown Soldier. The Pentagon just to the south and bordering the six hundred plus acres of national burial land, resting place of nearly half a million.

The cab kept heading south, then after four blocks took a U-turn of sorts onto North Lynn Street heading back the way we'd come.

Heading north.

Traffic was light so I gave them ten car lengths. The cab rolled past a bank and a drug store, brake lights showed though no cars were in front of it, then slowed, and pulled over to the curb. I was ready and pulled quickly into a parking space and leaned back into my seat, eyes peering through the opening under the steering wheel.

The man got out, walking methodically, limping on his right leg, around the corner of the grey oblique concrete structure into a mezzanine with metal picnic tables, topped with folded up umbrellas, spread throughout the middle of the courtyard.

I waited a moment and followed through the parking lot that was next to me. I was hidden from his view but could see his movement through the mezzanine towards a store front.

Big block letters over the front glass entrance

read Coding Dojo. It was some type of martial arts training center. The literal translation of Dojo is 'place of the way'. It could be any type of physical training facility, wrestling, judo, karate, or all of them rolled together. Coding must be the name of the owner of the dojo.

I walked closer, found a spot where I could sit and see the entrance, a park bench near the outskirts of the mezzanine. I expected to be there for a while and made myself comfortable, pulled out my phone and pretended to look at it so I wouldn't attract any unwanted attention.

At half past seven after sitting for nearly ten minutes the front door opened and out walked half a dozen young people, chatting as they disbursed into the mezzanine, some walking together, while others broke apart from the group, headed their own way.

Strange. They didn't appear to be normal martial arts students, swaggering with self-confidence, boisterous and muscular. None of them wearing or carrying a gi.

Most were either carrying briefcases, or wearing back packs, dressed as though they'd just gotten out of a college chemistry class. Half of them were wearing eyeglasses, and for lack of a better description looked like high school or college nerds.

One of them, an especially gangly young man, suffering the facial skin pangs of pubescence was walking directly my way. Unabsorbed with the world around him, he walked while looking down at his phone, somehow able to navigate the world with some type of inner radar, through feel alone.

When he was a mere ten feet away, still seemingly oblivious to the world outside his cell phone, and unaware that I was sitting in his path, I greeted him.

"Hey buddy, how was the class?"

He stopped and looked up. "Huh?"

"I saw you coming out of the Coding Dojo, so I was wondering what type of martial arts they teach, what type of classes they have there. Karate? Judo?"

He stood still, staring at me as though he hadn't heard a single word I said. His face was blank, mouth hanging halfway open, then cracked at the edges with a bit of a wry smile.

"Hey mister are you making fun of me?"

I held up the palms of my hands in defense, sitting still, apologetically backtracking my question.

"No, of course not, I'm not from around here, I was just wondering what type of dojo that this guy Coding runs."

He turned and looked at the entrance to the dojo, pointing at it, then gave me a surly answer.

"There's no 'guy' named Coding. They teach software coding there. There's a chain of them around the country. Software coding, for computers, get it? We're learning how to be software developers. It's like a boot camp."

It was my turn for a blank face. It was a computer school. Of course, dojo could mean any type of training. He turned to walk away, ready to be re-absorbed into his phone.

"Hey what time do they close up?"

He was polite enough to turn back to me with the answer, sans the surly.

"They're closing up now. We were the last class of the day."

He waited, tilting his head slightly to see if that was the last question I had for him.

I held up my left palm in farewell.

"Thank you."

Then he turned and continued on his way.

Someone stole something from Palo Alto. From a research facility. Something that made people do things they wouldn't normally do.

I waited.

The lights on the upper floors went out, one by one, until there was only light left, inside the entrance, and that one also went dark.

Two men exited the glass doored entrance. One of them locked the door with a key while the other, the one I'd been following waited to the side. I snapped two quick pictures with my phone, one while they were both looking to the side, and another as their faces were pointed straight at me. They started across the quad following the same path as my new friend who just left my side.

Heading to the parking lot behind me.

Turning my back, then getting up slowly I followed the computer student, looking down at my phone as I walked. Blending in. Same, same.

I clicked the side of the phone so the screen stayed blank, black shiny glass reflecting the scene behind me as I walked away. They bisected a one eighty degree path where I'd been sitting just a few moments ago. I turned on the phone and took another couple of photos for good measure. Then turned the screen black again. I could see the man I'd been following glance my way briefly as they walked. Then they continued on, deep in conversation. The man from the coding school was agitated. His body angles tense, disrupted.

They disappeared out of sight so I stopped and waited. The sound of two car doors, an engine, tires sharply rounding the corner of a slick parking lot.

I waited behind the trunk of a tree nearby, lining up my body, peering around the edge of it as the car exited the lot and headed up North Lynn Street, the man in the passenger side looked towards where I was hidden. Though he was suspicious there was no way he could see me. It was a late model family van, white and tall, easy to follow. When it was past the edge of the building I jogged quickly back to my car.

21.

His knuckles turning white on the steering wheel as he gripped it at the proper ten and two positions, in the comfortable driver's seat of the family van heading up North Lynn Street. Eyes unwavering on the road ahead. Watching for trouble, ready to take swift action if someone might step out into the street, or a car should cross into his lane too hastily. Always be ready. Always be careful. Safety first, even though he wanted to take both hands off the wheel and throttle the person sitting beside him in the passenger seat.

"Where are we going? Where do you want me to drive us?"

"Let's go to your office at the university."

"I'm very angry about this Dmitri. When I heard the device had been stolen I was a little shocked. It almost seemed comical in a way. I actually laughed, because I thought it had to be some kind of a joke. I even checked the calendar to make sure it wasn't April the first and someone was pulling my leg. Why would someone go to such lengths to steal something that was still in the research and development phase. It wasn't even close to being operational. Why not wait until it was completed? Who would even do such a thing? The big question for me was how did they even find out about it? Only a handful of people even knew about the project. Less than a handful, only four myself included. My first inclination as always with something like this is that the government stepped in to shut it down, or take it over, and was doing a cover-up. Those bastards will do anything to have complete control. My second and laughingly far fletched inclination was that if it was indeed stolen that it had to be an inside job, because no one outside of our little circle even knew about it. But of course that would be impossible because everyone who was working on the project were like brothers. More than just brothers, like conjoined twins. Joined at the hip no less. And now for crying out loud you show up unannounced at my company asking for help to fix it."

The man in the impeccable suit shrugged his shoulders, and shook his head in acceptance. "All true."

"I trusted you!"

"What's done is done and there's no turning back."

"I'm an idiot!" He took his right hand off the wheel for a split second and slapped himself hard against his forehead with the palm. "All I did was mention in passing a line of code we were working on. I didn't even say that I was working with anyone on a project. But somehow you put two and two together it."

"Two things you need to know John. First off your project was way farther along than you realized..."

"I'll go to the police."

"That wouldn't be wise."

"Why not? You're not above the law. Who the hell do you think you are anyways?"

"It's not me you have to worry about."

"Who then. Who's behind this?"

"You don't want to know, believe me. One thing you should know however, and I don't want to make this like some overused cliché, but these people are ruthless. They've given me a little bit of leeway to work out some of the kinks to your device. A minor issue, something that you and I with a little bit of brain work can figure out."

"Is it the government?"

He shook his head. "Not the government. Way worse than that. So let me finish what I was saying. Number one is that the project was a lot farther along than you knew. Number two is that it was also a lot bigger than you knew. Much, much bigger."

"I was a silent partner. They wanted it that way. We all agreed that it was safer, just in case we were successful and something happened to the rest of us. They all lived on the west coast, because they like it there, and I live here in D.C. because I prefer this city. We did all the work in our enclaves and uploaded to an encrypted smart vault. I fed them code as needed and they proceeded with the hardware portion of the project on their end. We haven't met in person in over a year. We kept our separate distances just in case."

"In case what?"

"Well for one thing, in case the government or someone else came along and poached our idea, which is exactly what happened."

"You are naïve."

"What..."

"The government was busy monitoring your project from the very beginning. The only thing you did right was covering your tracks as far as keeping your personal identity secret. You're the only one of the group they were unaware of."

"How do you know that."

"The other three are in federal... well we can't call it custody, we can just call it protection. You however managed to evade detection."

"You know this for a fact?"

"Has anyone from the government, or any other entity questioned you? Police, private investigator?"

"No."

"Are you in custody?"

"Does it look like it?"

"Well there you go."

"How do I know that *you're* not with the government?"

"I'm just an independent contractor. Like you. I saw an opportunity and took it."

"Well, there's no way I'm helping you."

"You don't have a choice."

"So you're a spy. You hang around research facilities at universities, make friends, look for ideas to steal. Seducing people into revealing secrets."

"Well you must admit, fresh minds and new ideas tend to flourish in settings such as this. Let's just say I got lucky. I had no idea that it would be you that could lead me to the promised land so to speak."

"It was one line of code."

"Ahh, yes, but a very important line. A key to hypnosis I recall you saying, you wrote it on the board that evening, proud as a peacock with the magnificence of it. And it was intriguing to say the least. But then when I pressed you on it, you quickly erased it from the board, clammed up, changed the subject, refused to talk about it anymore. As though in a fine bright moment of utter bliss and happiness you came forth with one of the most incredible feats of your academic life, showering it upon me with unrestrained pride, and just like that expunged it, deleted it with the most rapacious secrecy. It was then and there that I realized there was much more to it than just a line of code on a chalkboard. There was something bigger and deeper behind it, and with the short amount of time we'd spent together, I realized that you were incapable of big ideas. Only small ones."

"But then how did you find my friends?"

"Now that was not luck, my fine little insatiable friend, but hard detective work. One line of code led me to four friends from college who won an award for their senior project at MIT. Three of those friends were now living in close proximity to each other in another high tech research oriented neighborhood on the West coast. Now why, I asked myself, would they be living so close together after graduating from such a prestigious school such as MIT. Normally when college buddies graduate, they split and go their separate ways. But not these three."

"You bastard."

"So we have three fairly successful professors working at a research facility in Palo Alto who seem to be doing very well, while you, the fourth friend, toil away working two jobs, one at this university during the day, and another job at a code camp down the road."

They pulled up to the two story brick lined building near the center of Georgetown University and got out of the van. Jonathon fuming while he walked up the steps to the front door, while Dmitri scanned the street around them, then followed, up into the building through the mezzanine to the wide staircase that led to the classrooms on the second floor.

No one else was in the building as Jonathon unlocked the door to room number two ten, and flicked on the lights. His heels clicked on the hard floor, echoing as he walked across the classroom then sat in a chair near the front.

Dmitri walked over to the chalkboard and began to write a line of code in small white letters from one side to the next, then when he got to the end of the green board he started on a second line, stopping halfway across.

"You see, I know the code by heart. The integral part of the equation is here." He pointed to the end of the second line. "And this is what I need your help with."

It was more of a giggle than a laugh, a nervous outburst that Jonathon tried to hold in like a sudden uncontrollable sneeze, leaping out of his mouth before he could contain it. Then he was somber again, sitting quietly. "I wouldn't help you if my life depended on it."

Dmitri smiled, a ravenous full white toothed grin, from ear to ear. "Ah, but dear Jonathon my poor detached friend. Your life does depend on it."

He took out a small round black object from his left pocket, the length of a cigar, threaded on one end, with a small deep opening on the other. Then from his right pocket a square silver plated gun emerged, the two hands came together with a task, the left hand carefully screwing the black cigar onto the barrel. Dmitri's eyes never wavered from his gaze down at Jonathon. It was apparent that he could thread the silencer on the gun blindfolded if need be.

Jonathon was stuck to his seat. He wanted to move but was suddenly frozen, paralyzed in fear. He'd only seen a real gun once in his life.

Long ago he was in a bank that was being robbed when he was a teenager. It happened so fast that he was paralyzed with fear back then too. He thought for sure the man would shoot them all and he tried to mouth the words help, help, but nothing came out then and nothing came out now.

An electric static seemed to envelop him, standing every hair on end, adrenaline surging, wanting to run but unable to so much as pull a single breath through his rigid lips.

"Ever had your knee shot out?" asked Dmitri.

Jonathon tried to shake his head no, but at the moment he was having a hard time breathing.

"I can attest that it's actually quite painful." Dmitri continued. "It's like having your entire body stuck upon a flaming metal skewer, and that skewer begins at the knee and goes all the way throughout every inch, every sinew, every nerve ending. I don't recommend it. So all I need you to do, in order to avoid that fate, is to come up here and complete the code. There's one piece missing, and I know that you have it." He tilted his head and limped to the side. "Or I promise you that I'll shoot out one knee first, and then the other. Why should I have to endure this pain after all, without sharing it with you?"

22.

I spotted the white van parked in front of a two story brick office building on 36th street.

The small bronze plaque on the wall next to the green door read 'Center for International Studies'

We were in Georgetown, and I'd been across the Francis Scott Key bridge twice in one day to get here. Blue banners hanging from the building across the street read Georgetown University Department of Art & Art History.

There was a lot of money here, you could feel it saturated in the red bricked sidewalks, and tony buildings that reeked of old cash. There was a lot of money to be made and a lot of money to be spent in this old college town, by the people running it, the pocketbooks of the parents paying astronomical amounts to send their kids here, and the kids themselves. Graduate from Georgetown and you graduate straight into the old boy network, government business, if you want it, and you'll be set for life. There was a reason why the highest per capita earners in the country were in this particular zip code.

The last bits of sunlight had long since departed, globe street lights lit the area with a soft ambient illumination.

I was late to the party and had no idea which building they could have gone into, so I parked in the first open spot I could find and waited.

The art department across the street had a wide ranging Wi-Fi signal for their well-heeled student population, and I was able to access it for high speed internet on my phone. Might as well stay busy. I typed in the license plate of the van.

Jonathon Myles Stepenvich. Thirty eight years old, unmarried, graduated from MIT at twenty four years old with a degree in computer science. His parents emigrated from Russia in the mid-nineteen eighties, part of the exodus after the fall of the Berlin Wall and detente. Both were math professors for MIT. His father specialized in statistical analysis, while his mother taught spatial calculus, whatever that was. A lot of brain power it seemed.

He bounced around the country doing stints at various computer software companies, high tech firms, start-ups, gaming companies, search engine wanna be's, and was now currently employed by the coding college where I picked up his trail.

This tells me nothing, sort of a dead end.

He didn't seem to have a very illustrious

career for a graduate at MIT.

Why does the dapper foreigner have him in a meeting.

I looked deeper. School records. His senior project won first place in the school's aerospace competition. A team project with three other students. I researched their names, put them in boxes on the side of the search engine. What made them alike, what traits or accomplishes brought them together.

For one thing it looked like they shared a dorm all the way though school from their freshmen years to graduation.

Two were software engineers, one was a mechanical engineer, and the forth graduated with a degree in physics.

So where were they now. I clicked the boxes one after the other, and was pleasantly surprised to see that they all now resided in the little town of Palo Alto, California. How cozy.

I decided to put a tracker on the van.

Got out, stretched my legs, yawned, locked the car door, walked down the brick sidewalk, thought about whistling a tune, just a joyful unassuming guy out for an evening stroll, then remembered what my Dad used to say. "Never whistle at night. That's how the ghosts find you."

Scared the beejeesus out of me since I was a little kid. No need to whistle, especially not in this old town, it was probably filled to the roof tops with spirits.

I walked, unassuming, not looking at anything in particular, the magnet backed tracer palmed in my right hand. When I got close to the van, I decided to cross the street, and at the rear bumper seemed like as good a place as any. I stumbled a bit going off the curb, falling to one knee gently, while quietly cursing my bumbling way of walking, brushing off my pants with both hands, sans the tracker, and kept on my way across the street, up past the Department of Art & Art History, tilted my head up towards the heavens, then walked back towards the little white sedan, sat back in the driver's seat and waited again.

There was one light on in the top floor corner of the International Studies building.

I could probably pull up the personnel directory for this building in the University's data base, then access the schematic of the floorplans to see who was the tenant in that room.

A couple of clicks later and I was in. Room number two ten. Classroom of none other than Jonathon Myles Stepenvich, assistant professor of computer science.

But who was the other man?

I had the photos when they were leaving the coding college. Pulling them all on the screen, it hit me. The younger military looking guy. He reminded me of the guy back in San Francisco, the one in the big black SUV who got out of the car looking for the phone of the assassin from the hospital. The phone I placed in the trash can.

I pulled up the photos from that night. They were dark and blurry, too far away to increase the magnification and get a definitive image. I focused on the one image where he was looking back down the street towards my car hidden in the shadows, increased the magnification. Same hair, same shape face. I was ninety percent sure it was the same guy, but my experience was that the photo was too blurry to use in facial recognizing software.

I went back to the photos from this afternoon at the Dojo. The ones I virtually took over my shoulder. I photo shopped the younger man's face out, till I had three distinct angles. One straight forward, one at a forty five degree angle, and one at a one eighty profile.

Then I sharpened the images, increased the white balance so the angles of the facial contours were most distinct and fed them into the FBI's facial recognition software.

Points of light appeared on the edges of the face; chin, nose, eyes, cheek bones, ears, distinct angles and measurements of percentages between them. A clock on the bottom of the screen showed the time left for the answers.

Ten matches. Two in Washington D.C. so I segregated them onto the screen one next to the other. Doppelgangers, but the one on the left looked older, not only with more greying hair, but deeper wrinkles on the forehead. Focusing on the one on the right, I pulled up the data sheet.

Dmitri Pavlovic, thirty four year old Serbian exchange professor, specializing in 'spatial software development as it relates to psychiatric developments in humans'. Now that was a tongue twister.

I pulled up his profile with the accompanying

color photo of a seriously unsmiling man with rounded features and slicked back black hair, greying slightly on the sides above the ears.

The grey looked out of place. I wondered if he painted the grey in there for effect. You can't be a respected professor after all unless you have a little grey hair right? How can you be taken seriously as an old wizen figure if you don't look like you're old enough. If you don't have a beard, you must at least have some greying hair.

I looked back up at the building, the light was still on in the top floor corner unit. Up there was my guy from the restaurant who had lunch with the gal from Black Op Security, and was probably the same guy from San Francisco.

Having a little meeting with the guy who was roommates with the geniuses at MIT, the masterminds who lost the device in Palo Alto.

Small world.

Or maybe the device wasn't stolen. Maybe it was a ruse to make it look that way.

What else has 'ol Dmitri been up in his travels around the world. An exchange professor from Serbia.

I dug deeper.

He graduated from the University of Belgrade with a degree in software engineering when he was just twenty years old. A whiz kid.

Then he got caught up at the tail end of the great Yugoslav war that lasted from nineteen ninety one to two thousand and one, resulting in the breakup of the Yugoslav state.

NATO bombed Belgrade, seriously injuring him with shrapnel from a bomb that nearly destroyed the Chinese Embassy. A coin sized piece of metal popped through the wall of his apartment while he was sleeping, going straight through his right knee. He was evacuated to Moscow where he recovered with a full knee replacement, and was immediately hired by a private security firm, specializing in military surveillance.

It had been two long hours since I'd been sitting outside the Center for International Studies. The light upstairs in the top floor corner room went unceremoniously out. Now the whole building was dark.

The front door opened a few minutes later. Out popped a man with a limp. Dmitri. He closed the door behind him, then without any unnecessary movements made his way to the white van. Jonathon's van.

He opened the front driver's side door, hoisted his frame into the seat, closed the door, turned over the engine and drove away.

I was never one to trust tracking devices and followed far behind. The van was easy to see. Unfortunately he parked it just a few blocks from the university. Streetlights poured light through the windows of van and I could see him wiping down the interior. Getting rid of the evidence. He flagged down a cab that took him deeper into the city. Around DuPont Circle, then straight up New Hampshire Avenue into the Cardozo. A swank area just north of the Capitol Rotunda. The cab stopped short of the church district, in front of a row of stores, The Cha-Cha Club, and Bandito Taquito stood out.

He paid the cab, walked across the street and went into a low rise apartment building.

I checked the address and matched it against his profile. This was his place of residence.

Now that I was fairly sure that Dmitri was settled in for the night, his address confirmed, I decided to go back and check on the other guy who did not leave the Center for International Studies. The agitated Jonathon.

Maybe he slept in his office.

I travelled back to the university and parked far down the street.

Sometimes it was better to just go right through the front door rather than going around the side or the back and trying to be crafty about it. That's how you get caught in a place like this. Motion detected lighting was usually set up on the sides and backs of buildings, while the front had constant lighting. Make it look like you belonged there, so I walked right up the steps to the front door then with a single deft movement lock pick hidden in the palm of my hand opened it and strolled in.

As I passed the threshold from outside to inside the air quality diminished. It was a faint aroma lingering on the edges of the air.

I sniffed the air lightly, lifting my head like a bloodhound.

I was familiar with the odor.

Modern bullets have a distinct smell. If you could think of a mix of ozone and ether with an edge of burnt rock you would have that fragrance. Home remediation companies had ozone machines that knocked out any type of smell with this apparatus that pumped ozone into the entire space, it actually burst the scent molecule, and was useful for homes that had been burnt, or had mold, or dead animals. Put an ozone machine in there, close up all the doors and windows, get out for the night and you'd come home to a scent that bordered on machine shop.

It wasn't an overwhelming scent as though an actual ozone machine had been hard at work, but I could sense the residue as I climbed the stairs and went down the hallway to the front right room. It was unmistakable.

I used my pinpoint light red light shining it conservatively forward as I moved quickly. No sense in dilly dallying someplace where I hadn't been invited.

The door to the room was closed. A large etched glass window sat in the top middle of the door. Stretched across the middle in bold black letters; PROFESSOR STEPENVICH – PHD.

The door was unlocked, the room inside dark.

I made my way to the front of the classroom, past rows of chairs with half-moon desks over the seats.

He was a asleep alright. For the rest of eternity. Slumped at the foot of the chalkboard, legs at odd angles, head tilted back with two little red filled holes at the back of his head. Probably never knew it was coming. One minute writing on the chalkboard, then the next moment darkness.

It must be the kind of low velocity bullet that makes a clean entrance and then bounces around inside the cranial cavity for a while and does not exit.

You can even have a low compression, low velocity projectile that's slowed further with a silencer, which is what I determined must have happened here.

Probably had the end of the silencer right up against the back of the head for less splash effect.

It was not a fine sight to see.

He still had a piece of chalk in his right hand, clutching it with his last grasp. His skin was a pale white matching the piece of chalk he was holding.

The chalkboard itself had been wiped, you couldn't say clean, as it looked as though it had been hurriedly smudged from end to end with the eraser on the ground next to Myles.

Maybe a highly trained crime scene inspector could take a thermal photo of the chalk board and pull out the indented markings. It's what I would do if I had the equipment and the time.

I looked at my watch. It was a quarter past midnight. And as my Dad used to say, nothing good happens after midnight. That's when the capital letters Shit Hits The Fan.

Time to go.

23.

So, Dmitri Pavlovic wasn't just a professor. He was a killer.

I would treat him as such.

It was a little after three AM when I parked in front of the Cha-Cha club. They were still going strong with another hour before they closed up for the night.

A trio of semi drunk guys in suits stumbled out of the front door, cursing and singing at the same time. Thumping music followed them echoing out of the blue and red tinted showroom bar, then as the door closed it was quiet on the street again. One of the trio stopped to light a cigarette, standing there wobbling on his legs as the puff of smoke wafted around his head, circling up into the black night sky, back lit by street lamps. He inhaled the poison as though it was an elixir.

An oriental woman leaned against the lamp-post, pulling her skirt to the side, showing me her leg up to her hip. She looked experienced. She knew I wasn't a cop, and the drunk guys would just waste her time. She'd soon find out she was wasting her time with me also.

She was an American, but tried to act like she was straight from the Saigon Delta with a fake accent.

"Hey baby? I love you long time. You like?"

I walked across the street without looking her in the eyes.

The Hillcrest Apartments. Two miles from the Lincoln Memorial. You had high end housing mixed right in with the dregs of the world. There was a secure front door and you needed an electronic code to get in. No problem. There were three hundred units at the Hillcrest.

All I needed to do was wait till someone exited, and be there at the exact same time as though I belonged.

I stood by the side of the road, near the curb. The oriental woman on the other side of the road studied me, wondering if she should give it another try. Then a long car came along, pulling alongside her. She leaned through the open window at the back seat, then climbed in, and the car continued down the road.

Twenty long minutes later I saw the elevator open, out walked a light grey suit, this guy was in better shape than the suits exiting the Cha-Cha Club, he looked stone sober, hair neatly combed, eyes bright, carrying a thin black briefcase, walking crisply for the front door. He was in a hurry. Trying to get a jump on the other suits in the city.

I made as though I was walking for the front door also, timed it so I'd get there at the same exact moment. The door would have to swing outward and I was blocking his exit. I'd have to punch in the code while he waited.

I saw too late that it was Dmitri.

It was also too late to turn away from the door as if I never intended to enter the building. That would be a dead giveaway.

I'd made a mistake. It was late, I was fatigued from not sleeping. I forced my outer demeanor into non-aggressive passive, semi bumbling, eyelids drooping, not really aware of my surroundings, possibly drunk. Completely non-threatening. A poor slob out late just trying to get home.

Maybe he'd recognize me as the guy sitting outside the Coding Dojo and try to take me out like he did to the guy back at the college, with a silencer on the front end of a pistol.

His eyes however told the story, he was agitated. Unnecessarily so. I was in his way, and that's all that mattered to him at that particular moment in time.

I noticed he was holding the briefcase in his left hand, that meant he was right handed, which would come into play within the next few seconds. When carrying an object and walking it was a normal tendency to carry it in your free hand while keeping the dominant hand ready for action. If he was carrying a gun it would be in his right pocket.

I pretended to just then notice my bad timing, as though I'd just woken out of a walking slumber, holding up my hands in the universal sign of 'I'm so sorry', and backed away from the door. I put my open left palm forward in the other universal sign of 'after you'.

"You go first!" I said loud enough so he could hear through the double paned glass.

He smiled tightly, pushed against the crossbar, unlocking the door and tried to walk right by me without a word.

Too late his eyes widened as he realized that he'd seen me before, twice actually in the past few hours, sudden adrenalin, his entire body exhibiting a frantic movement as he tried to back away from the door and reach into his pocket.

I stepped in front of him, grabbed his Adams apple in a pincer between my thumb and forefinger of my left hand, and waltzed him back through the doorway. He grabbed the pincer with his right hand, his dominant hand, a normal reaction in a fight to the death as the wind was abruptly cut off from his pipe.

He dropped the briefcase, as he stumbled backwards losing balance, reaching for the pistol which unfortunately was in his right pocket. He tried to switch hands on the pincer but it was too late. I danced him straight back into the stairwell next to the elevator, and threw him into the first set of stairs like a sack of potatoes. Cracking his head on the metal stairwell.

He blinked hard, jackknifed off the stairs, not trying to grab for the gun, just trying to create some space so he could reach for it again, kicking and clawing, one kick caught me on the shin, the left one that was nearly broken. Stifling a shudder of pain I backed up an inch to give myself room to attack, he lunged forward, caught me under my cracked ribs with a left handed undercut. His chin exposed, left hand extended, I caught him with a straight right cross to the side of his jaw. I could feel it dislocate out of the socket. He went down on his side, legs splayed in odd angles, out cold. Or so I thought.

The gun with the silencer was halfway out of his pocket, I kicked it all the way out with my foot, sliding it well behind me, then reached down, grabbed him by the ears, shaking his head, slapping his face to wake him up.

"Where's the device?" I whispered. His eyes fluttered, but did not open. "Palo Alto. Where's the device? Is it in the briefcase?"

I didn't want to take my hands off him just yet to retrieve and search the briefcase.

"Where is it?" I repeated.

He was playing possum. With his eyes still closed he reached his left hand up towards my face as though it was a natural reaction of his unconscious synapses. I pushed the hand back.

He reached up again, I pushed it back again, his eyes still lightly shut.

It was a slow motion feint. Slowly moving his right hand along his side towards his ankle. I didn't see it coming, he gave a quick twist of his torso, bringing his ankle up into contact with his fingers. Too late to prevent it, the tiny gun from the ankle holster was in his grip. Small caliber, smaller than the palm of his hand, a one shot derringer, perfect for a fight like this, fitting in so tight that there was no way to dislodge it, I could only try to make sure that the barrel didn't point at me. One shot and it would be over.

Now both of my hands clamping down, circling his right wrist struggling to maintain control. Both of us gasping for air. His legs like serpents leveraging around my thighs, twisting me off, and I with no leverage, taken by surprise.

I fell on my left side, the point of my hip grinding on the concrete. The hand with the gun pushing against my grip with all his might, getting close to having a shot at my mid-section.

No way around it, reversed leverage from pushing against the gun hand to pulling straight up in the air then down into his side. The sound of a muffled pop and he went limp, this time for good I imagined. The bullet must have pierced his heart, or a good enough portion of it to stop it. He shuddered once more and was still. Eyes half open, pupils dilating as they rolled back into his skull.

There was no mistaking the body language. There's knocked out cold, and then there's dead. He was the later of the two.

I searched his pockets. All he had was a thin wallet, a cell phone, and a set of three keys on a small simple ring. I put the wallet in my front pocket and left the phone and keys where they were.

I stood up and left the pistol in his hand, thought about picking up the larger one with the silencer attached and tossing it a storm drain but realized that I hadn't touched it. No prints.

Not that it would matter.

They had motion detecting sensors and cameras all over this building, inside and outside the front door, where most of the action normally took place. Top of the line motion detecting, passive infrared radiation sensors, high definition wide angle lenses.

I was on another camera with a dead guy nearby. They were starting to pile up in my wake.

Walking towards the exit, picking up the briefcase, I almost felt like waving to the camera, but that would be immoral. I didn't choose this fight. It came at me. Now I was reacting to it.

The Cha-Cha club was still going strong when I crossed the street for a second time heading for my car. The lovelorn oriental woman with the long skirt was long gone and there was no one to take her place.

I settled into the driver's seat, fired up the engine and did a U-turn down the street two blocks then took a left turn. The nearest lamp post was twenty feet away so I was in a bit of shadow. The briefcase was locked.

This is one of those instances where maybe you shouldn't go poking your nose into places they didn't belong. For all I knew it could be booby trapped. It was unlikely, who in their right mind would walk around with an explosive armed briefcase. It could accidently just open up on you and then, kablam.

If it did have a trigger, it would be on the front. Wrong guy opens it up without putting in the correct code, kablam.

The funny thing about locking briefcases is the fact that they don't think anyone will see the flaw in the design. Grabbed my boot knife, popped off the rear hinges and carefully pried the top off a quarter inch. Just enough to poke my little pen light into the crack and look at the front. No wires, no bulges, just the normal smooth inside faux black leather interior, with brown stitching along the top edges. Opened it up a bit further and pulled out the contents laying them on the passenger seat.

The usual; pens, notepads, calculator, handgun with a silencer. This made three guns the professor was carrying. One in his pocket, one on his ankle, and one in his briefcase.

The paper on top had a mathematical equation: X=201-030400+5060-00330.

Maybe this was the equation that was on the chalk board. There was a stack of more papers dealing with psychology, human anatomy. More papers on hypnosis, case studies of human behavior while in a hypnotic trance.

Then a schematic of a military base, buildings, roads, live fire ranges, check points, a train station, barracks, even a little golf course, all bordering the Potomac river to the east and curving away down and to the right. In tiny letters at the top of the page: Marine Base Quantico.

Training ground for the Marines, FBI, Secret Service. I always wanted to go there, but never had the chance. You could fire any weapon in the world on the ranges they had scattered throughout the creek filled Virginia countryside.

I kept flipping through the papers.

Towards the bottom of the pile of papers,

wedged in between two pages of mathematical calculations, a single ruffled page torn from a yellow legal pad. In the middle in big bold black letters:

NUKE TEHRAN

I looked closer at the two papers that bookended the yellow paper.

Mathematical equations dealing with the weight and price of gold, lift capabilities of helicopters. The physical structure of a steel plated bank vault door and the explosive force per square inch needed to breach it.

Looked like someone was planning a heist.

24.

Yuri sat in the hard backed chair at his desk on the top floor of Black Op Security. The one way silver tinted windows looked out onto a small city park to the east. There was a basketball court, swings, benches. A grass area to walk a dog or throw a baseball. The black of the night sky was beginning to lighten on the edges of the horizon, heralding the impending dawn less than an hour away.

Dmitri needed to ditch his clothes, so he texted a few hours ago with the code. Walter was inserting the language into the software in his office downstairs, and soon they'd be ready to go to war.

Yuri's office was bare bones, solid tile floor, light stained redwood walls, tongue and groove ceiling. One chair, one desk, one computer screen, one keyboard, one phone, one yellow legal pad, one pen, one pencil. No trophies, no pictures on the walls, no vases with flowers. If someone came to visit or debrief, they stood at the front of the desk.

He looked down at the phone, checking the time print on the face. Four twenty five AM. Five minutes from now he'd receive a call on the satellite line. Untraceable.

In Iran, at the edge of the desert, one hundred miles from Tehran sat two sleek attack helicopters, and one giant heavy lift helicopter in an old crater the size of a warehouse.

Camouflage netting that resembled the sand and rocks surrounding them covered the crater, propped up by telescoping poles, giving them invisibility and air flow to survive the torrid desert heat for the three days they'd been in hiding.

Two forklifts were strapped into the belly of the heavy lift copter. The two attack choppers, armed with Gatling guns on either side of the nose, also had two AGM-114 hellfire missiles mounted under the small wings that jutted out from the fuselage. Five feet long, one hundred eight pounds in weight, cobalt black with three bright yellow bands around the seven inch diameter.

It was a precision missile designed for soft targets such as buildings, tanks, bunkers. This particular design was modified for a tight blast window and minimal collateral damage. They needed to blow through a ten inch thick steel plated door, and not bring down the entire building around it.

Not included in the official descriptive uses for the precision missile, but one that they felt confident would work was against a bank vault.

One that held half a billion dollars in gold bullion. Each missile cost seventy thousand dollars to procure and even if they needed all four to complete the job, it would be money well spent.

Yagiz Kaplan, Turkish Air Force retired patted the rounded nose of one of the missiles.

All system checks were completed, with just one more right before they lifted off.

The time on his watch read one o'clock. It was afternoon in the desert, the sun still directly overhead and hot in the crater even though shaded by the netting.

He pulled out the satellite phone and dialed the ten digit telephone number. It rang once.

"Conduit," said Yuri.

"Copper," replied Yagiz completing the code.

"You are ready?"

"All systems go," said Yagiz.

"Remember our procedure."

"Yes," said Yagiz. "Any changes?"

"None yet. We have the device prepared. Our meeting is in ten hours."

Yuri hung up the phone.

Nothing else needed to be said. With the helicopters airspeed at three hundred miles per hour, they were twenty minutes from Tehran.

If all went well the nuke would explode at eleven o'clock at night, two hundred feet above the center of the city, while nearly everyone was either asleep, or headed there.

They needed to stay hidden deep in the crater until a few moments after the nuclear blast to protect the sensitive electronics on board the aircraft from the resulting EMP, the electromagnetic pulse that would fry any gear that was turned on with a voltage surge.

Five minutes after the blast, while the mushroom cloud was still rising into the atmosphere, in the frantic minutes after the shock wave had passed by, they would fly in low to the bank vault, blast the door off the hinges with the Hellfire missiles, then with the forklifts load up twenty pallets of gold into the heavy lift helicopter, and five pallets each into the attack helicopters.

They wouldn't have to worry about any survivors getting in their way. With their protective radiation suits, and air tanks, they'd be able to move at will throughout the compound, clearing a road if needed for the forklifts through the rubble from the mother lode to the choppers.

Twenty five minutes after the blast to the bank vault, half hour at the most to load the freight. One hour after the disaster, five minutes before midnight, they'd be flying straight south to the rendezvous site on the coast.

Now where was Dmitri?

He should have been here fifteen minutes ago. He looked at the security cameras outside the office. No movement had been recorded in the past half hour. He called down to Walter.

"Any word from Dmitri?"

"None."

"Are you finished with the software coding?"

"Yes, it fits seamlessly."

"Be ready to leave in one hour," said Yuri and hung up the phone. He picked it back up and dialed Dmitri's cell phone. It rang five times then went to a robot voice asking the caller to leave a message.

Hair raising on the back of Yuri's neck, he turned to his computer, logged into the camera system and pulled up the security camera link to Dmitri's apartment complex. The screen was empty. He looked back at his phone, scrolling through his messages, the one from Dmitri said he was leaving his apartment in five minutes. That was at three ten AM.

Over half an hour ago.

Three camera angles edge to edge on the screen. One camera on the outside of the building with a super wide lens showing the street running from end to end. One on the wall by the elevator looking directly at the front entrance. The best angle is the camera with a wide lens that points towards the elevator and the front entrance from inside the lobby. A few people coming and going through the front door. Then at three fifteen AM, Dmitri walking swiftly from the elevator to the entrance, trying to get by a seemingly drunk, wavering man on the outside who is blocking his way. The door opens. They tangle, Dmitri drops the briefcase and is pushed backwards into the stairwell next to the elevator.

Two minutes later, the other man leaves the stairwell, picks up the briefcase and exits the building.

All three of the cameras are mounted high on walls looking down. It's a flaw. You have to install them that way to make it harder for punks, hooligans and drunks to rip them off their base. The man on the screen who ambushed Dmitri must know this and keeps his head pointed down the entire time. There is no clear shot of his face.

Yuri's forehead turns red as the fury builds inside, but he quickly calms his emotions. Takes a long deep breath, slowly releasing it. Rage solves nothing. Pure calculated thought takes over. There are other security cameras that he can access. They take more time to locate, but nothing is impossible. He has access to a wide array of government cameras. It took a few quick clicks till he found the right set.

The man leaves the building walking to the right, there's a camera on the corner, he walks straight towards it, head angled down, crosses the street, there's one on that side also, same result head down, no clear shot, gets into a white sedan wedged in between two other cars. As the car pulls out Yuri freezes the frame, zooms in on the license plate, writes down the number. The man's face is hidden by the visor that's pulled down, even though it's still night and there is no glare. The guy is a pro. The car pulls a U-turn, heading south. Yuri pulls up the corresponding cameras. One block, two blocks, heading south.

The car takes a left turn into a residential neighborhood with single story homes and disappears. All the cameras on this block are private.

Yuri calmly breaks a pencil in half to relieve some stress and throws it in the wastebasket on the side of the desk. Looks down at the license plate number, pulls up the DMV database, inputs the number. Registered to a rental car company. Pulls up that database. The car was rented just yesterday morning to a Stanley Carpenter of Snohomish, Washington.

Yuri shook his head. Not a chance that someone named Stanley just took out his number two agent. There was a copy of the license in the file. The photo is blurred. You can make a copy of any type of document and photo of a person, but if there's a smudge of dried sunscreen, the sensor on the copier machine is defrayed.

A lone wolf.

Yuri recognized the pattern. He could see it if he looked in the mirror. Someone was stalking them from the shadows.

The same person from the hospital who broke Antoine's neck.

None of it mattered, he was reminded with a single dulling thought. As though a black cloud drifted through his mind. The others could have the gold, it was but an afterthought and meant nothing to him. A means towards an end. Nothing more.

Dangle two tons of gold on the end of a stick and men of a certain nature would do any bidding. Go to any length to get their hands on it, as though it would cure all the ills that afflicted them.

Not for Yuri. Unfortunately. If only it was that easy, he could have ended his suffering long ago.

An endless stack of gold and money wouldn't quench the thirst constricting his throat. Squeezing his soul. Like a boot on his neck that he couldn't get out from under. Nothing except revenge mattered. Without it the world could stop spinning for all he cared. Everything good about the Earth and everything in it died in the car bomb.

He picked up the phone and dialed Walter.

"Be ready to leave in five minutes."

"What about Dmitri? He's not here yet."

"He's not coming. I'll explain in the car."

He opened the top drawer, lifted out a silver plated service gun, settled it in the palm of his hand, feeling its weight, then picked up the phone and dialed another number.

The voice of the man on the other end was not pleased.

"I told you not to call me on this number."

"You know who you're talking to," said Yuri. "I don't make mistakes."

"So why start now?"

"Your guy from San Francisco. The one in the hospital."

"What about him."

"You tell me," said Yuri.

"We knocked him out of the sky last night east of Memphis."

Bob was silent for a moment. Anger building. He suppressed it. Then he continued. "We didn't give you clearance to kill the man, and try to kill the mother. That was a useless mistake. You left yourself open for surveillance."

"He's here in D.C." said Yuri. "Probably outside my office right now."

"I'll take care of it. I'll send some people over."

"You think I need your help with this?"

"Isn't that why you called?"

"I just called to remind you of our deal."

"You don't need to remind me of anything," said Bob. "Are you ready to go, yes or no."

"We're leaving in a few minutes. The question I have for you is; are *you* ready."

"You just bring the device to me and stand by. I'll make sure it gets delivered to the right eyes."

"We're going to adjust our plan just a bit."

"What are you talking about."

"I'll be at the meeting at Quantico."

"There is no reason for you to be there. Your presence is not needed."

"Make it happen."

"I don't have clearance for you to be there."

"Get it."

"It's too late."

"Not for you it isn't. The number two man in the CIA can get me clearance. I'm your advisor on private military affairs."

"Why do you want to be there."

"I want to see that bastard push the button."

"You understand there is no actual button to push."

"Let me rephrase that; I want to be right there watching when the order is given."

"I'm not even sure I'll be able to observe it."

"Get me as close as you can then. You owe me."

"And you're going to owe me."

"Yes," said Yuri. "And that day is coming my friend, when I will gladly pay you for what we are about to accomplish."

The phone on the other end clicked.

25.

Bob hung up the phone. He turned it on the side, grabbed a paperclip from a cup on top of the desk, pulled on one end till it was sticking straight out, stuck it in the tiny key hole releasing the little drawer and pulled out the sim card, placed it in a new phone, then got up, walked across the room, placed the old phone in the electronic incinerator and zapped it.

When this is all over, thought Bob, I'll have fifty million dollars' worth of gold bullion in a safe in Switzerland.

Black Op Security be damned.

They were a necessary evil, but they got a bit sloppy on this one. He sucked air through his teeth. Of all times to lose focus.

Take your eye off the big picture for one tiny moment while you're walking next to the precipice, one false move, and you fall off the cliff.

They didn't have to try to kill the mother. She wouldn't have remembered a single thing. The professor also could have been left alone and was like the domino that led to the mother.

They were acting like small time crooks. It

had taken over a year to put this project in motion and they had to screw it up by letting Badger see an opening, and find a way to follow them to D.C.

There's no way he would have gotten a trail if they hadn't tried to kill the woman. And how did he get the info that the woman with the children was one of the test cases?

I'd like to know the answer to that, thought Bob. I did everything I could to steer him away from San Francisco. And now one day later he's in D.C.

Eyes on the prize, he thought. Stay calm, we're almost there.

Eight hours from now sat the apex they'd been working towards.

Two goals.

One; to end the regime in Tehran once and for all and pay those bastards back for the Marine barracks in Beirut. Pay them back for his Dad who was there and who perished along with two hundred twenty other soldiers.

The other; half a billion dollars in gold.

In a way they considered it payment in kind for the work that needed to be done. By a government with the wherewithal, but without the courage. With the device they could nudge the key pieces of the puzzle into their proper role.

Eight hours from now three of the necessary players would be primed and in place.

The Secretary of Defense, and the President would be together in private, while the third, the Joint Chief of Staff would be on a satellite link with them. At a critical moment in time when tensions were running high. Tehran was rattling it's saber, and was being helped in its rattling by units within our own security apparatus. Heightened, Bob thought, by my own team with a single hidden purpose. The sound of the rattling magnified, enhanced. Brought to the ears of our civilian and military leaders.

Not since Truman on August 9, 1945 had a sitting President ordered a nuclear strike. In fact, no one in history had ordered such a strike since that fateful day.

The world had come close though. More than a few times some known and well documented, while it was also true that none of the closest calls would ever be known, hidden from the general population to prevent a malaise. One false move from complete disaster.

The fact remained that for the United States of America, the President had sole authority to order a nuclear strike at any time for any reason.

There was a procedure in place. He would notify both the Secretary of Defense, and the Chairman of the Joint Chief of Staff. They would review the options; whether a single cruise missile, or multiple ICBM's. The target location and delivery vehicles would be decided on. In this case two nuclear armed cruise missiles from a destroyer in the Gulf.

Since they would be outside a fixed command center, the so-called nuclear football would be accessed. The bulky aluminum suitcase in the black leather jacket carried by a military aide would be opened and four items would come out; the black book with hardware options, another book with classified site locations, a manila folder with procedures for the emergency alert system, and a three by five inch laminated card with authentication codes.

There was a two man rule at the nuclear launch facility, in this case the USS Ingersoll stationed in the Persian Gulf. The President would give the order, and it would be verified by the Secretary of Defense. The Defense Secretary has no veto power and must comply with the President's order. The order would be reverified by the commander of the destroyer and the missile would be armed and launched. All within minutes of the order being given.

There were procedures in place, and for survival they needed to be secure, decisive, and quick. The survival of the country might be in the balance, and a single person needed to have the authority to step forward, not a committee which might take too long to decide a fate. If a foreign power launched missiles and they were in-bound, there might only be a few moments for a retaliatory strike before it was too late. The trust for launching a nuclear weapon was instilled in the commander in chief, it made sense to put the trust with the top civilian elected official, rather than with a military commander.

The military served at the pleasure of the civilian leaders, not the other way around. For that would be a military dictatorship. The United States for all intents and purposes was still a Republic, ruled by the citizens.

26.

It had been a long day for Amber. With bone tired feet she climbed the stairs to the second floor apartment in cozy fogged in Dana Point. Badger had been gone for two days without a word. In many ways that was to be expected.

The worry that she suddenly felt however was not expected, and began to overwhelm her like a slow tide moving over the shore.

Throughout the day from three in the morning till just now well after sunset, the demanding nature of her job precluded anything except sharp focus on the task at hand.

They'd delivered five babies at the hospital, all within the same hour, although the journey to that specific hour dragged on from the proverbial early morning till just after lunch time.

Two were breached and cesarean sections were done with no complications.

Two others were normal deliveries, nothing out of the ordinary except for the new mothers who had to endure seven hours of labor each between them.

One however was the most difficult of all. The mother was in labor for fifteen hours. The baby did not have an abnormally large head, but the mother was small in comparison, and they both had a tough time. The baby's face was also facing towards her abdomen rather than the preferred back placement. He was in essence stuck in the birth canal.

She was a young woman in her early twenties which was in her favor strength and endurance wise.

Pricilla was from a small island outside of Manila in the Philippines, she emigrated to southern California, meeting and marrying Tavita Kava, a large Tongan brick layer nearly three times her size as sometimes happens in life.

Their strict religious rules forbid an emergency cesarean. So the labor went on through the day.

As with any natural birth, the mother needed to squeeze and push with all her might to force the baby out of the uterus through the cervix.

Fifteen hours had taken its toll. She was weakened by the effort, yet still held onto Amber with one hand and Tavita with the other.

"Don't leave me," she whispered to Amber during an exceptionally long and excruciating contraction.

"I'm not going anywhere," Amber replied. "Stay strong and push."

For such a small woman, Amber felt as though her hand might be about to break from the squeeze.

Pricilla began to bleed out from her womb stretched for so long of a time, virtually cracking on the edges, rupturing capillaries and vessels.

Her essential fluids leaking out from the tears inside her body, blood pressure dropping into a dangerously low zone, the doctors were ready to override any religious restrictions, take the father out of the room, and go into emergency procedures when all of a sudden the baby miraculously decided to make a grand entrance.

Once the largest part of his head, maybe an ear or two made it past the smallest part of her cervix, he popped straight out like he was shot out of a cannon, the surprised doctor caught him with both hands as though he was catching a line drive in a baseball game, cradling the baby in the nook of his arm.

The nurses quickly wiped the baby's face and body, suctioning out his mouth and nostrils, then as they heard the loud cry with the first breaths leaving the newborn's lungs they all exhaled in relief.

The young mother however went into shock. Her face turned chalk white and she stopped breathing at the same instant that her newborn baby started his. The attention turned quickly to the mother. The doctor did everything he could to save her but she went into cardiac arrest. Five times they revived her, and now she was on life support, barely hanging on, yet she was still hanging on, still in the land of the living.

The baby was incredible, nine pounds, nine ounces and the envy of every nurse in the station. Already tan in complexion with curly black hair and little bulging muscles he was destined to be a heart breaker from day one.

Amber stayed with the new mother, never letting go of her hand as promised, sitting in a chair next to the bed ready to jump into action, while her husband slept on a cot next to her, until the head night nurse came up and patted Amber on the shoulder.

"There's nothing more you can do honey, why don't you go home and get some sleep, you've been here twenty hours. We don't want to admit you as a patient next now do we?"

She was right and Amber in a fog reluctantly agreed. Now, standing in front of her doorway with key in hand she thought about her Badger, and wondered how he was. The neighbors on either side of her apartment must be asleep, the windows were dark so she put the key in the door quietly and opened it even quieter.

She blinked her eyes, sighing with relief at finally being home and when she did, it seemed as though a flash of light hit the corner of her right eye.

"I am really tired," she whispered and closed the door behind her.

The volume of air in the room seemed to shift, the emptiness that should have prevailed in that section of the house, the open space by the front door with nothing in front of it changed as a shape filled it, she could feel it, she knew someone was suddenly behind her. Before she could turn and scream out two large hands with tight fitting gloves grabbed her, she could smell the rancid leather in her nostrils, one slapped across her mouth cutting off her breath, while the other wrapped around her neck pulling her backwards.

Instinct and training crashed into being. She lunged forward biting hard through the leather on the hand across her face, then with both of her hands reached up to the hand on her neck, located the thumb, wrapped her right hand around it, and bent it back and sideways quick just as Badger taught her, back and sideways twisting it at an acute angle until she heard the popping sound as the metacarpal bone broke.

The muffled screaming sound didn't come from her, it came from her assailant as he pushed her away then kicked at her to gain more distance, opened the door with his unbroken hand, then ran out and down the stairs.

In the darkness Amber located her purse, pulled out the stun gun then reached up and latched the door in case he decided to come back. Pulling aside the curtains just a crack at the front window she saw a man jump into a black sedan parked down the street from the apartment complex and speed away. Chills ran up her spine as she pulled short bursts of air into her lungs, hands shaking.

They'd never had a burglar in the complex the entire ten years that Amber had lived there. Unfortunately she had a feeling this was no normal burgle job. She double bolted the front door, keeping the stun gun tight in her right hand, turned on every light in the apartment, looking in every nook and cranny in the entire place from one end to the other, under beds, in closets, the shower, even under the bathroom and kitchen sink and in the dishwasher.

Nothing had been touched, no drawers were opened, no papers shuffled.

She sat down in the hallway and steadied her breathing. As a nurse she was accustomed to a wide array of odors. A hospital was a complex arrangement of cleanliness and disease. When a person's body was decaying, or fighting off illness, there was almost no hiding it. And yet the hospital staff, highly trained cleaners stayed ahead of the curve, mopping and wiping every surface throughout the day. The scent of scrubbing solvents overwhelming all else.

Here at home, she tried to maintain a neutral aroma. No air fresheners, just plain air.

The acrid scent was still hanging in the atmosphere. She could smell it clearly. There hadn't been a man in this apartment for a few days, yet now it was lingering within the walls. A mix of testosterone, sweat and bad deodorant.

She suppressed her gag reflex and got back to her feet, all thought of being tired had vanished.

She headed for the back bedroom. In the closet to the back right hidden behind a row of clothes was a four foot high safe. Where Badger kept his bag of tricks as he liked to say.

She spun the dial at the front of the black cast iron door. 060175. Badger's father's birthday. June 1, 1975. He held onto the little things in funny ways. The silver lever clicked smooth into place, the front of the safe swung open. Two rifles leaning against the back corner, a black Kevlar backpack taking up most the rest of the space. She pulled it out and unzipped it.

It was heavy. Full of metal things. Handguns, a silencer, bullet proof vest, gun tripod, barrel scopes, night vision gear, ammunition. Cartons full of bullets. Weapons of destruction. She passed over them, looking for a specific little box. Black onyx with a latch on the front, you flipped the latch, then pulled the top portion off, rubber seals around the edges, waterproof to protect the electronic device inside. The little box itself was high tech, designed to withstand three hundred feet of underwater pressure, or being dropped from an airplane a mile in the air and bouncing off the ground.

Designed for the Navy Seals to take behind enemy lines, whether parachuting from a jet, or ejected from a submarine off the coast. Code name EID, electronic identifying device.

He showed it to her once. Showed her how to use it. About the size of a cell phone, it actually did look like a smart phone. Dark black screen with a single button at the front bottom to activate it.

She pushed it. No beep, no lights to give you away in the dark of night on the wrong side of the border, just a tiny red pinpoint of light in the top right corner showing that it was activated. She touched the pinpoint of light and the screen showed the walls of the bedroom she was in like construction blueprints in light red.

She used the tip of her finger lightly touching the screen and pulling it down to scroll over to the room next door, the adjacent bathroom, then the living room, the large space with the eight picture windows, and the kitchen. There, in the top corner of the living room that faced the kitchen was a blinking pinpoint of red light.

An electronic signal.

She set the device down, got to her feet and walked slowly to the living room, eyes wide yet not focused on any one item. Walked to the center of the room, turning in a circle, looking first towards the kitchen, then staring towards the picture windows, yet with her peripheral vision searching the top corner of the wall directly across from the kitchen.

She had to be sure.

Smaller than a flea, white like the walls it was set into. A tiny bump in the apex where the two walls met the ceiling, a tiny white bump with a black spot directly in the middle of it. She swept her eyes quickly across the area, but did not linger. Yes, it was there. Whatever it was. A camera, a listening device, a cell phone signal tracker, or a combination of all of them.

It was time to go. She walked to the kitchen, got out a cup, filled it with water from the tap, took a slow drink, then set it in the middle of the sink. Leisurely unhurried motions.

Walked back to the bedroom, sat down next to the backpack, staring inside it. Thought for a moment. The smallest handgun would do. A Berretta, a .38 special with a matching box of bullets to go with it. Since she wasn't a very good shot, whatever happened, if she needed to use it, would have to be done at short range. She checked the safety, it was on, then slid the clip out of the bottom of the handle, it was full, seven bullets.

No sense in lingering. She grabbed a small flowered carry bag from the closet, her day bag, the one she usually took to the park to work out or have a picnic with a book under the shade of a tree, put the box of bullets on the bottom, then filled it with spare clothes, a couple pairs of pants, shirts, socks, running shoes, underwear, enough for a couple of days on the run.

Went into the bathroom, grabbed a new bar of soap, her toothbrush, toothpaste, shampoo, and two rolls of toilet paper. Back to the closet, placed the EID carefully on top of the clothes, then the handgun even more carefully next to it, zipped it up.

Anything else? She looked at the war chest of goodies in the Kevlar bag. Badger would take the whole thing, and the rifles, but she wanted to be nimble and ready to run at a moment's notice, and not stand out when leaving the apartment in just a few moments from now.

She zipped it up, placed it carefully back in the safe, pulled the silver lever closed and spun the dials, thought twice and set the numbers at her birthday, 022796. If she never made it back here and Badger did, he'd know where she went. Back to the home she was born in. The safe house they'd discussed during their 'talk'.

Out to the living room, grabbed her purse where she'd left it a few moments ago while being attacked, not a single glance at the camera/listening device/tracker in the top corner of the wall, then opened the front door carefully.

Whatever they were going to do, it would probably be outside in the dark, not here on the landing where anyone could see. She locked the door behind her and closed it tight.

Down in the parking lot sat her little blue sedan, tucked neatly into its rightful space in between her two neighbors giant silver SUV's.

She slung her purse over her left shoulder, and the day bag over her right, unzipped the day bag just enough for her hand to fit, slid it in inside and grasped the Barretta ever so gently, wrapping her bottom three fingers around the handle on one side and her thumb on the other, securing it tight, then with her trigger finger unlatching the safety, pulling back, clicking it in place, keeping the index finger on the outside of trigger housing, pointing the barrel out and to the right.

She remembered Badger's instructions at the gun range, the one she did not want to go to but reluctantly agreed. Crouch and fire, he said, crouch and fire, don't point, extend.

"Why do I have to learn how to fire a gun?" she complained. "I'm a nurse, I save people's lives, not end them."

"Humor me," he said without a trace of a smile. She could see that it was important to him.

Crouch and fire, steady your legs, keep your balance extend your arm and squeeze the trigger, like you're squeezing a little tube of toothpaste.

"You might never need to fire a gun, but it's not a bad idea to at least know how," he told her.

"Think of it this way, you're never going to be on the Pro Bowling Tour, or be in the NBA, but you know how to bowl, and how to shoot a free throw."

He had a point.

She headed for the stairway, then down one step at a time, until she was down at ground level. Listening, watching. Finger next to the trigger housing.

A lonely car went by on the road bordering the apartment complex. Red tail lights fading out of sight around the corner.

Up on the top third floor of the apartment building, on the northwest corner, a flickering blue light filtered by thin drapes pulled loosely against the windows, someone watching TV at this late hour. All the rest of the windows in the entire building were dark.

She walked quickly towards the giant silver SUVs surrounding her little blue car. No sense in lingering now out in the open.

Her left hand deftly unzipped her handbag, pulling out the car key, while keeping a lookout for someone who might be ready to jump out at her from behind or under a car. Finger on the trigger now.

She unlocked the driver's side door, with her left hand, pulled the Barretta out of the day bag on her right, and crouched next to the door, listening, waiting.

If something was going to happen here in the parking lot, it would happen quick, before she could drive away.

She threw her purse across the interior of the

car landing it on the passenger seat, rose from her crouch and slid into the driver's seat with one swift motion leveraging the day bag on top of the purse, pulled the door closed, locked it, set the gun on her lap, took the key in her right hand, started the ignition and backed out of the stall.

Quick now, she told herself heading down the row of cars towards the exit, steering with her left hand while pulling the EID out of the day bag and setting it on her lap next to the gun. She thought twice and placed the gun on the passenger seat, barrel facing away. No sense she thought, of grabbing it suddenly, or have it fall on the ground out of your lap and shooting yourself. Last thing now would be a trip to the ER, it was time to get far and fast away from here.

She stopped for a moment at the exit, looked all around to make sure her perimeter was clear, then down at the Electronic Identifying Device.

It was still on. Light red lines showed the outline of her car. There at the front right, in what would be the location of the wheel well was a tiny blinking light. They put a tracker on her car. So be it. She turned right and sped out of the parking lot, heading north, through the center of Dana Point.

She zigzagged through the nearly empty city, looking for the right spot to pull over. Up ahead on the left side was a twenty four hour gas station and convenience store. A large dirty truck was in one of the gas stalls, with no one in sight. She pulled in, rolled down all the windows keeping the handgun on the passenger's side seat where she could get to it quick if needed. She always kept a small flashlight in the center console and grabbed it in her left hand.

Somewhere out in the dark behind her was a car, with people watching and waiting, down some side street, behind a parked car, maybe around the corner just out of sight. Waiting for her to get to a secluded spot where they could ambush her.

She opened the little door on the side of the car, put the gas hose in, pretended to drop something and scrambled towards the front right wheel with the flashlight searching up under the fender.

A small circular object the size of a silver dollar attached to the metal behind the wheel. She pried it off with her fingernails. It was a coal black magnet with the device attached to the front. She palmed it, shuffled back to the gas hose, stood straight up, removed the nozzle from the car replaced it in the gas pump, and pretended to take a receipt from the machine and read it.

The door to the convenience store opened, out walked a burly construction worker, bright green shirt, long baggy pants, big clunky work boots, from head to toe as dirty as the truck he was heading towards. He nodded and smiled through his bearded face as he passed her, kind gentle hard working eyes crackling on the edges.

"Howdy ma'am."

She forgot for a moment what it was like to have a civil interaction with someone, while a gun sat on the seat of her car ready for defense.

She managed a slight "howdy" back, and went around to her driver's side door ready to get in, still palming the tracker in her left hand.

He got into the truck, shut the door, the engine rumbling to life, grey black smoke billowing from the tailpipe as the engine idled.

She walked over to the passenger side of the truck and tapped on the window. It rolled down.

"Yes ma'am, can I help you?"

She leaned her hands against the side of the truck.

"Do you know how to get to the freeway from here?"

"Yeah sure, you go straight down this road till you get to Golden Lantern, turn right and head down the hill to the harbor, and take a left on Pacific Coast Highway...." He tapped the front of his gnarled brow. "What was I thinking. I'm going that way anyhow, just follow me. But in case you fall behind just take PAC Highway south, it turns into Camino Las Ramblas then meets the San Diego Freeway I-5."

"Thank you."

He smiled at her hoping there was something else she needed. But she turned away, headed back to the little blue sedan closed the door, flipped the lock button and started the engine. Her left hand was empty. There, on the side of the truck, just under the handle and blending in nicely was the tracker.

Her plan at the moment was no plan. Somehow she needed the trackers to follow the truck without knowing she'd made the switch.

The truck lurched forward out of the gas station, heading down the highway. She followed close behind at first, then faded back. Up ahead the signs pointed to the freeway entrance, he got into the right lane, the one heading south.

"I need to go north," she whispered. There was no way to get out of it. She followed far behind the truck and merged onto the freeway. Traffic was light at this time of the early morning. The white truck stayed in the slow lane lumbering along. She stayed ten car lengths behind. The left lanes were busy, packs of cars, the speeders would overtake the slow cars in bunches, whizzing by at close to eighty miles an hour, like race cars on a track heading for the finish line trying to edge the other guy out on the final turn, then it would be quiet again.

Her friend in the white truck was nestled close behind a giant freight truck, a sixteen wheeler.

Up ahead two miles away over a slight rise in the freeway the lime green exit sign for Camino de Estrella was hanging over the right lane. A long wall started where the sign was located, running along the freeway. She remembered that wall. It wasn't too long ago that she'd had a flat tire and pulled over right at that spot.

She remembered it not only since it was a wide open spot, perfect for filling the tire with flat fixer, but for the fact that behind the wall way down the line, someone had set up a little camp site. It was so far down along the wall that it was out of sight from everyone travelling on the freeway.

Another pack of racers was coming up behind. She punched the accelerator and swerved two lanes over to get in front of them.

Horns honked, tires squealed, the speedometer read eighty five. Now suddenly out in front of the white truck and the sixteen wheeler she swerved right in front of the freight truck and hit the brakes till he was on her tail, horns blaring, the man in the cab looming above her little car.

She turned off her lights as they got closer to the wall then she pulled off the freeway zipping on the other side of the wall praying that there wasn't a campsite, downshifting the auto transmission to slow the car without braking.

All was quiet on the other side of the wall. There were houses to the right of her, each with its own hollow tile wall at each back yard, then in between the two parallel walls a twenty foot buffer zone of scrub grass and eucalyptus trees. A buffer zone maintained by the State.

She moved forward over the bumpy ground. There must be a way out. No lights yet behind her, she'd lost them. Or maybe they figured it out and were doubling back. She rolled faster, bottoming out on rocks and moving forward. Past ten houses, then ten more.

Finally on the right there was an opening, a house with a driveway that meandered near the buffer zone, then after that a sidewalk and a small park with trees and benches. She turned towards the opening, there was a low chain link fence in between her and the street. She brought the front bumper up against it, slowly applying the accelerator till it fell in front and she was free. Rolling the car forward over the fence.

The sign on a lamppost in front of the last house read Calle Paloma, double yellow lines heading north. She followed them.

27.

"She broke my thumb."

"What'd you let her do that for?"

"Let her? That bitch is strong like a man, hell for all we know maybe she is a man, and she had some kind of technique, I'll tell you that much. I never saw that move coming. Damn bitch."

"Stop your whining. Do you want me to take you a hospital so you can get your booboo looked at?"

"It's broke. I could hear the cracking."

"You're an idiot."

"At least I got the bug planted."

They were watching the screen on the laptop sitting on the dashboard. Wide angle lens with the living room spread out in front of them.

"Yeah, you got it planted alright. Did you see that? She walked right underneath it and looked right up at it. Great job."

"We should have timed it better. They didn't give us enough time to get this set up."

"We get what we get. She knows it's there. I'm sure of it."

"They didn't give us enough time, I could only

plant one bug, and now I've got a broken thumb."

"I warned you she was on her way up. You could have figured something else besides attacking her from behind."

"I was trying to throw her off. As far as she knows I was just a burglar."

"Then why did she walk right under the bug and look at it?"

"Maybe she has a signal locator."

"Ya think?"

"Doesn't matter now. Look there she is."

From their vantage point in the parking lot next door they could see her at the front door of her apartment. Both men with tiny binoculars watching her.

"She's on the run."

"Let her run. Doesn't matter since we have the tracking device on her car. Run as far and fast as you want lady, or man, whatever you are. Thumb breaking bitch beast."

"What do you think the chances are that since she found our bug with a signal detector, that she'll find the tracker?"

"Turn it off remotely."

"It's not that kind."

"Constant beacon? We're screwed."

"Just keep a close eye on her, if she takes it off we'll know immediately. I'm driving, you keep an eye on the tracking map. If she stops and pulls over and takes it off and the device isn't still on the vehicle, we'll know right away."

"And then we run her off the road right?"

"What the hell are you talking about?"

"Run that bitch off the road for breaking my thumb."

"If she finds the tracking device, we just follow her the old fashioned way, by line of sight. And when she gets to her point of destination we bug her again. Or if we can't get close enough to physically bug her we use the microwave antennae."

"What if she finds the tracking device, tosses it in the bushes, and then out drives you."

"Out drive me? Are you crazy? No one is going to out drive me buddy. Especially not some chick."

"Thumb breaking bitch is what she is."

"Okay, she's at the bottom of the stairway, looking around. C'mon lady we're not gonna jump you again. She's at the car. She's inside. What is she doing. What's taking her so long. Now turning on the ignition. Backing out. There she goes. She didn't find the bug Darrel. We're in business."

They followed far behind in the old junk sedan. Rusty on all the edges, broken fenders, cloudy windows, frayed rubber molding.

No one would mistake them for operatives for the CIA. More likely they'd get ID'd as a poor unsuccessful drug dealer's car, or a homeless persons mobile pad.

The only things new on the vehicle were the important ones, the engine, transmission, suspension, and tires. Both the engine and suspension were race car quality, four hundred horsepower able to go from zero to a hundred in four seconds, and able to corner at a hundred forty with just a few degrees of sway. The tires were covered in dirt on purpose to make them look old, and even they were top of the line five hundred dollars each, puncture proof. The tail pipe had a special modification to exude grey smoke to make it look like the engine was old and burning oil.

"She's stopping at the gas station."

"Yeah."

"Getting gas at a time like this. When she's on the run. Doesn't make sense."

"Maybe she's low on gas, and it's a good place, lots of light, open spaces. No room for someone like us to come sneaking up behind. How's the thumb by the way?"

"The size of a potato, thanks for asking."

"What's she doing? Did she just bend down by the front wheel well?"

"Yep. Wait, maybe not. Looks like she dropped her credit card and just stooped down to pick it up."

"Yeah, we'll see."

"Who's that guy coming out of the store."

"Some bum by the looks of him."

"They're talking, what are they saying. Can you read lips."

"I could only see his lips moving and it looked he said 'Hey man'. See I knew that bitch was a man."

"Okay, he's getting in his truck, and she's getting in her car. Now what's she doing? Knocking on his window, asking him a question. Damn I wish we had a bug on her right now."

"They're both driving off. Let's go. How's the

signal Darrel."

"Right on target." The laptop sitting on his knees showing a schematic of the road ahead, and a bright ruby red circle just where the tagged car was in front of them. "Straight down Golden Lantern."

They followed far behind. Jake was a retired stock car and street racer. He could tell when a light was about to go yellow, the cross walks had timers in big numbers letting walkers know how much time they had before the lights changed. He'd give a little tap of the accelerator and the big engine would rumble to life, speed them through the light in time, then he would fall behind again.

She was headed for the on-ramp, the San Diego Freeway headed south. She settled for the slow lane at first, then suddenly bolted for the fast lane in front of a pack of fast movers.

"Man, she is one crazy bitch, gonna get herself killed before we can get a tag on her. Put a tag on a body bag first the way she's driving. Look at her, now she's swerving over in front of the sixteen wheeler."

"She can swerve all over the place for all I care. She aint getting away is all I can tell you. The big rig almost took out her back bumper though, man that guy must be pissed. He's still sitting on his brakes, you can hear him honking his big assed horn at her."

They drove on in silence for a while.

"How's the tracker signal?"

"Steady."

"She must be getting tired of having that big

rig on her tail."

"Why don't you move up a little so we can see how close he's riding her."

Jake tapped the accelerator and moved into the second then third lane over, passing the back end of the big rig. No little blue car in sight. His heart sank.

"Uh oh..."

"We still have a signal though." Darrel was looking down at the laptop, the red dot was still shining bright but now it was behind them. "Yeah, uh oh." He looked back and to the right, at the dirty white truck that was nestled in behind the big rig. "Isn't that the truck that was at the gas station back at Dana Point?"

"Son of a bitch, yes." Jake tapped on the brakes and they slowed down till they were parallel with the truck. "Signal?"

"Yep. How long's it been since she swerved in front of the big rig?"

"Three, maybe five minutes. We're doing seventy so about four maybe five miles back. Here's an exit."

"It's an easy job they said. Put a nice little bug in an apartment, she's a nurse, she always works the night shift. She's never home. Now we're in trouble."

"Forget about that. Find the general location where she got off. We'll ask for help. They'll acquisition the cameras and we'll find her."

"Marking our location now. Four to five miles back is just before Camino de Estrella, we'll start there. Maybe she got off the exit?"

"Not a chance, the exits are long and visible.

She got in front of the truck and zipped off behind some sort of obstacle. Look for a row of bushes, or a wall."

Darrel backtracked on the computer and pointed at the screen.

"There it is."

28.

"Top assets huh?"

"Supposedly"

"This order came straight from the top. We give these guys a simple job. Put a wire on a basic unsuspecting civilian. A nurse for crying out loud. All we want to do is find out if she has any communication with her boyfriend. See if we can track his location through her. It's not rocket science, or something that's never been done in the history of the world. It's how we catch nearly every fugitive on the planet. They always go back to the honey pot. Always."

"You want me to pull them?"

"No. Keep them on the case for now. I don't want any more fingers in this than are needed."

"They're at a dead end. They lost her. We had her pinpointed with our traffic cameras, and then she went off onto a country road on the east side of the freeway. Basically heading north."

The man behind the desk tapped his finger slowly. "Heading north. First she was heading south when they lost her, and now she's heading north. For how long? Maybe she'll change course and go east, or backtrack and go south again, or west. The main thing is that we lost her. Unless she goes by a camera that auto-detects her make model color of vehicle there's no way we'll find her again. Alright, let's try something different. What's her full name?"

"Amber Melanie Tavares."

"Spell it."

The man sitting behind the desk punched the name onto the keyboard as the other man spewed out the letters. "Tavares. Spanish?"

"Portuguese."

"I have ten matches in the country. Let's narrow it down. Two in California. One is in Eureka. And here's our perfect match, currently residing in Dana Point. Amber Melanie Tavares. United States Citizen. Twenty nine years old. Here's her passport, driver's license, tax returns. Let's see her birth certificate. Well look here, it's just a county clerk form. She was not born in a hospital, she was delivered at a private home. By a mid-wife with the name of Tavares. Her mother's maiden name is also Tavares. No mention of a father on this document."

"All in the family."

"No doubt."

He kept typing.

"The mother's name is Rose Calina Tavares." He shook his head when the screen showed the answer. "Deceased." He kept typing. "The mid-wife's' name is Rosarita Tavares, no middle name. Fifty seven matches. Great." He tapped the desk with his fingers, thinking. "Let's go back to the birth certificate. The house she was born in is located in the little town of Big Bear,

California. 2013 Boysenberry lane to be exact. Let's look up the owner of that house."

His fingers pecked away at the keyboard.

"And bingo. Here we have a Rosarita Tavares currently residing at that exact same house. She gets a tax exemption as a resident occupant, and an additional one for being elderly. Seventy three years old to be exact, which I suppose could make her our little runaway nurse's grandmother?"

He pulled the calculator from the side. "Seventy three minus twenty nine is forty four divided by two equals twenty two. That's about the right age for both the deceased mom and the grandma to have kids. Let's take a look at the deceased mom's birth certificate." He tapped his finger again while waiting for the answer. "And bingo again. County clerk certified birth certificate. Rose Calina Tavares, born in the same house on Boysenberry lane, mother is Rosarita Tavares age twenty two, father Romero Tavares aged thirty three."

He tapped again at the keyboard.

"We do not have a birth certificate for grandma. But we do know that she was born in Punto Santo Thomas in Baja California, maiden name Santos just like the town she was born in, immigrated to the United States when she was sixteen and became a naturalized citizen when she was twenty one and married Romero. They've owned that house for fifty two years."

"What do you want to do?"

"Let's get our two operatives up there to Boysenberry lane, and tell them not to screw this one up. No bugs on the inside of the house. We don't want her flying the coop again if she's there. Just stake it out, nothing more, nothing less. Get confirmation that our nurse is there, if possible. And if she is maybe they can get close enough with a microwave receiver that will pick up her cell phone signal. All we need is a split second trace."

29.

Bob McCade, assistant to the head of the CIA walked resolutely down the hallway of the Pentagon towards his appointment, black leather folder under his left arm held tight, shoes clicking on the polished light grey granite floor with the light reddish square inserts, symbolic of the hardened certitude and sacrifice of a battlefield.

Past the River Entrance, through a pair of glass security doors, stopping at the door whose bronze plaque on the wall to the side read simply CJCS in bold letters.

Chairman of the Joint Chiefs of Staff.

He waited politely in a hard backed chair in the anteroom with the secretary, a solid woman in her early thirties, sharp features, jet black hair tied tight in a bun at the back of her head, neat pressed navy blue jacket, light blue buttoned shirt with tie, knee length skirt, busy typing a handwritten memo that was sitting on the desk in front of her. Her demeanor was calm and precise, yet Bob felt that if he tried to get past her without permission she'd flip him to the ground and put him in a headlock.

The buzzer on the phone rang lightly, barely audible, she picked up the receiver, speaking softly into it so that no one could hear what was being said. Then she turned to him with a slight smile.

"The General will see you now."

Bob nodded, said a polite thank you and headed through the white metal bomb proof door to the inner office.

The general was seated at a simple square desk with a computer screen on the right side. He was busy writing a memo on a yellow legal pad. He rose when Bob entered, a tall semi-thin man, short light black grey hair trimmed well above his ears which stood out on the sides like sails in the wind. He was dressed in his Marine Corps work uniform. Pressed green slacks, light khaki belt, light khaki shirt unbuttoned without a tie, four silver stars on each lapel, gold eagle on the left chest, then below that five rows of service ribbons.

With a quick eye Bob recognized many of them by their colors; Sinai, Panama; Haiti; Iraq; Operation Enduring Freedom, Afghanistan.

One ribbon that was missing, and Bob was fairly certain that the General had been assigned to that theatre during the troubled time when Clinton and NATO decided to bomb Belgrade, was the ribbon for Bosnia-Herzegovina.

Many servicemen from that era refused to wear it. Disgusted at the outcome.

The general motioned to the set of chairs in front of the desk. Bob sat in the one on the right side to have a straight view of the general without being impeded by the computer screen.

"Good to see you again General."

"Thanks for stopping by Bob. Where's the Director?"

"He couldn't make it. Last minute call that couldn't wait. He sends his apologies."

"Alright well fine then, let's see what you have."

Even though they were in a small office, his voice was solid and direct as though he was barking orders on the drill field to a platoon full of soldiers. So ingrained was the need to make certain that your specific orders were heard by everyone in the unit, no matter how far away or hard of hearing the soldier was, the battle could be won or lost with a single missed syllable. Communication on the battle field was of utmost importance to the commander.

Bob unlatched the lock at the top, unfolded the briefcase on the desk, unpacked the stack of photos and slid them across.

"Two days ago we see that tankers with liquid rocket fuel departed Iran, heading for Lebanon. They disguised them as old dirty diesel gas trucks. These are photos from our sources in Tehran this morning. Achmed Parzid is the head of the missile development division. Here he is arriving at their military headquarters. At the very same time we have satellite imagery showing that very same liquid rocket fuel being transported to their proxy army units in Lebanon. Here it is arriving at the rocket launch site this morning. And here's the radiation tracker from one of our people on the ground."

"What's your prognosis."

"This is either a miniature nuclear device loaded onto the top of the missile, or it could be radioactive material loaded into a warhead. A dirty bomb."

The general picked up the phone and spoke into it, lowering his normal battlefield voice to a dull roar.

"Jill get commander Lewis on the phone for me, have him give me a call ASAP."

The General pulled out a magnifying glass from the desk and looked closer at some of the images, shuffling them back and forth.

"You think they're getting ready to do something stupid?"

"We think they're getting ready to launch a missile towards Tel Aviv, or towards our forces positioned in the Gulf."

"That would be suicide. First off, the Israelis would shoot that missile down the moment it showed velocity and angle towards their state, then destroy the missile site and launch their own counter attack. Secondly, if it showed similar angle and velocity towards our ships. Well, we'd make them wish they were never born. Maybe it's a bluff. We've seen this before."

The General looked closer with the magnifying glass then sat rock straight, a frown forming.

"Is this it? Or is there more."

"Well yes, there's this little memo of sorts that we pulled up from one of our intelligence sources." Bob slid the single page across the desk. Five paragraphs of single spaced print. At the top was a title in bold letters. QUICK READ."

"What is this?"

"It's some sort of short story that we found embedded in a courier package from Iran."

"What in blazes does a short story have to do with a potential missile launch?"

"Just read the first few paragraphs General, it will all become clear to you."

The frown on his face deepened, then as the General reluctantly began to read the document, the pupils in his eyes began to dilate, large black holes, glazing over on the edges, unblinking. His breath became slow and steady.

Amazing, thought Bob. He reached over, slid the paper back across the table, placing it carefully in his briefcase, locking the top latch.

The General looked up and across the table.

"Why are you here again?" he asked.

"I'm not here," replied Bob.

"That's right you're not, so I'd better get back to work." He took a deep breath, shook his head, blinking his eyes to focus them, and looked down at the satellite photographs. "What are these doing here?"

"A courier from the CIA dropped them off. Tehran is getting ready to launch a nuclear tipped missile."

"That's right." He tilted his head, as though listening to a far off sound, lost in a train of thought.

Bob got up, turned and left the room. As he was walking out, he took one last look at the General who was still trying to listen to the far off sound. Soon though, within seconds, he'd snap out of it with no recollection of the past few minutes, and his meeting with Bob would be wiped from his memory banks with a simple precise order that he'd received while staring blankly at the metal shrouded words printed as a short story.

Next on Bob's list was the Secretary of Defense, and he headed down the hall to his office.

30.

I needed access to Quantico. Whatever was going to happen, was going to happen there.

Staff Sergeant Duke Cranelly was going to help me get in there, even if he was still in the hospital recovering from a wound to his foot.

Especially since he was still in the hospital.

I needed his uniform and his ID, from all reports he wasn't going to need it for a while.

I looked at the number on my phone, the text between Mr. Aloha Josh Hailey, myself and Duke. I punched it into the software and pulled up his personal details. No criminal offenses, a credit score of seven eighty, and two addresses, one in California that belonged to two people with the same last name, most likely his parents, and one in D.C. that belonged to someone without the same last name. Most likely a rental.

Cross checked the address of the DC residence, it was an apartment complex at the north edge of Georgetown near the Naval Observatory and two blocks over from Georgetown University. On the same block was a deli, a bagel shop, an escape room, and the Chinese Embassy Visa Section office. Typical

D.C. hodgepodge.

I parked by the bagel shop. It was nine AM on a Sunday morning. There was a line out the door.

If I was going to impersonate a Marine, I needed a haircut. My hair was touching my ears. I might pass on an Air Force base, but the Marine MP's at Quantico would probably throw me in the stockade.

One block over from the deli, a barber shop pole stuck out from the side of a building. The red white and blue pole was spinning within a glass cylinder, and the light was on. I was in business.

The sign on the door was blunt. Military cuts fifteen dollars. It was a short wait and I sat in a seat by the window and told the barber what I wanted. High and tight. Sixteenth of an inch on the sides and a quarter inch on the landing deck topside.

"Going into battle?" The old man joked.

"Just going back to work on the base, so in a way yes."

He worked fast, a line had formed outside the door and time was money. Ten minutes later I had the look I needed and put the palm of my hand on top of my head, brushing it lightly, it felt like a baby porcupine, the hair standing at attention, the sides were virtually bald. I gave him a crisp twenty, then headed back to the apartment building feeling twenty pounds lighter.

There were a lot of reasons why an enlisted man would prefer to stay off base rather than save money by staying on it. Someone might take an accounting on the number of wine or beer bottles in the recycle bin outside your quarters, and there was always the possibility of guests of the gentler persuasion deciding to pay a visit without the hassle of acquiring a pass.

On the outside it looked like a high class dump. It was an aged building, I estimated it to be at least eighty to ninety years old, which for D.C. was sort of young, if it had been maintained. Pinkish walls, rusty metal fire escape ladders down the sides that looked ready to peel off the sides and fall into the street. Large square trash bins right below the ladders. You could jump onto a bin and swing up to the ladders like a monkey and easily gain access to the upper floors.

If it was the dark of night that's the route I'd take, but I didn't think it would go over so well on a sunny Sunday morning with everyone in the building all around us sitting at home, having a cup of coffee and watching the world out the windows.

The front entrance was simple, double glass swinging doors leading to a bank of mailboxes to the right of a single elevator, while to the left was the entrance to the stairwell. The floor at one time polished concrete, yet now etched over the decades with millions of shoes and cleaning solvents, it looked nearly identical to the sidewalk bordering the street.

I went inside. Two cameras were positioned to capture the front door and the elevator.

There was a numbered list of rules and

contact numbers next to the bank of mailboxes enclosed in yellowed plexiglass, framed and hung on the concrete wall. At the bottom of the list in bold letters was the superintendent's name and cell phone number.

Walter 'Wally' Naimens.

I could only hope I didn't run into 'ol Wally. Or anyone for that matter who might know Duke Cranelly and could possibly spot me for a fake.

The elevator was on the move, heading down from the third floor. You could hear the steady whir of the motors winching the car down to ground level. I made my own move for the staircase and started up to the fifth floor, unit number five oh three. My first few steps were too violent and echoed in the close confines of the stairwell. I softened them, going slower now. It didn't matter.

The light sounding ding announced the elevator landing at ground level. A voice shouted out.

"Duke! Yo Duke, where'd you go?"

Then the voice shouted up the stairwell.

"Yo Duke, you up there?"

Busted.

"Right here," I shouted back. It seemed as though Duke was a boisterous sort, so I hoped that my voice conveyed it. "I'm coming down."

I came around the corner, remembering to limp since I just got out of the hospital from a mortar hitting me in the foot.

There at the bottom of the stairwell, a wide grinned ruddy face beaming up towards me, dressed in blue overalls, workman's clothes, a middle aged janitor, black hair greying on the sides.

"Hey Wally," I said. "What's up?"

"The rent, that's what's up."

I froze. Maybe Duke was a deadbeat and never paid his rent. But Wally just laughed, slapping his leg when he saw the look on my face. Then I knew it was just an old saying he used, same as like Dad whenever I'd ask him what's up. The rent. Real funny.

"The rent's always up, that's a fact of life Duke. Hey I heard you were in the hospital, when'd you get out?"

"Today actually. I was just heading up to my apartment. Thought I'd get some exercise by taking the stairs."

"Yeah I saw you on the camera come in the front door. Thought I'd come down and see how you're doing. I'll walk up with you. Hey you're limping."

"Yeah, little mis-hap on the gun range." I enhanced the limp for good measure.

""So what'd you do, shoot yourself in the foot?"

Funny guy. "Well, I hate to admit it, but I got winged by a mortar round."

He whistled.

"Yeah, setting up the targets in a no fire zone, and sure enough some green horn sits on the button, the warning siren goes off, I'm running for my life and diving in a safety pit, then wham! Half my toe is gone." I smiled. "They re-attached it. Gotta hand it to the military surgeons. Top notch."

We were on the fifth floor. I limped down the hallway to number five oh three, and reached into my pocket for the key but only found the lock pick that I was planning to use until 'ol Wally showed up.

"Dang." I patted my pants front and back, stuck my hands in all four pockets, turned in a circle, looked at the ceiling in deep thought. Then, "I think I left my keys at the hospital."

Wally was unsympathetic. "You sure you didn't hit your head when you were diving into that pit?"

I frowned.

He studied me closer.

"Man, you just look different."

"I'm tired, I just want to go inside and lay down. Think you could help me out?"

"Oh yeah that's right," he nearly fell over with the realization, reaching to his side and the giant jangling ring of keys. He looked through them quickly then held one up with self-satisfaction. "I have the master key."

The door opened to a darkened interior hallway leading past a kitchen to the living room. The drapes were shut and the smell was dry mold.

"Well I'd invite you in Wally, but maybe some other time?"

"Yeah no problem Duke." He seemed let down, still studying my face. Maybe he was beginning to suspect something wasn't right. I held my left hand down by my waist out in front of me and stared down while flexing it as though trying to relieve pain or stress, squeezing the knuckles with my right hand index fingers so he'd look down and see the white scar that I'd drawn across it with a thin white magic marker. So he'd see the scar that the real Duke got from a crazy inmate in the brig many years ago.

Yeah, that's right Wally, it's really me.

"Maybe tomorrow we'll get together and have some drinks what do you say?"

He beamed at that. "You got it!" Then popped me on the right shoulder and headed to the elevator. "I gotta head down to Mrs. Kendal's. She clogged her toilet again."

I half grimaced half smiled. "Well I'm glad she's on a lower floor." Then closed the door behind me and got to work.

Without an ID nothing else mattered so that was the first order of business. Straight to the bedroom and the tall chest of drawers opposite the foot of the bed.

The air was stale, like bottling up used air and letting it sit for a couple of weeks on top of dusty cloth. Though musty, the place was neat. Bedspread tight, military right, only one item on top of the dresser, the obligatory picture of a young man with what looked like his parents standing in front of a snow covered mountain peak in some glacial setting. Maybe it was Denali in Alaska. He looked like he was probably a good son, had a name and a life, and I was going to borrow it for a while if I could only find an ID.

The top drawers were a little more jumbled. Filled with the hardware necessary for life.

Coins, fingernail clippers, a money clip, keys, charging devices. No ID.

I searched the lower drawers. Underneath all the socks, shirts underwear, ties. Still no ID. The closet. Shoes placed neatly in order on the floor, dress shirts and pants lined up on the hangers. Military wear on the left, civilian on the right. Formal military dress uniforms on the very left, then every-day service, then the Combat Utility Uniform. I searched all the pockets down the line, and there in a Combat Coat, tucked into the left pocket a laminated CAC card, a common access device.

The back of the card had a ghost image of Duke's face, date of birth, blood type, Geneva Convention category. The front of the card was white signifying active duty armed forces, a full color photo on the top left, then writing indicating name, rank, pay grade, service affiliate being The Marine Corps, federal identifier, and expiration date.

Since the card was found in a Combat Utility Uniform, I chose that style: one coat, one pair of trousers, a green T-shirt, a starched Utility Cover, and one pair of Suede Combat Boots. Pray that they fit. Sitting on the ground now loosening the laces, slipping toes into the top of the boots, now standing up, wedging the toes forward while pushing the heel down.

One size too large. Perfect.

If I was on a forced march, more than five miles I'd be in trouble at the end, too much room meant sure fire blisters on the heels. I didn't plan on any long marches. Get in, and get out.

Get in and save the world. Then get out, and hopefully not in a body bag.

Duke had an empty garment bag hanging in the closet. I loaded the 'Utes and Boots' and the Utility Cover into it. There was a palm sized tin of three color war paint on the shelf and I stuck that in one of the boots, zipped up the bag and headed for the front door.

If I was lucky, Wally would still be unclogging Mrs. Kendal's plumbing and I could slip out of the building without having to explain myself.

31.

I sat in the back of the cab as we were stuck in traffic nearly a mile from the main hub bus and train station, Union Square. I could see it in the distance. It was mid-morning and the first slam of commuters riding the inner city buses had come and gone with the rising sun that was nearing the apex.

A new crowd was beginning to form. A lot of uniformed personnel along with a mix of civilians heading to the base.

I checked my watch. Ten forty five AM. In less than twenty minutes if it was on time, the train to Quantico would arrive, fill up with passengers and head out of the city south to Virginia.

Once I got on that train there was no turning back. Since I knew they were trying to flush me out, I needed to know if they had their hands on Amber. Not that it would make any difference to the mission I was on, but I needed to know. I waited until I saw the train make the long winding turn to the station.

It was time to make the call. I pulled out my last burner phone and dialed the number. It was four hours earlier on the west coast, so six forty five AM. I could only hope she wasn't at work without her phone nearby.

Three rings and she answered.

"You're okay."

"Yes," I replied.

"How much longer before you come home?"

"I'm just about finished here."

"I'll keep the coffee on the kettle. Love you."

"Love you too." Then I pressed the red button ending the call. I looked at the time line. Five seconds.

If I was being traced they'd have to be quick.

She'd keep the coffee on the kettle. Her Grandma's favorite expression.

So she escaped Dana Point for whatever reason and went to the safe house.

I could envision the scene. Six forty five in the morning. The sun still not risen over the Sierra Nevada mountain range with the little cabin settled into the shadow of a grizzled peak at the base of a rock jumbled arroyo.

Grandma would have the coffee on the kettle and the rifle nearby just in case any coyotes were still prowling around after a night of howling on the hillsides. She'd have the rifle nearby just in case she could get a shot off to start her day with a bang.

The train pulled into the station. Somewhere in the middle of the terminal people would be piling off, and new passengers would be lining up to get on. I had about twenty minutes to get there. Even from here I could see the cameras mounted on the edges of the buildings. Everybody was being watched and filmed, every minute of every day. If the phone was traced, they'd pinpoint the signal here to the inside of this cab which was fine with me.

"You can let me out here," I told the driver. I could easily walk the mile in less than fifteen minutes.

His English was halting. He pointed out the window. "We go station sir." He obviously was disappointed in the loss of an extra dollar for the fare.

I insisted. "Let me out here please."

I set the volume to mute, dialed the marine weather report in Dana Point and pushed the phone under the seat. From experience I knew that the weather report would play endlessly in a loop, and if somehow they pinged the phone and triangulated the location, they could follow this cab around for a while.

The fare on the meter read fifteen fifty, I handed him a twenty. Told him to keep the change, then closed the door and started walking towards the station. The cab pulled into traffic, then turned left away from the station back to the inner city where the driver hoped to snag longer fares and bigger tips.

32.

Amber put the phone down, her racing heartbeat slowing after the brief call. He was okay for now. But all the most dangerous things seemed to happen at the end of his jobs.

Three things then happened all at once. The kettle on the stove reached the critical boiling point and whistled out, steam billowing in a thin line from the black cap to the ceiling. The dog barked twice, his golden retriever mane flowing out as he put his all into it. And a rifle popped loud as a firecracker on the front porch. She rushed past the dog and he followed her.

The sound of the gunshot echoed around in the canyons surrounding the cabin.

Grandma was sitting in a sturdy high backed chair, looking through the scope on the barrel. She cackled loudly.

"I think I winged it! Ha-ha, you bastard. I'll get you yet."

Seventy nine years old, still nearly as feisty as she was when she was twenty. And maybe it was because she was so fiery in her younger years, that some of it naturally flowed with her into old age.

The rifle was a recoilless sniper gun mounted on a turret attached to the railing that surrounded the porch. Long ago she decided not to risk the kickback associated with holding the weapon against her cheek, and opted for the mounted method.

She allowed herself one shot per day. The bullets were two dollars a pop, and she was on a fixed income. She preferred the Winchester manufactured M-14 since it had a heavier stock than the M-16, and had a twenty round magazine in case she got surrounded by a pack of coyotes. It had a gas operated re-loader and a rotating bolt that ejected the spent cartridge, making it easy on her old hands. The barrel was chambered for 7.62×51mm NATO rounds, a rimless bottleneck cartridge three inches long, a comparable width as a double AA battery.

She couldn't get her hands on the military grade rounds anymore and used the commercial grade Winchester .308 instead.

They were loaded to higher pressures than the NATO rounds and there was talk about the safety aspect, but she paid it no mind, they worked just fine.

The rifle had been in their family since her dear sweet husband brought it back from serving in the Army in the late fifties.

The effective firing range was about five hundred yards, or just over a quarter mile which was about the distance to the nearest ridgeline to the east, where the mangy scum dogs came from. Out of the mountains.

She hated coyotes more than anything. They

killed her cats and her dogs and almost killed her one day, middle of the winter ten years ago when she let her guard down, out to get the mail and forgot to bring a firearm.

She hadn't seen or heard of one for a couple of weeks and must have forgotten they even existed, or maybe it was a senior moment, until one came out from around a snow blind, hungry and crazy for food, eyeing her up like she was a sirloin steak, stalking her, ready to leap when her good old dog Mason came growling along. They tangled right there by the road while she ran back to the cabin for the rifle, but it was too late. Mason drove off the mangy animal but was mortally wounded in the process.

Took her half the day to dig a grave in the frozen soil. Now she kept the rifle on the porch covered in an oil sheath ready to deploy at a moment's notice if needed. She also carried a handgun on a holster rather than lugging the heavy rifle if she had to walk around outside the house for any reason. Better safe than sorry.

"Grandma," whispered Amber as she came out of the front screen door. "You scared the pee out of me."

"Sorry honey, you know how I hate those mangy bastards."

"Did you get it?"

"Have a look. My old eyes get tired looking through the scope for more than a few minutes."

Grandma scooted over to the side while Amber settled her eye socket over the end of the scope. The view was crystal clear, jumbled round granite boulders on the top of the ridge just to east. Dried brown sage brush and dark green cactus growing in the cracks between rocks.

"I don't see anything Grandma."

"Well, I'm pretty sure I winged it. I saw the fur flying in the air, and the varmint head straight over the hill."

"Grandma I'm really worried about you shooting this rifle at your...." She stopped herself from saying old age, nothing pissed off Grandma more than that.

"At my what?" Her grey eyes flared, white eyebrows arching. She was bristling, ready for a fight. Latino blood about to boil over.

Amber thought fast.

"At your...no I don't mean at *your* ridge since you don't own it, but at *the* ridge."

She smiled at her brilliance. That was a close one.

Then continued.

"Because after all, what if a hiker for instance just happened to be up on *that* ridge, and you mistook the hiker for a coyote."

She scoffed. "I think I can tell the difference between a human and a dirty damned varmint."

"But what if they were wearing some sort of camouflage that made them *look* like an animal. What if they were hunters dressing up like a coyote in order to hunt them and you mistook them for an *actual* coyote."

Grasping at straws now.

"Look," said Grandma. "If you think I 'caint tell the way a coyote moves around compared to a human being, then you don't know me at all."

She thought about spitting on the ground for good measure, then thought better of it. Wouldn't be lady like.

"And if you think I'm too old to be shooting this rifle that I've had for the past sixty years, then just say so."

Daring her.

"Oh never mind Grandma," said Amber reaching over and putting her arms around her shoulders and hugging her. "I'm your guest after all. I shouldn't be coming up here and telling you what to do. I'm just glad to be here."

They both turned their heads to the cabin.

In all the commotion, they forgot about the kettle on the stove, which was still lightly whistling. Amber raced through the front door to take it off the heat.

33.

"We got it," cackled the voice over the radio. "You can come on down now."

"That old bitch almost shot my head off," whispered Darrell, gingerly rubbing the top of his scalp.

The bullet ripped through the camouflage hat that he was wearing, with such force and velocity, that in the process a few strands of hair got caught up in the front flap, tearing a bit of hair and scalp from his crown, and sending everything flying backwards through the air.

"Well what are you doing sticking your head up over the ridge for?"

"I had to line up the receiver didn't I?"

"Dang that should've been done a long time ago."

"Well, I had to double check it."

"You sure you weren't trying to get a look at that young nurse walking around in her night gown? Or maybe you just wanted to get a good look at that old dried up Grandma." He chuckled over the radio.

"Damn you Jake, you sonofabitch."

"C'mon get down off of there, it's lined up and

we got a signal. At least we captured one. We linked it to command and it's in their hands now. You better make sure it sure it was only you that got nicked, and not the receiver right?"

"The hell you say. You think I'm sticking my neck out over that ridge with that crazy assed old hag with a sniper rifle you got another thing coming."

"Okay, well I think we're done here to be honest. They asked for a cell phone signal, and we got it for them. Now we'll just have to wait for them to confirm and call us out of here. One thing we can be happy about is they didn't ask us to put a wire on the inside of that house."

"That's a fact," said Darrel. "Ok, I'm coming down the backside."

It was about a two hour hike down the back of the ridge and around to the side road where their car was hidden. Damn the sun was bound to be hot in just a while here on the east side of the ridge facing the sunrise.

Luckily he spotted his hat in a crevice in between two boulders twenty feet below, happily scampering like a crab down to it. A ragged round bullet hole went through the top of the khaki colored hat, and sure enough, there was a piece of his scalp dangling under the front of it, stuck in the elastic band.

34.

Sitting at a bank of computer screens in a small room in the middle of CIA headquarters in Langley, Virginia, Kyle Rasmussen traced the five second ping signal to a location right nearby in Washington DC.

"Well I'll be damned," he whispered. "That phone is only about fifteen miles away."

While the source ping that they traced it from was on the other side of the country, over two thousand miles away.

He patched into Capitol security, releasing the hounds. Code Red. A roving pack of armed personnel driving unmarked black cars in the general vicinity of the target listened to his instructions.

"It's on the move," he said into his lapel mic. "Heading west on Massachusetts Avenue, passing Cobb Park, now going across Fourth Street, turning left on Hook and Ladder Alley, damn this guy knows how to get around the city, now he's turning left onto Fifth Street, heading south, stopping in front of a bar called the Irish Pub, you got it? It's a cab? Okay the signal is stopped right there." Kyle smiled. We got him.

A voice came over the headphones. "We've got the vehicle secured. Engine off, the driver is exiting the vehicle, hands up, no passengers. This guy can barely understand what we're telling him. Sounds like he's Pakistani, we might need an interpreter."

"Only the cabbie is inside?"

"Affirmative. We're searching the car," came the voice over the headphones. "Okay we found the phone, it was hidden under the seat. It's still turned on, some type of weather recording."

Kyle's smile had vanished along with their target. He didn't like to lose.

"You bastard," he whispered.

"Ask the driver where he let the last fare off."

"He keeps saying Union Square, this poor guy is ready to crap in his pants."

"What's the license number."

"WAN576," came the answer.

"You want us to hold onto this guy?"

"Yes, get an interpreter over there and get everything we can from him."

Okay, so Union Square. His teeth flashed white but Kyle wasn't smiling. It was more like a wolf that had his dinner in sight.

"Let's just pull up some cameras from the exact moment and location that we got the first ping."

He looked on his map then quickly typed in three sets of numbers and coordinates. On the screen to the right was a still shot, a camera angle looking straight down Massachusetts Avenue at the exact moment the ping was received. There in the screen was the cab with the matching license plate. There was the shape of a head in the back window.

He pushed a button and the film rolled on, the cab faded out of sight. He pulled up the next camera down the line. The cab pulled over to the edge of the curb. A man got out carrying a garment bag draped over his shoulder, and walked away towards the park that bordered Union Square.

Kyle froze the image, and marked down the time. Then he pulled up his map of camera locations and accessed one that faced south towards Massachusetts Avenue, punched in the time code, the still image came up on the screen. The man exiting the cab. He fast forwarded till the man was standing straight up and facing straight ahead. He zoomed in, took a snap shot, then put the image on the side panel, clicked on the facial recognizing software for a match.

Two images and profiles came up. Badger Thompson, and Duke Cranelly.

"Gotcha," whispered Kyle.

He clicked on the camera banks lining the perimeter of Union Square, and punched in a time frame of twenty minutes from when the man exited the cab.

The software pulled up the image heading into the west entrance, and then he was lost in a crowd. He pulled up the interior cameras and punched in a time frame plus the image, and came up empty.

Time was becoming an issue. It was twenty minutes since they received the first ping. They should have this guy in cuffs by now.

Cameras were a great tool in surveillance and tracking, but they had weak spots. If someone was particularly savvy, they could elude immediate detection by the facial recognition software just by looking down at the ground. They didn't have software that could determine identity by the top of a head. Yet.

"Alright you sonofabitch, I'll do this the old fashioned way."

He clicked on the perimeter camera, scrolled ahead till he saw Badger head through the front doors, then clicked on the camera on the other side of the doors. There he was, head down, following close behind a large sweaty man carrying a briefcase in one hand, while pulling a suitcase on rollers in the other.

Badger zigged to the left, under a row of arches bordering convenience stores. Kyle clicked the camera up ahead and rotated the view towards the storefront. Badger was buying a newspaper, then held the paper down in front as he walked.

Kyle sighed. This might take forever. Union Square was huge, so wherever this guy was going might take just as long now or more to follow him.

He knuckled down and scrolled through the cameras, switching them as Badger zigged and zagged through the station.

He stopped for a moment and noted the time on the line below the footage. All this happened fifty minutes ago. Kyle was falling behind.

He tried to skip ahead, but lost him again, and had to backtrack to the footage where he was visible and just took it now, scrolling ahead and jumping to cameras that could keep up with the target.

Finally, he stopped at an entrance.

Kyle nodded. Of course he wasn't sure but it was possible. A man with a severely short haircut carrying a garment bag, and heading south. He clicked a still shot, saving it to his desktop, then checked the schedule.

A train was about to depart, and one of the next stops down the line was Marine Barracks, Quantico.

Kyle looked up the arrival time for the station at Quantico, then clicked on the camera in that location while imputing the time.

A small crowd got off the train. Dozens of people of all shapes and sizes, a handful of Marines, one of them with his head down hiding his face from the camera. Impossible to tell for sure if it was their guy. Suddenly a space in the crowd, and there draped over his forearm was the garment bag.

Not hiding anymore. Or maybe he was hiding in plain sight. A Marine at the most secure barracks in the country.

Kyle clicked the picture link and forwarded it in an e-mail, then picked up the phone to the chief.

35.

The director of the CIA, Jack Pellegrino sat back in his leather chair, in the simple wood paneled office. Like a triage unit at a hospital, his team needed to choose which volatile situations to focus on. There was usually a half dozen or more at any given time that if untended could see the world spinning out of control. You never knew what was going to happen next, and you had to be ready to move quickly at a moment's notice.

The stack of problems were always piling up. Put one fire out, and two more sprang up. And you never knew which one was going to turn out to be the big one. Sometimes they started out small and cartwheeled out of control. Fan the flames of discontent and it could engulf the entire planet before you knew it. One thing for certain, you couldn't say it was a dull occupation.

Now there was a situation brewing in the Middle East, big surprise there. Fuel transports captured by satellite surveillance along with eyewitness accounts on the ground indicated that Iran was getting ready to launch some type of ballistic missile. Or maybe it was a bluff. They needed to verify the information, quickly.

He looked at the source. Bradford Longman's office was in charge. Based out of Tel Aviv. One time years ago he was on Bob McCade's team in Cairo. Small world. He was about to pick up the phone and call the station chief in Tel Aviv, when the red light blinked and the phone rang.

It was Kyle from logistics tracking. On another, separate matter.

He picked up the phone quickly.

"Did you find him?"

"I think so."

"But you're not sure."

"He got on a train heading south, and I'm pretty sure he gets off in Quantico. This guy is pretty savvy. I'm sending you the photos now."

Jack hung up the phone, while looking at the photos on his computer. Getting on the train at Union Station, then getting off at Marine Base Quantico. The hair was shorter, a Marine cut, but it was him, no doubt about it. This was his man from Catalina.

"I've still got a few tricks up my sleeve," he said to no one in the empty office, as he studied the photos of Badger dressed in civilian clothes but carrying a garment bag. Looking for some tell-tale sign in body language.

"What are you up to?" he thought as he tapped the side of his head with his forefinger.

He flipped through the binder on the desk. It was the daily threat awareness briefing. Who was going to be where, and when they would be there. Key times and destinations for the top officials in the country, Supreme Court justices, top Senate and Congressional officials, the President of the United States of America.

The President.

Breakfast at the White House with the governors of Oregon and Idaho. Photo op with the Ambassador from Chile. Lunch with a group of donors. Then a trip away from the Capital for the second half of the day. A short flight aboard the Presidential helicopter Marine One, taking off from the White House lawn at exactly thirteen oh five for an aerial tour of Arlington, then straight south for a stop at Marine Corps Base Quantico in the afternoon for another photo op with the troops. There'd be an award ceremony at fourteen thirty five, then a live fire exhibition at fifteen hundred. Also penciled in was a nine hole round on the base golf course with the Secretary of Defense after the live fire exhibition. Busy day.

He looked at the dial of the clock on the wall. One hour till the live fire demonstration.

This was getting a little too close for comfort.

He touched the intercom.

"Brenda, any word back from Bob?"

"Sorry Chief, he must still be in the air."

Of all times to take a trip in an aircraft without Wi-Fi.

He dialed a number that linked him direct to Marine Corps Quantico.

"Get me the base commander."

36.

I hadn't been on a military base in over two years, not since the day I was discharged and sent packing into the real world.

Now here I was at Marine Base Quantico. The crossroads of the Marine Corps. Training ground for the Marines, FBI, Hostage Rescue Teams, the Drug Enforcement Agency, Defense Intelligence, Counterintelligence. You name it. Just about every law enforcement agency in the country sent their personnel here. Everyone wanted to come here. And for good reason.

Fifty four thousand acres of live fire ranges and raw training grounds. Entire villages to invade, houses to both defend and attack. You could fire just about any weapon or missile in the U.S. military arsenal. Blast away at tanks, personnel carriers, moving targets, do bombing runs, get the hell scared out of you by a forced march, then crawling through a simulated battle zone complete with machine guns and bombs exploding right next to you. The acrid smell of smoke burning your nostrils as you burrowed your way through a disaster zone while trying to avoid claymore mines and snipers.

Here you could be placed into situations both exhilarating and frightening. This place was used to train a human being in behaving calmly amidst loud sounds and destruction that you would normally try to run away from.

Storm buildings, throw grenades through windows, blast away with machine guns, pistols, grenade launchers, shoulder fired missiles.

It was both comforting, but at the same time un-nerving. There was something about the rigid platform that was laid in front of me that was appealing, that without being sentimental, maybe I'd missed since turning civilian.

Comforting in the fact that a military base had a rigid set of rules and regulations.

Un-nerving because if you stepped out of line, it was shackles, and the brig. Not to mention the fact that nearly everyone had a gun and was a pretty good shot.

I however had no weapon, since I didn't want to have the metal detector at the gate both sing out and single me out as well.

Here I was about to set foot across the border into hostile territory, since I was in essence doing so in someone else's skin. The man I was pretending to be, Duke Cranelly, was a Staff Sergeant, a non-commissioned officer but an officer in the Marine Corps non-the-less. Staff Sergeants lead by example. They are typically in charge of a platoon of 40-50 Marines and they are primarily responsible for its training.

The penalty for impersonating a military serviceman outside of a base was severe. For impersonating an officer on base, it was prison, if they let you live.

With great respect for the military, and especially for the Marine Corps what I was about to do couldn't be helped.

I remember clearly the very first day in boot camp while the drill sergeant was yelling in my ear as I stood at attention, the veins sticking out of his neck that was in itself the size of an elephant leg:

"THIS ISN'T YELLING SON, THIS IS MOTIVATION!"

The thing I liked about being on a military base is there was no BS. At least not out in the open. It was professional. Drilled into a soldier in the beginning with a lot of motivational yelling that carried over into creating a calm disciplined soldier that could handle just about anything.

Tuned to near machine grade perfection through rigorous, sometimes cruel training, that compartmentalized command structure. Do as you're told and everything will be okay.

You didn't see people lazing around out in the open anywhere on the base. That could get you 'volunteered' for a project that you might not necessarily take a liking to.

You get to your destination, get to your task at hand and mind your own business.

I had my orders. Report to barracks company one for training. Pure and simple. Or at least that's what I would tell anyone who asked me where I was going.

I reverted back to my post military bodyguard

training. Blend in to the perimeter. Become transparent, unremarkable. It was actually easy to do on a base where just about everyone wore the same clothes, and had the same haircut.

I stopped at the gym, changed into the utilities and boots in an empty bathroom stall, loaded the civvies in the bag, put it in the back of a broom closet, and continued on my way, out the front doors into the bright afternoon light.

A hundred feet onto the base and my cover was blown.

A jeep with a silver Eagle placard travelling down the road slowed down. The passenger told the driver to back up till I was face to face with an officer staring intently at me.

I stood rigid at attention with a crisp salute and held my position, eyes forward ready for orders. On both collars of his shirt, wings perpendicular to the deck, silver eagles, heads facing to the right, a shield on their chest, in their right talons bunched together were olive branches while the left talons held a slew of arrows.

He was a full bird Colonel.

"Well I'll be damned," he said. "At ease Marine. Staff Sergeant Cranelly when did you get out of the hospital?"

"Just today Sir," I lied. I could feel my face getting hot. He thought I was Duke.

"You got out today, and you're already back at the base? What's the matter with you son, didn't you want to take some time off, get some R&R?"

I thought fast. Never disagree with the brass.

"Yes Sir, I think there's something wrong with me. Well to be honest Sir, I've been getting plenty of R&R on my backside in the hospital so much so that I've been going stir crazy, and with all due respect I just wanted to get back to the action."

This is the kind of stuff the brass liked to hear.

"That's the spirit. How's the foot?"

"Still attached Colonel."

"Fine, where are you heading?"

"Mess hall Colonel."

"You want a ride?"

"No thank you Colonel, I'm enjoying walking again."

"Well, I'd like to get you back on the live fire range. In fact we have a little demonstration this afternoon. We'll be at range eight. We have a demonstration of the AT-4 rocket launcher. We'll also have the 25mm Bushmaster in action. Some real VIP's from DC. I may have to check with the Range Safety Officer, and the Officer in Charge if you need to be re-certified after your accident. Check in with the range C.O. at 1300, and we'll get you back in the action, okay?"

"Thank you Sir." I stood rigid at attention again with a crisp salute, face resolute.

He casually returned the salute and pointed forward for the jeep to continue.

I would have breathed a sigh of relief, but now I'd been given an assignment, and there was no way out of it.

One of the rules about being on a military base, when the brass gave an order, you followed it, or it was the brig.

Right now I couldn't afford to spend any time behind bars.

I had to go with the flow, following the trail of the mysterious wind wherever it took me.

As my old kung fu instructor said, sometimes the path chooses you, and you need to follow it.

I brought a detailed map of the base with me, stuffed into my back pocket, and got it out to get my bearings.

37.

I stopped outside the training room, took the tin of war paint from my front pocket, dipped my fingers one by one into the three colors and swiped them across my face. I'd put on the camo paint about a hundred times before, and since this wasn't a beauty pageant I knew it would be sufficient without using a mirror, then walked into the room dressed in my full Combat Utility Uniform with camo paint on my face, green, black, and brown streaks across nose and cheeks, blending into my neck.

However, none of the other people in the room were wearing war paint on their faces. I stood out like a sore thumb.

Ten Marines were standing around a ledger holding a large aerial photograph of a firing range. They were receiving a briefing from a staff sergeant who had a long wooden pointer placed on the photo to designate locations.

There was a tower next to some low buildings. Long red arrows marked the firing lines towards the top of the photo. An open rugged field in the middle bordered on three sides by varying depths of forest.

In the middle of the rugged open field was a bold black line marking a circle, a single word in the middle also in bold black said targets. Tanks and personnel carriers were placed to the right and left of center. A blue star on the top left of the photo had a single letter N on one of the top points, marking north and tilting, pointing slight to the top left, the target range was facing directly North East. On the right side of the photo in bold orange letters, Range 8.

I was in the right place.

They all turned to face me. Not one of them gave me a single look of recognition. The officer giving the briefing had a nametag stitched above his right breast pocket. In black bold letters: SKULLY.

"Sorry I'm late, Staff Sergeant, but there was a paperwork release foul up at the Hospital." I walked forward to join the group.

Skully looked to be about thirty years old. Nearly bald head with a quarter inch smidgen of black hair on the very top, black eyes, dark skin with a smattering of freckles across his thick flat nose.

He took one look at me, unsmiling. Shaking his head slowly from side to side.

He was a burly bear of a man, probably weighed in at over two hundred twenty five pounds on a six foot frame, not the normal size for a Marine used to long marches. More like someone out of the World Wrestling Federation.

The bulky combat clothing increased his girth. If you could boil down one word to describe his appearance, it would be imposing.

"And who are you again?"

"Staff Sergeant Duke Cranelly."

He didn't budge. Cocked his head slightly to the side. Walked closer to me until we were nearly nose to nose.

"No, who are you really?"

The blood left my head, bunching down into the pit of my stomach. I was busted. It was over.

Ten heavily armed Marines were in close quarters, looking intently at me, ringing me in. The seconds dragged on. Then I remembered. Said the words slowly.

"I'm just a meatball."

His stoic face cracked, wide smile ear to ear, pounded me on the shoulder with a bear mitt.

"Now that's what I'm talking about. Damn son you worried me. You really don't look the same for some reason, must be all the nurses patting you on the backside all day long telling you how pretty you are."

The other Marines chuckled.

"How's the foot?"

"Still attached." It never got old.

"Well let's keep it that way." He got back to business. "Gentlemen we have been assigned to entertain the top brass in the United States Military. We will enlighten, delight, and enthrall them with the finest display of munitions deployment and marksmanship that the world has ever seen. We have been assigned because we are the best of the best. We have forty guests in total, and three guests of particular note. The Secretary of Defense, the Chief of Staff, and the Commander in Chief."

You could sense a palpable shift in the atmosphere of the room.

"It may come as surprise to find this out at the last minute, but that is how these things work. We're professionals and can handle last minute details."

"Now the President, from what the Chief of Staff told me directly, has an extremely tedious job, meeting with dignitaries, signing bland declarations, meeting with a hostile press, day after day after day. He has been looking forward to this event for quite some time now because he gets to have the kind of fun that you gentlemen get to enjoy every single day. Fire some weapons."

"Hoorah," murmured the group.

"Now he wanted to launch some shoulder fired missiles and fire some machine guns. Time constraints, training requirements, safety concerns being what they are we were able to narrow it down and eliminate the shoulder fired missile. We'll demonstrate that weapon on one of the tanks. After that we'll put the President behind the twenty five millimeter Bushmaster single barrel chain driven auto cannon. With a bullet the size of a small water bottle, and a gun able to fire two hundred rounds per minute, that should him give some of the thrill he's looking for. We'll fire three rounds of the AT-4, blow the hell out the tank, then let him get behind the barrel of the Bushmaster and fire a couple hundred rounds to completely finish it off."

"Hoorah," they murmured again.

"We have a total of one hour to complete the mission from receiving our guests at the firing range. Fifteen minutes to brief the guests on what they are about to witness, fifteen minutes to train the President in firing the auto cannon, fifteen minutes to destroy the tank with the shoulder missiles, and fifteen minutes to let our Commander in Chief go hog wild with the cannon. Are there any questions."

The room was silent.

"Now listen up, let's put on a good show for them. Duke had the right idea and beat us to the punch by wearing camo paint. Everyone put on face paint camouflage, it'll look more authentic that way. Duke I want you next to the Range Safety Officer, as an extra set of eyes and ears. Let's make sure we get our commander in chief out of here in the same shape we got him. That clear?"

The room rang out, 'Hoorah.'

38.

A contingent of five secret service agents had already swept the area, which seemed duplicitous since we had enough firepower on hand to take out a division. They were mostly concerned with the area behind and to the sides, looking for someone not on our team who might be hiding in a tree or in a fox hole.

My guess was that they also had snipers set up in a few different locations just in case something, or someone, went awry. A few years ago a former President with a very poor standing among military personnel used to insist that all service personnel be disarmed if he was in range.

A little tough to do if you're on a military base, or near a warship.

This President however ran his show a little different. He was born into a working class family, went straight into the military after high school for four years, never went to combat, never rose to a higher rank than corporal, but enjoyed his time in the corps, then was honorably discharged, used the GI bill to go to college, won a seat on a local board, then rose steadily through the civilian leadership ranks. A true American success story.

His nickname was the big dog because of his booming voice and his propensity to barking out orders. He had a barrel chest and a loud voice.

He relished the ability to get back in the dirt with the troops and utilized his Commander-in-Chief rank every chance he got. The military embraced him back, you'd have to go back to Eisenhower to find another President as well liked and respected.

The President would arrive by Humvee with the rest of the guests after taking a driving tour of the base, then he'd leave in Marine One, the helicopter parked to the side in the landing zone.

We were lined up with our weapons at the firing line at range number eight when the Humvees arrived. Ten of them, camouflaged tan low slung wide wheel base troop transports, each with four passengers and a driver. The first car had a contingent of secret service and they jumped out first and scanned the area, the second vehicle had the President and his aides, one was a firm faced woman, one looked like the Base Commander with a chest full of ribbons, and one carried a large square briefcase covered in a leather bag. I recognized this as the football, the nuclear football that went everywhere with the big dog.

The other Humvees parked, ejecting more people of all shapes and sizes. I noticed a man in one of the middle cars, suit and tie, tall, black hair, steady eyes, stone like personality. Bob

McCade, my contact at the CIA. He wanted to bring me in two days ago, or was it two nights ago. The time blurred. He wanted to bring me in, he said, to protect me. Well here I was suddenly within range if he could pick me out from the other men in my platoon. I was confident that he would not be able to identify me with my camouflage face paint.

Forty guests in all, a hodgepodge of suits, military personnel, photographers, reporters.

Another one of the men in the group also looked familiar. He hung to the back of the crowd, short white hair though his face looked tan and too young to be grey. It was Yuri Ambrov, I was nearly sure of it. He was wearing silver reflecting aviator glasses, his face like a rock with no emotion.

Military.

From the way he was swiveling his head, slow and steady from side to side I knew that the eyes behind the glasses were studying the entire area, looking for details he could use to his advantage when the time arrived, like a commando behind enemy lines.

Like me.

This is the guy I'd been looking for across the entire country, and suddenly here he was on a firing range in close proximity to the President. I could shout loudly, point him out to McCabe and the secret service, and be done with it. He's the guy, I'd tell them, who stole the device. But that might not solve the problem. Maybe he wasn't the main guy after all. And even if he was, maybe he didn't have the device with him.

Why, I wondered, was Yuri Ambrov here with a group of people that included Bob McCade.

They all gathered together and walked onto the range, led by the Base Commander who was giving a walking tour of sorts, the history of this particular range, the weapons that were authorized to be used.

There was a viewing platform with chairs for everyone lined up in two rows well behind the firing line.

The Base Commander led the group straight up to us and turned it over to the officer in charge.

"Gentlemen and ladies, I'd like to introduce the Office in Charge Staff Sergeant Skully, and the range Safety Officer Sergeant McClan."

"Thank you General and welcome everyone to range number eight," said Skully. "This is one the most utilized ranges on the base due the wide array of weapons we can deploy. It's one of the largest in area ranges on the base. We have hardware targets as you can see at the three to four thousand yard marks. Here we can test all types of small arms, grenade launchers, mortars, machine guns, sniper rifles. Today we'll be deploying two different weapons, the AT-4 shoulder fired anti-tank weapon which we utilize on battlefields to disable and destroy bunkers, tanks, hardened targets. We'll also be demonstrating the twenty five millimeter Bushmaster, a versatile weapon that can be used on the dirt and also on the water. The bushmaster is heavily utilized on our naval vessels."

"Any questions so far?"

"I see that you all have your own personal set of eye protection and ear support. It's going to get loud."

"Please all have a seat while the Safety Officer explains the procedure."

"Thank you Staff Sergeant Skully.," said McClan. "The AT-4 is a non-chambered weapon, meaning that it does not have an enclosed back end, therefore it has no recoil which makes it ideal for controlling such a powerful weapon on the battlefield, however in return it has a tremendous back-blast that necessitates a forty meter safety zone. It is also an unguided missile therefore we actually have to aim it. There is a technique. One man can pack the weapon, however we normally use a second person as a spotter and to assist in carrying the munitions. It's muzzle velocity is two hundred ninety meters per second, it's effective firing range to a pointed target is three hundred yards, to a broad area target of five hundred yards, and its maximum range is two thousand yards. Several distinct projectiles can be utilized with this weapon. Today we'll be demonstrating a high explosive anti-tank munition which can penetrate sixteen and a half inches of steel, and we'll also be demonstrating an anti-personnel munition with an airburst detonation. The AT-4 is a one shot weapon meaning it cannot be reloaded and reused, compared to the heavier types that are built with steel. It is pre-loaded at the factory. The canister is built with fiberglass. It is both disposable and lightweight making it ideal for one man to carry it to the front line in battle. One well-placed shot is all that's needed in our fast mobile marine corps unit of today. Any questions?"

A woman sitting close to the front seemed perplexed. "You mean after you use it once, you throw it away?"

"Yes ma'am."

"You mean like littering?"

McClan was non-plussed. "Ma'am we clean every battlefield after the fact to the fullest extent possible. We have detachments whose entire job description is clearing the battlefield of any and all items left on the landscape. The most important item of business first and foremost of course would be the wounded, both friend and foe. Then they conduct the hazardous job of collecting every bit of unexploded ordinance that can be located. Unfortunately to this day, casualties from the First World War are still being found along with unexploded ordinance. Our purpose with this weapon is to avoid being a casualty and instead attach that description to our enemy. With all due respect ma'am."

"Dang Louise," said the President. "You're taking all the fun out of firing a rocket."

Everyone laughed. Except Yuri and the secret service detail.

"These Marines," continued Sergeant McClan. "Are all instructors here at the range. After each trainee under their command has gone through a dry run with an empty missile tube, they go through the live fire drill which is what we will conduct right now. I see that all of you have your safety glasses and ear plugs, please install these now and raise your hand when you have this task completed."

He waited until they complied, even the President held his hand in the air.

"Thank you," he said to them, then yelled at the top of his lungs. "Prepare to fire!"

A warning siren beeped one short high pitched blast.

Then he motioned to the team standing in wait.

Three pairs of men stood twenty feet to the side and perpendicular to the viewing area. Each one of the pair held the short tube hanging down from his shoulder, while the spotter stood next to him.

The Officer in Charge Staff Sergeant Skully shouted out; "Enemy tank in the open, two hundred yards!"

The first set of men raced forward twenty yards taking position in front of and angled away from the other men and the viewing platform. The man with the rocket tube crouched on one knee while the spotter stood close by watching the tank.

"Preparing rocket!" shouted the man kneeling with the tube, flipped an item on the front of the tube, put his fore finger on the red safety button, while placing his thumb on the red trigger button, then looked behind him shouting; "Back blast area all secure!"

The man standing next to him double checked quickly behind and also at the weapon, then said; "You're clear to fire when ready."

The man with the weapon yelled out; "Rocket!" then a moment later squeezed down on both the safety and the trigger. A shock wave of grey smoke, noise and dust took shape around the two man team as the rocket blasted out of the tube, searing through the air, then two split seconds later it hit the tank directly below the turret, exploding black acrid smoke billowing around the tank and out of the muzzle barrel. A direct hit.

As the back-up Safety Officer I was watching both the men with the weapon and the viewing platform. Half the people on the platform flinched when the rocket was fired. The secret service detail was unmoved, keeping their eyes both on the perimeter and the remaining men with the unfired weapons.

Most of the group clapped in appreciation. The spotter tapped the gunner on the helmet. "Good shot, secure the weapon, safety on."

Then they hustled to the rear making way for the next group.

"Prepare to fire!" yelled Skully to the crowd. The woman who asked about the litter placed her hands over her ears and got ready to cringe.

Skully went through the drill again.

"Enemy tank in the open, two hundred yards!"

The next pair hustled forward and went through the same exact pre-shot routine. This missile hit the tanks below the turret and just above the treads. Another direct hit. They hustled to the back and Skully began to go through the routine again, but first he addressed the crowd.

"This will be an airburst detonation. Set for two hundred yards directly above the tank. Prepare to fire!"

This time two split seconds after the missile left the tube the explosion burst directly above the tank's turret in a fireball of shrapnel and TNT, the ground beneath the explosion raising up in peppers of dust.

Applause from the crowd and relief from the woman that the missile firing was complete.

"That ladies and gentlemen concludes our anti-tank rocket demonstration. Mr. President if you would be so kind we'll now have you go through a short tutorial on the Bushmaster. I know it's been a while since you've fired one of these, but it's just like riding a bike."

"Just don't treat me like a baby okay?" he whispered to McClan.

The Marines standing nearby smiled at that.

McClan handed him a flak jacket and then a combat helmet. The President turned to the right at the behest of the photographer standing nearby and smiled with McClan next to him and the other soldiers behind. The flak jacket had a special presidential seal insignia sewn into the left breast.

The photographer followed as the president and McClan walked over to the Bushmaster. The entire weapon was the size of a small closet square at the base, half-moon adjustable shoulder supports fitted with shock absorbers. Blue tipped bullets the size of a soda bottle traveling out of the magazine on the left inside a snake like trestle over the top of the gun to the firing mechanism. The eight foot long barrel the width of a baseball tapering to the size of a golf ball at the end. It was mounted onto a swivel turret, the entire system weighing half as much as a car.

"Mr. President, honored guests, this is the M242 Bushmaster, one the most powerful weapons that we deploy along various factions in our military, from all types of naval vessels, destroyers, aircraft carriers, submarines, and land based vehicles such as the M-2 and M-3 Bradley Fighting vehicles, and the LAV-25 amphibious reconnaissance vehicle. It is a close range defensive weapon that is deployed as protection against enemy fast attack boats, floating mines, near shore targets, bunkers, tanks, armored personnel carriers, slow moving aircraft such as helicopters and fixed wing aircraft."

He held up a bullet casing nearly as long as his forearm with a blue projectile at the top.

"Today we'll be utilizing the M793 target practice round that's also equipped with a phosphorescent tracer. We use this type of round for training since it's a bit cheaper to produce than the armor piercing rounds, and our commander in chief has made it clear that we will be saving money whenever possible."

The crowd chuckled.

"That's right," said the President loudly enough for everyone to hear. "Let's save the real bullets for whatever enemy makes the wrong decision to test us."

Skully, McClan and I escorted the President over to the gun, we double checked the mechanisms, McClan adjusting the shoulder supports till they were the right width.

I walked back and to the right while they stayed put giving final instructions. In my line of vision I could see the whole field laid out in front of us, the line of fire, the stationary targets, the safety zone to the sides and behind the weapon.

The guests all standing in anticipation, photographers snapping away. Yuri Ambrov still stood to the right rear corner of the group.

A tall man with slick black hair wearing a dark blue suit was walking backwards along the edge of the crowd towards Yuri. I couldn't see his face, but then he turned when he got within an arm's length.

McCade. I could see him whispering, his lips barely moving. Yuri was still, not acknowledging or looking at the man walking past, as though no words were being spoken to him. McCade continued to walk away, then dialed a number on his phone, placing it next to his ear. Their interaction was brief, to the untrained eye they were strangers.

"Prepare to fire!" shouted McClan. He stood to the left of the President hovering over the canister holding the train of bullets. The warning siren beeped. "Any time you're ready sir," he said.

Five long seconds ticked off as the gun was carefully aimed, then a single crack erupted, the gun recoiling against his shoulders, the bullet pierced the air, tracer on a line to the tank in the center of the field. Short and to the right. The gunner adjusted the aim and squeezed the trigger again. High and to the left, the tracer sailing over the turret. You could almost hear the gunner cursing, but all was dead silence as he readjusted his aim, taking his time, squeezing the trigger a third time, gun recoiling, tracer flying to a direct hit in the center of the tank.

The crowd erupted in celebration.

"Now let 'er rip," said McClan, tapping the gunner on the shoulder.

The gunner squeezed the trigger and kept it squeezed, the Bushmaster turned into a giant machine gun rattling off three rounds per second, blowing the hell out of the poor tank.

Thirty seconds of blazing hell, and a hundred bullets later the gunner, with confidence and wind in his sail swiveled the gun along a line towards the target on the right, keeping the trigger down, bullets ripping through the dirt as the destruction zeroed in on the new target for another thirty seconds, blowing the hell out of this tank, it went on and on, I wondered what was going through the President's mind as he blasted away, what enemy was he destroying, then all was quiet, the last echoes of the gunfire fading through the air, an eerie aftermath ensued as the seconds ticked by.

Then the gunner gave out a hearty yell, nearly everyone in the viewing gallery cheered along with him clapping, the photographers clicking away.

Yuri however, did not celebrate. I could see

him calmly and deliberately watching the proceedings, studying the President. His attention unwavering.

McClan and Skully high fived the President who brought them to each side placing his arm over their shoulders while beaming towards the camera. I could almost envision him telling his political opponents to eat it as he soaked up the testosteronal windfall of personally destroying two enemy tanks and saving the world in the process while having the press corps record it all for the evening news.

He crisply saluted McClan and Skully then shook their hands, going down the line saluting and shaking all the men in our platoon.

Then the President, along with the Chief of Staff, Secretary of Defense, and the press corps walked to the helicopter, Marine One.

I kept the corner of my eyes on Yuri Ambrov, he turned abruptly on his heels, walking quickly to join the group of people crowding into the Humvees, not once looking around until the moment he was climbing into the back seat of one of the vehicles, then he turned to look across the dusty parking lot.

I was still watching him as the President's helicopter engine's RPM's increased in speed till it was humming with a fine tuned chord like a musical instrument all the sound coming together in unison, the giant blades spinning in an ever increasing velocity, the dust from Blackbird billowing in the air.

Our platoon waited, standing at attention until Marine One lifted off the ground, then the

Humvees as one unit pulled out in unison.

I watched as the train of vehicles headed towards highway six ten and was out of sight.

From the casual conversations that I could hear, the next stop for the President was a round of golf at the Medal of Honor course on base.

It seemed like a good idea to get to the golf course to have a look at the perimeter protection that they'd put around him, but for now I was stuck with the platoon. I needed to find a way out.

"Well men," said Skully. "I think that went pretty well. No one died except for two tanks that were already dead. Now we can stand around and pat ourselves on the back about how great we are, or we can hustle out of here and get to the bar. Our job here is done, what do you say we do a quick pack up and call it a day?"

In unison: "Hurrah!"

39.

The weapons technicians began to break down the Bushmaster while the rest of us picked up the discarded AT-4 tubes, and empty bullet cartridges.

"Don't want to piss off Louise," quipped Skully.

Ten minutes later we had everything packed in the trucks, ready to transport back to the base. Marines didn't screw around.

"Well that was a hell of a lot of fun," said Skully as we settled into the lead vehicle.

"Yes sir," I agreed. "Better than a kick in the tail with a steel toed boot."

"Unless you're the one doing the kicking. It sure was great seeing the old man blast the hell out of those tanks," he continued. "Did you notice how he seemed to take great pleasure in having the weapon on full automatic. I was even wondering which enemy he was destroying. The Russians, Chinese..."

"Speaker of the House," I interjected.

He turned to me unsmiling. "Well, he is one tough son of a bitch."

I didn't know whether he was talking about

the President or the Speaker.

He gave out a loud whistle, circling his left forefinger in the air out of the window. "Alright, let's get back to base."

Range 8 was twenty miles as the crow flies from Range Control and we were there within half an hour.

"Lunch and drinks on the house at the Golf Course Clubhouse," said Skully. "I just got word from the Commander, the President is buying."

I passed on the offer, told them I wasn't hungry but wanted to get back to the base to get a haircut and pick up some items from the PX.

They gave me a ride back to the center of Quantico, and let me off in front of the barber shop on Potomac Avenue. Before I got out of the jeep I grabbed a small towel from the back, splashed some water from a canteen on it and wiped my face clean. Even though I was on a Marine base, you couldn't just walk around town with war paint, you'd probably get arrested. As soon as they turned left around the corner I headed east over the railroad tracks and took a right on Barnett Avenue heading north.

The golf course was less than mile away.

Barnett turned into Fuller and angled to the east again. My legs were beginning to ache with the walking although I'd only gone a little more than a quarter mile. A car pulled stopped next to me to ask if I wanted a ride. I politely declined and evened out my gait, eliminating any hint of a limp. No need to draw attention to myself. I was a Marine on base in a Combat Utility Uniform just walking up the road, nothing out of the ordinary.

The elevation increased, going up a slight hill. Geiger Road was on the right. Bordering it was the first golf green on the course. It was nearly perfectly round with one long peanut shaped sand bunker next to it. I had no idea what hole it was. I could see a creek cutting across Geiger road heading towards the sea. The sun was hanging lower now in the west, filtering through the elm forest, the air had a scent of newly mowed grass hanging in the breeze from the north.

I continued on for another three hundred yards. Somewhere off to the right through the thin forest was a long section of the golf course. I could hear voices and golf carts carried towards me along the breeze. I waited until there were no cars either behind or in front of me, then slipped into the low bushes out of sight heading north.

Settling into the dense brush, I made myself still as a rock, then scanned the surroundings and listened.

There was the unmistakable sound of a dog panting as it was heading through the brush, through the forest I made out the shape of a man leading a blood hound through the woods. He had a rifle slung over his shoulder as he worked through the thicket. He wasn't hunting for animals, he was hunting for men. This was the advance team and I let him pass well to the right.

A little more than a hundred feet through the thicket I came to a little creek. Ironically its name on the map was 'Little Creek'. The shape varied from ten to twenty feet wide with low sandy banks as it meandered downhill with slow moving clear green tinted water. I found a narrow spot with some flat rocks to cross without getting sloshed.

I was in a bend in the creek, on an island of sorts, the creek rounding behind me, in the middle of mound covered with thick bushes and twenty foot tall trees.

The paved golf cart path was fifteen feet in front of my position, with a large forty foot tall tree on the other side of it.

A fairway stretched out in front of me going from left to right towards another green, this one more of a long oval shaped with another peanut shaped sand bunker to its right side.

I found a place in the nook of a tree and settled in to watch and listen.

This was the perimeter, and I felt comfortable here.

I pulled out the binoculars and surveyed the scene all around me, then across the fairway through the woods that bordered this hole.

There was movement directly across from me. It looked like a small bush that was scuttling along. It had legs, and I could see the muzzle of the barrel of a long gun. It moved up the fairway and took up position two hundred yards further up towards the green.

I saw another movement on the other side of the fairway, just behind and to the left of the sniper who had settled in to his hiding spot. Even though this man was not wearing camo gear, he was dressed in black, and seemed to have stealthy movements, using the trees to his advantage, blending into the shadows. The sniper did not seem to know that he was nearby. I zoomed in on the face. Flat nose, deep tan, etched furrows on a face too young to be wrinkled.

It was Yuri.

To my left leaves rustling, a branch breaking, light footsteps. I melded low into the trunk of my tree, pulling a branch over my back and setting my cheek against the bark.

It was another sniper, dressed like a tree. He scanned the bushes as he passed but did not see me hunkered down. If I had gotten here a few minutes earlier I would have been sniffed out by the blood hound. They must have another dog team on the other side of the fairway leading the way for the other sniper. This was the perimeter protection team for the President of the United States and so far they were doing a piss poor job.

The voices that I heard were off to the left and about two hundred yards away, hidden by the curve of the fairway. Somewhere over there must be the tee box. Boisterous laughter, a loud booming voice. Then quiet and the cracking sound of a golf ball being hit. Close to my location in the center of the fairway a little white ball thumped to the hard ground, rolling forward a few extra yards.

Another crack of the golf ball, then loud swearing as this ball rolled past the first one.

Minutes passed with no sounds.

Two golf carts moved into view with the President in one cart, and the Secretary of

Defense and the aide with the nuclear football in the other. Well to the rear, over a hundred yards back was a third cart with a single secret service agent. The President was renowned for distancing himself from his protection force, and in this case must have wanted them as far away from his golf swing as possible.

The President and the Secretary got out and surveyed the scene, looking down at the golf ball, then towards the green off in the distance down the fairway, while the man riding with the President remained seated, shaded by the cart roof. The President pulled out a club from the bag at the rear of the cart, approached the ball and took a couple of practice swings. His pre shot routine complete, he settled in, head down, ready to take a mighty hack.

He was stopped mid back swing by an approaching cart coming from the rear. It stopped briefly next to the secret service agent, then continued full speed towards the golfers.

There was a single man in the cart, and he appeared to be agitated. He stopped quickly then hopped out of the cart. He had slick black hair, wearing a dark blue suit. It was Bob McCade.

The three men huddled together, having a discussion. Meanwhile the other man who was riding with the Secretary of Defense got out of the cart with a large leather briefcase and set it on the passenger seat.

I focused the binoculars and watched.

40.

The Presidential aide, unsmiling, opened up the nuclear football, and spread four items on the passenger seat of the golf cart. Two black loose leaf notebooks filled with papers, one detailing launch options, the other detailing classified site locations where they would head to for safety, a manila folder with stapled papers detailing the emergency broadcast system, and a three by five inch laminated card with launch codes.

Two other men besides the aide stood around the President as he sat in the golf cart driver's seat looking down at the papers. The Secretary of Defense, and Bob McCade.

The President was livid.

"You've got to be damned well kidding me if you think I'm going to launch a nuclear attack on Iran while at a golf course."

"Sir this is threat level one," said the Secretary.

The President frowned. "Missile launch eh?"

"Imminent threat sir," said the Secretary. "A nuclear armed missile is about to be launched at our fleet in the Gulf."

"Can't we just shoot it down?"

"We're not a hundred percent sure we can guarantee success."

"How much time do we have?"

"Five minutes."

"Not much time."

"No sir. This is why we have this protocol in place."

"What's the recommendation?"

"Two quick strikes sir. One on the missile site in Lebanon, and the other in the center of Tehran. We don't know how many more weapons they have and this should take care of the threat once and for all."

His face contorted in disgust, turning red in anger.

"Son of a bitch!" he yelled. "Some kind of options you're giving me." He got out of the seat, took one step and threw his golf club to the side, it bounced a few times, the shaft wobbling in the air till it came to rest in the middle of the fairway. He leaned his head against the cart's top.

"Dammit it all. Remind me the procedure."

"You sir," said the Secretary. "As President have the sole authority to launch a nuclear strike. You are the only one, in fact who can authorize it, unless you are somehow incapacitated, in which case the responsibility transfers down the line to the Vice President, then Speaker of the House... "

He was agitated. "Yes, I know that part, now get on with the rest."

"It's a multi-tiered process, but really consists

of two steps, you and me. The entire procedure is geared to ensure the identity of the one giving the order, you sir, and the authenticity of the order itself. We have the Chairman of the Joint Chiefs of Staff on a satellite phone ready for your orders. You as Commander in Chief give the order for the nuclear attack and produce the launch codes, I verify the authenticity of the order and your identity. We contact the destroyer in the Gulf who verifies the launch codes. The order is re-verified once more, and the missiles are launched. The whole process takes a few minutes."

The President took a deep breath and released it slowly crunching his lips together.

"Gentlemen, with all due respect I'm going to have to say no. This is too sudden and brutal of a response for something that may not even happen. As much as I dislike the regime in Tehran, destroying the entire city in a pre-emptive nuclear attack would diminish our country forever. I think we should wait and double check our intelligence."

"Sir we don't have time for that," said Bob McCade. "I need you to read this paper." He handed it to the President.

"What the hell is this now?" It was a single piece of paper. He turned it over to look at the back which was blank. He turned it around to the front, looked at the heading at the top of the page. In bold black letters:

QUICK READ.

"Quick read. What the hell is it?"

"Threat alert sir, you need to read that paper

immediately."

The President was about to look back down at the paper, when he was abruptly interrupted.

A voice shouted out from the woods, echoing down the fairway.

"Don't read that paper mister President! It's a trick!"

A loud shot rang out from the opposite tree line ricocheting off the woods where the voice came from.

41.

I watched in amazement as the scene unfolded in the middle of the fairway. They were two hundred yards away from my cubby hole in the tree line and yet with U.S. Military top-of-the-line binoculars I could just about read their lips and tell what was being said. I could see tiny drops of spittle flying from the big dog's lips.

Even from this distance you could hear the yelling. Booming voice bouncing off the stratosphere.

The President was pissed off.

Pretty sure he said son-of-a-bitch just now and threw his golf club. It rattled off to the side.

The other man was calmly explaining something to him while Bob stood silently to the side holding a piece of paper. The aide with the nuclear football also stood silently to the side, while the contents of the briefcase that he carried sat spread out on the seat. This was not good. The contents of the so-called nuclear football had been emptied, and they weren't discussing how to make paper hats out of it.

They were trying to talk him into launching a nuclear attack, that much was clear to see even from this distance. But the President wasn't buying what they were trying to sell.

In the back of my mind I could still see the bold black words on the legal sized paper from the briefcase. NUKE TEHRAN.

I increased the binocular magnification. Bob was holding a single piece of paper that seemed to have a slight metallic sheen. It waffled in the breeze for a moment obscuring the title. The heading on the left ruffled into sight, bold black letters:

QUICK

Then the word at the top right came into view ever so slightly:

READ

Bob was waiting patiently to get his two cents in. I could see him fidgeting with his feet. The other man was just about done with his pitch. It was a no-go.

The President looked firm. He frowned and shook his head in the negative, followed by the universal hand gesture that meant a definitive no, end of discussion.

Bob made his move, the other man gave room for him to lean in, and he handed the paper to the President who frowned even deeper, his facial expression clear. He'd obviously been through a few charades in his life. Still trying to sell him a bag of goods. His eyes settled on the title. I could see him mouth the words. Quick Read. He looked up from the paper. What the hell is it, he asked Bob, who attempted to explain with eloquent hand gestures.

The President was about to look back down at

the paper.

Someone stole something that made people do things they wouldn't normally do.

This I knew, was the moment of truth.

I made my move, stood tall stepping away from the tree, made a megaphone with my hands cupped around my mouth, and shouted out at the top of my lungs.

"Don't read it mister President! It's a trick!"

The sound of my voice echoed through the tree lined golf course. Everyone down in the fairway looked my way.

Then I ducked tight to the ground because I knew what was coming next.

Whoever the sniper was, picked out my location pretty quick, but was either a really poor shot, was just trying to warn me off, or maybe point out my location with a bullet.

It ricocheted off the bark of the tree about five feet higher than my head. I scurried to the left, then farther to the left through a line of bushes.

Another shot rang out, but it had a distinctly different sound, this time it was a pistol shot in the same general location of the sniper, muffled as though the muzzle of the gun was pressed against something soft. I hustled to the front of the bush line and sought out the sniper on the other side of the fairway with my binoculars. He was down. In his place, crouching over him, a shape. It was Yuri who picked up the long rifle.

There were two snipers protecting the President, one on either side of the fairway, each one mobile to keep up with the golf party, while the perimeter of the course was cleared of all other personnel.

One of them was just ambushed by Yuri. The other one, on my side of the fairway and about fifty feet from me opened fire on Yuri's position, too quickly in my opinion, he also missed badly by just a few inches, which might as well have been a mile, exposing his location to Yuri who did not miss from the sound of it. A hollow thump and an anguished cry.

The secret service agent standing next to his golf cart well to the rear of the President was caught flat footed when the shots rang out.

He jumped in the cart, punching the accelerator to get in front of the President. The Secretary of Defense stood in place unmoving like a docile cow in a pasture, blank face, eyes like saucers, while the President jumped into his golf cart, huddled down as low as he could manage in the seat, stomping on the accelerator attempting to flee. A shot echoed, the back end of the golf cart exploded with plastic and metal shards, the battery powered engine disabled.

The secret service agent yelling into his microphone got within a few feet of the President, but fell tumbling in two heaps with a quick shot. The military aide fell in a separate heap at the front of the cart.

Somewhere nearby on the safest military base in the world, soldiers were scrambling, sirens were blaring, help was on its way.

In my judgement it would be too late. As far as I knew the nearest live soldier with a weapon was nearly half a mile away.

Yuri tossed the rifle to the side, and with

pistol in hand ran across the fairway towards the President who stumbled to the rear of the golf cart and tried to grab a gun out of the dead secret service agents hand to at least have a chance.

It was too late. Yuri came quickly up next to him, pistol whipped him against the side of his head, then pointed the weapon at Bob McCade who seemed frozen in fear, yelling instructions. He pulled the President to his feet, dragging him back to the cart.

I hustled to the right, fifty feet is not very far to run if you're jacked with adrenaline. I could not run and see what was happening at the golf cart at the same time. I needed the sniper rifle.

He was laying on his side, I couldn't tell if he was alive and there was no time to check for a pulse. His index finger wedged into the trigger guard. I carefully pulled it out and lifted the long gun away from him, checked the chamber, one bullet was in the barrel, another waiting in the magazine below.

I turned my attention to the golf carts in the center of the fairway. Bob was now laying on his side, I couldn't tell if he was alive. The Secretary of Defense was still standing like a statue, as though nothing out of the ordinary was happening around him, while Yuri held the pistol against the President's cheek.

I aimed and fired at Yuri's head and now I missed badly, hitting the top of the golf cart, it shattered plastic shards flying through the air. The two men lurched to the ground, Yuri using the President as a shield while still holding the pistol next to his cheek.

"I'll kill him!" he yelled. "Back off!" He put the satellite phone next to the President's head and yelled into his ear.

I had no doubt that if the President was able to order the nuclear attack, he was dead anyways.

I could only hope that the old man still had some of the spunk that he showed on the firing range when he was gunning down the enemy tanks just a couple of hours ago.

I checked the rifle again, one bullet in the barrel, one in the magazine, then aimed and fired, hitting the top of the golf cart again, then jumped up and sprinted towards them as the two men crouched at the sound of the bullet fragment ripping through the cart.

In my mind I was sprinting, but in reality limping on bruised legs, zigging and zagging, rifle held low. If I could only get closer to them.

Halfway across the center of the fairway, Yuri pulled the pistol away from the President's cheek, firing at me. I tried to zig, but my legs disobeyed, the bullet punched through the top of my right shoulder, just above the flak jacket as though a foot long nail had been driven through me. I stumbled and fell, rolling with the rifle clattering under me. It was just the moment that was needed. The President, the big dog, held Yuri's hand with the pistol with both of his hands clamped around the wrist, bent his head down and bit the thumb that was wrapped around the handle of the pistol. Yuri's head twisted back as he yelled in pain, exposing his upper torso. From a sitting position I fired the rifle taking the top of his head off.

Now, bullets from another source were splattering the ground around me, kicking grass and dirt into my eyes. I pitched the rifle as far away as I could then threw myself chest on the ground, laid still, arms and legs spread eagled, face straight down nose first into the grass, dead to the world for all intents and purposes.

Vehicles roared nearby, a helicopter thundered overhead, feet racing towards us. I stayed still as a dead man until I felt a boot on my neck and the barrel of some type of weapon dig into the tip of my cheek bone. Then all went black.

42.

Yagiz looked at his watch for the fifth time in the past five minutes. It was now twelve thirty in the morning. They should have gotten the word thirty five minutes ago.

"Maintain silence until you receive final confirmation," was the last communication from base.

Confirmation wouldn't be with a radio signal, it would be a sudden bright light over Tehran.

They took the camouflage netting off the crater well after sunset. Swept up every bit of evidence of their presence, burying it in the pit they'd prepared the day before. When they left this crater, they would leave for good, and if someone someday should ever find a scrap of their stay here it would be too late to connect them to any of it. There would be bigger problems to tackle, much bigger than some empty food tins, and military gear in a hole over a hundred miles from ground zero.

The helicopters were ready, checked and re-checked over the past two days, and the past two hours. Five minutes after the blast, Yagiz kept telling himself to calm his nerves. Five minutes after the blast and we start the engines. The two attack helicopters leave first, then the heavy lift chopper follows. We travel to ground zero and steal the gold. It's waiting there for us.

He looked at his watch for the sixth time and cursed at his stupidity. He hated the number six and tried to tell himself that it was number seven instead. He skipped number six with a glance at the watch a few moments ago, and now he was on number seven. He always hated the number six because that was how many sides a coffin had.

He gazed up at the lookout scout on the top edge of the crater who was facing Tehran far to the north. The steady night glow of the large metropolis lit the horizon. The man waffled his hand. Nothing yet.

When the explosion happened, the resulting electromagnetic pulse would knock out all power in the city. Not only would there be a sudden bright light indicating a successful strike, complete darkness would quickly follow, confirming the fact.

When the explosion happened, Yagiz kept telling himself. When it happened.

There were nearly always delays in military operations. You hurry up, get ready for battle, then wait. And then wait some more.

This however was something much different.

A tight window of opportunity. A plan so foolproof that the only thing that could throw it off kilter would be complete failure on the other end.

It was now nearly an hour since they should

have seen the bright light.

Negative thoughts crept into the back his mind. Thoughts not of attack, but of escape.

The back-up plan was to leave the heavy lift helicopter behind, get everyone into the two attack helicopters and make a bee-line for the border. Save the aircraft if at all possible, they were the ticket, the transportation out of the county.

At any rate, the confirmation to go to the gold would come from the definitive nuclear explosion over Tehran.

An order to retreat would need to come from a radio signal. They would need to maintain a steady posture of readiness in case the explosion was delayed. It was after all no small event that was planned.

There was an atmospheric inversion over the desert. Two separate layers of slow moving clouds, one in the jet stream thirty five thousand feet above the surface, stratocirrus heading to the east, while at two thousand feet a separate layer of low very slow moving mottled low level cumulous coming from the south.

The sounds were faint at first, whispers in the wind. The crater facing straight up into the clouds which acted as a sound board, bouncing the faint whispers into the crater as though conical speakers in a stereo. Whispers coming from the south. The lookout on the edge of the crater heard them first, turning his attention from Tehran to the north, and facing south towards the familiar sound.

The whispers quickly becoming steady,

separate staccato vibrations. Jet engines driving metal propellers that beat against the air causing lift and propulsion.

It would take over five minutes to fire up the attack helicopter jet propulsion engines, five minutes to get the power steady enough to gain air flight. Five minutes that they now did not have.

The lookout instinctively fled to the other side of the crater rather than leaping back down into it. Leaping towards potential safety rather than certain death.

The first helicopter flew straight over the crater, tilted into a wing-over circling well to the left, half a mile away now, hovering while pointing a green laser beam at each of the three aircraft sitting useless in the crater. Painting each fuselage with a beacon, a signature that a laser guided bomb would soon track, efficiently and precisely.

Yagiz watched calmly, this is after all what it meant to be on the front line of a military operation he told himself, then took a deep last breath as three separate missiles followed the laser markers, sweeping in so quick that he barely heard them.

43.

The headquarters of the Central Intelligence Agency is located in the north east corner of Langley Virginia, next to the lazy winding Potomac river.

A sprawling complex of steel, glass and high tech security on two hundred and fifty eight acres of land. The sprawling complex consists of two and half million square feet of covered space, thousands of miles of wire, cable, and over twenty thousand employees. On the other side of the river is Maryland and farther east the outskirts of Washington DC.

Eleven thousand years ago Native Americans chose this very site for its access to steady flowing water, and the wealth of natural resources, fish, deer, and quartz, which they used to manufacture tools and spear points. A lot had changed since those days. While in many ways the basic premise remained the same.

Survival.

The director of the CIA, Jack Pellegrino sat back in his leather chair, took off his reading glasses and rubbed his tired eyes.

He looked up at me from across the leather

topped desk and folded his hands in front of him.

His face was unreadable. Firm, without a trace of emotion. It had all been squeezed out from the events of the past few days.

"We owe you a debt of gratitude."

I was about to shrug my shoulders, but was reminded of the bullet wound that went straight through the collarbone and decided against it. Why stir things up. Plus I was angry with them.

"You used me to flush out your mole."

"We had to."

"You could have told me what was going on."

He shook his head no, but did not elaborate, then thought better of it. What did it matter, now that it was over. Might as well level with the guy.

"We didn't really know what was going on. That's why I took a big chance and gave you a free wheel to go wherever you wanted. We didn't know who was involved. We had no idea Yuri Ambrov and Black Op Security had control of the device. We knew someone on our inside was involved but we didn't know it was Bob McCade, and we certainly didn't know he was going to be on the golf course. I called the base commander when I suspected you were heading to Quantico. We had an extra security detail for the President's golf outing. That guy sure loves to play golf, but hates to have security tagging along. The two snipers in the tree line were on a hair trigger alert."

"Everything happened pretty quick."

He nodded and pulled up a piece of paper,

reading from it.

"We analyzed the audio from the secret service agents microphone. From the first shot till the last a total of three minutes elapsed. A lot can happen in a short amount of time."

Three minutes riding on the edge. It was all a blur now. Whatever hair trigger the snipers were on paled in comparison to what I must have been tapped into. I remembered bits and pieces of it, yelling, then running with the long gun, getting shot, then pulling the trigger. I wondered if they might have wiped my memory somehow. I wouldn't put anything past these guys.

"What about those two snipers," I asked. "And the other people? The last thing I clearly remember there was a boot on my face, then I blacked out, and woke up in the ER."

His eyes remained steady.

"The President's military aide and the Secret Service agent will both survive. The snipers are in serious condition but are expected to pull out of it. If you weren't there, or would have stayed silent at that critical moment in time, no one on the golf course would have gotten hurt, but we'd be in a different world right now."

"And the device would still be with Black Op."

"The great thing is that you succeeded. It could have gone either way at the end there."

"I got lucky."

He shook his head while studying me.

"Yeah, I guess you can call it that. We all got lucky. From the President, to the Chairman of the Joint Chiefs of Staff, Secretary of Defense, the nine million Iranians and everyone else that was in Tehran yesterday, probably the rest of the planet for that matter. We came close to starting world war three. All because of greed for gold and revenge. Although the gold seemed to be an after-thought. It was revenge that was the real driving force. At the end, when Yuri realized he wasn't going to escape, he gave up his life trying to get that missile launched. It's the only thing that mattered to him."

Jack tapped his forefinger on the desk then continued.

"For the other people in the group, they may have wanted to see Tehran burn for their own sick reasons, but it was really only the gold that they wanted. And they were willing to inflict all that collateral damage to get it. Unbelievable what some people will do."

"What about Bob?" I asked.

"What about him?"

"Well for one thing, what's going to happen to him, I mean what are you going to do with him in the long run. I'm sure in the short run you'll turn him inside out a few times, find out what other little tricks he had up his sleeve. I know you have your ways."

"He's an American citizen, and as such has rights. But I'll answer your long run question as far as he's concerned. That guy's not going anywhere for quite a while. Maybe a few decades. Treason, espionage for a foreign power, attempted assassination of a sitting President. We're not letting him out of our control. That I can guarantee. He's not officially in the military which would carry a death sentence from a firing squad after a military court-martial, but we'll find ways to keep him behind a locked door till the end of his time."

"He's a fairly young man. It could be very long time."

"Yeah, well I'm not going to lose any sleep over it."

"You used the President of the United States as bait to catch these guys. I didn't think you people did that sort of stuff."

"There's a lot about us you don't know, but I'll say on the record that is something we would never do." His eyes narrowed. "You have to admit though, he handled himself pretty well."

"I saw him get pistol whipped. Must have left quite a bruise on his face."

"The official word is he got hurt playing golf. His playing partner hit a bad shot, the ball ricocheted off a tree and whacked him in the cheek bone before he could get out of the way."

My shoulder was throbbing. It was time to end our meeting and he realized it from my facial expression. I hadn't slept in two days.

"You know," he said. "You can just about write your own ticket now, with the agency that is. Pick any spot you want. You can take any office in the building. Move right in. We'll put you to work. I know how you operate. We have the biggest bag of tricks in the world."

It was my turn to shake my head no.

"All I want right now is to go home to Dana Point. Go home to my fiancé. Go home to a nice quiet, simple life." My mind drifted. Go home to

Amber, I thought to myself.

He nodded. "We'll still need to do an official off-the-record debriefing. Something for our files that we can look back on, and maybe we'll learn something from it. It'll take no more than an hour, I promise. Then we'll put you on the fastest military jet that we have, whenever you're ready. We'll fly you non-stop right to Camp Pendleton, and chauffeur you up the road to your home."

Home.

I'd only been away for two days, but it seemed like years.

"So what now?"

He didn't answer me right away, studying me.

"That's a big question."

"I'll be more specific. I know what happened to the main player Yuri. He's dead. Bob's about to be locked up for life. What about all the other bit players of this little drama."

He was quiet for a moment, making up his mind.

"I'm going to level with you Badger. Everything that transpired the past few days. As far as the world outside of this agency is concerned..." He paused. "None of it ever happened. We're going to put a tight lid on all of this. We don't want our enemies to have any knowledge of what just happened. And what might have happened. We'll generate cover stories for everything. The Secretary of Defense and Chairman of the Joint Chiefs of Staff will both retire with honors. The Black Op company will cease to exist. We'll sweep up all the other little crumbs from Beirut to Tehran. We'll do what we have to do."

I'm sure they would. When it was all boiled down, it wasn't a very friendly world that we all lived in.

"But that's not everything though. Is it?" I asked.

His rigid face slackened. "You mean the technology?"

I waited.

He nodded slowly then continued, his voice taking on a tone of resolve. "Yes. We're going to have to collect every bit of that also. Every notebook, scrap of paper, experiment, computer chip, monitor, wire, phone call, every nuance of anything and everything to do with that technology, the research, every single bit, gather it up, bottle it tight. We don't want any of it to get into the wrong hands."

My eyes narrowed as I studied him. I had a question.

"Are there any right hands?"

He was silent, then turned slowly in his chair to look straight out of the window that faced east over the Potomac River, over the little town of Palisades, then over Georgetown, towards the vast skyline of white marbled buildings on the horizon. Washington DC, nearly five miles away, looming in the distance, the edges of the buildings darkening as dusk approached.